IN ALL DIRECTIONS

eSpec Books by David Sherman

18th Race Series
ISSUE IN DOUBT
IN ALL DIRECTIONS
TO HELL AND REGROUP
(with Keith R.A. DeCandido)

DemonTech Series
DEMONTECH: THE LAST CAMPAIGNS

eSpec Books
including David Sherman

DOGS OF WAR REISSUED
BEST OF DEFENDING THE FUTURE
THE WEIRD WILD WEST
AFTER PUNK

THE 18th RACE
BOOK 2
IN ALL DIRECTIONS

DAVID SHERMAN

eBooks
Pennsville, NJ

PUBLISHED BY
eSpec Books LLC
Danielle McPhail, Publisher
PO Box 242,
Pennsville, New Jersey 08070
www.especbooks.com

Copyright ©2014, 2017 David Sherman
"Down to the Wire" Art Copyright ©2017, Mike McPhail

Previously published by DTF Publications, an imprint of Dark Quest Books, 2014.

ISBN: 978-1-942990-44-4
ISBN (eBook):978-1-942990-45-1

All rights reserved. No part of the contents of this book may be reproduced or transmitted in any form or by any means without the written permission of the publisher.

All persons, places, and events in this book are fictitious and any resemblance to actual persons, places, or events is purely coincidental.

Copyediting: Keith R.A. DeCandido
Design: Mike and Danielle McPhail
Cover Art: Mike McPhail, McP Digital Graphics
www.milscifi.com

This book is dedicated to the memory of:

Hospital Apprentice First Class
David E. Hayden

Awarded the Medal of Honor
While serving with 2nd Battalion, 6th Marines
Battle of Saint-Mihiel
September 15, 1918

On being told that his regiment was surrounded at Koto-ri
during the withdrawal from the Chosin Resevoir,
Colonel Lewis B. "Chesty" Puller,
commander of the 1st Marine Regiment,
is reputed to have said,
"We've got them right where we want them.
Now we can shoot in all directions!"

ACKNOWLEDGEMENTS

I want to thank the members of 17th Street Writers of Fort Lauderdale for their very helpful comments during the writing of *In All Directions*, particularly Anita, Christopher, Fatima, Gregory, Mona, Pat, Roy, and Stu—the irregulars.

PROLOG

A wormhole, 30 AU from
the Semi-Autonomous World Troy

A NON-HUMAN FLEET BEGAN DISGORGING FROM THE WORMHOLE.

Because of its location before the Scattered Disc of Troy's system, and due to the fact that the fleet waited until all of its ships were assembled, it was nearly a month before the human fleets close to the planet noticed it.

Firebase Zion, Company I, Third Battalion,
1st Marines, West Shapland
Semi-Autonomous World Troy

"First squad up!" Sergeant James Martin called as he approached his squad's area. Two nervous-looking strangers carrying rifles and full field packs followed him. The packs looked new.

It took little more than a minute for the ten Marines of his squad to gather in front of their leader. They cast curious glances at the new men.

"Listen up," Martin said. "We're a skosh bit under strength. Or we were. This is PFC William Horton." He indicated one of the strangers who stood off to one side behind him. "He's the replacement for Zion." A cloud briefly washed across his face at his mention of the Marine who'd been killed in an earlier action. He looked at Corporal William Button, the Second fire team leader. "Can't give him to you, Bill. Two Williams in the same fire team might make for confusion." To Horton, he said, "The William we've already got has been here longer, and he's got stripes on you. So if we use first names, you're Billy. Got that?"

Horton grimaced, but nodded and said, "All right, Sergeant, I'm Billy. But I'd rather just be 'Horton'."

"Good, that's settled. Mackie, he's replacing a man from your fire team, that makes him yours."

"But Sergeant Martin," Corporal John Mackie objected, "Zion was in First fire team, I've got Third."

"Shitcan that, Mackie. What was First fire team is now Third. You and Orndoff are still in the same fire team, and you're short-handed. I already gave you Cafferata, now you get Horton to get back to full strength. No more crap. Got it?"

"Yes, Sergeant," Mackie said. "You," he pointed a finger at Horton, then at his feet, "over here." He ignored the look Martin gave him.

"Continuing," Martin said, "Button, you get PFC Herbert Preston. Go," he told Preston, and gestured toward Corporal William Button, the leader of Second fire team.

Martin looked at his squad, at full strength for the first time since their initial combat on Troy. "You're probably wondering where these replacements came from. No, more Marines haven't joined us. Lieutenant Colonel Davis is reassigning support personnel to keep the rifle companies up to strength. Horton was a clerk in the battalion headquarters company, and Preston was a mechanic in the battalion motor pool."

He raised a hand and patted the air to quell any protests before they were voiced. "As you were, people," he said loudly. "No matter what their duty was yesterday, they're Marines. Remember, every Marine is a rifleman. It's been like that ever since Marines were climbing the rigging of wooden ships on water seas and firing down at the decks of enemy ships, shooting enemy officers and cannoneers. Every Marine goes to the rifle range every year to fire for requalification, so you know that they know how to shoot."

"But do they know how to duck?" Lance Corporal Hermann Kuchneister blurted.

"Don't sweat it, they'll catch on in a hurry," Corporal Joseph Vittori said.

"Duck, hell," Mackie said, looking askance at Horton. "Do they know how to snoop and poop?"

"As you were!" Martin roared. "They're Marines, they've been trained. They know what to do."

"Trained but inexperienced," Lance Corporal Cafferata whispered to Mackie.

Martin ignored that and other quiet remarks from members of the squad. "They're with us now," he said. "We're back up to strength. I want you to return to your positions and get acquainted with the new Marines." His mouth twisted before he added, "Your lives might depend on how well you know the new men."

✪

Their positions were three bunkers, one per fire team, inside the wire of Camp Zion, which was named after the first member of India Company to be killed in action on Troy.

"Inside, Horton," Mackie said when Third fire team reached their bunker.

Horton dropped into the beginning of the entrance tunnel, a meter-deep pit. The tunnel itself went in two sandbags deep before taking a ninety-degree turn for a meter and a half, then another ninety-degree turn to the interior of the bunker.

Mackie followed Horton while Cafferata and PFC Orndoff went around to the front of the bunker and sat on its forward edge, facing the land beyond the perimeter.

"Stow it there," Mackie said, pointing at an unoccupied section of wall. "There's the grenade sump." He pointed at a hole dug in the floor of a corner. Any hand-held explosive thrown into the bunker could be knocked into the hole and its explosion contained. That was the theory; none of the Marines ever wanted the chance to test it.

Horton dutifully dropped his pack where Mackie indicated, then uncertainly stood waiting, hunched over because of the low overhead.

Mackie studied his new man in the dim, uneven light that the bunker's firing aperture offered. "You were a clerk, huh?" he said before the silence became uncomfortable.

"That's right, Corporal Mackie."

"Just Mackie. Unless an officer is nearby. We don't stand much on formality here."

"Right, Corp—, ah, right, Mackie."

"Do you have *any* combat experience?"

Horton shook his head. "No."

"Did you even come under fire anytime?"

Another headshake, another, "No."

Mackie stared at him for a moment. "Pay attention to me, Cafferata, and Orndoff. Do what we do, and obey my orders immediately. That's your best chance of making it through alive and uninjured. I already lost one man. I don't want to lose another."

"Yes, Corp—,ah, yes, Mackie. I'll do my best."

Mackie nodded curtly. "Let's go topside and meet the rest of the fire team."

✪

Horton's meeting of the rest of the fire team was brief, not very in depth, and not in any particular order.

"Where are you from?"

"Illinois."

"Have you ever been in a rifle company before?"

"No."

"Are you married? Do you have a steady girl?"

"I used to, but she broke up with me right before we got orders to Troy."

Nobody remarked on that, but they all thought it was a bad sign. A Marine who just lost his woman might make a serious mistake that could get him or someone else killed. Or maybe it wouldn't be a mistake.

"Who were you with before Three/One?" Mackie asked before Cafferata and Orndoff could dwell on Horton's recent break up.

"I joined Three/One right out of school." They understood the school was Marine administrative training, not Horton's civilian school. And it begged a follow up question:

"How long have you been in?"

"Twenty-one months." Which explained why Three/One was his first duty station; he hadn't been in long enough to complete a tour at one station.

"How do you like getting assigned to the real Marines?" To most infantry Marines, anybody who wasn't a trigger-puller—infantry, recon, artillery, pilots and air crew of armed aircraft, and anybody else whose duties put them in the line of fire—wasn't a real Marine, no matter what uniform they wore or how much rank they had.

"Kind of nervous. It's why I enlisted in the Marines, but now that it's real...."

"Damn skippy, it's real. It doesn't get any realer than this."

"What did you qualify as on the range?"

"High Sharpshooter." That was the second highest marksmanship level.

"You've seen the vids of the Dusters?"

"Yes."

"They move too fast for you to aim at them, but you have to do better than just spray-and-pray," Ordnoff said. "Spray and pray," put out enough rounds fast enough and you're bound to hit something sooner or later.

Then it was time for chow. The sun had almost reached the horizon by the time First squad finished eating and moved into their overnight defensive positions, which were the same bunkers they slept in, the same bunkers facing the perimeter and the cleared ground beyond.

Overnight

"Have you stood much perimeter duty?" Mackie asked Horton once Third fire team was in its bunker; he'd assigned first watch to himself and the new man.

"Not since Infantry School." Horton swallowed to moisten his suddenly dry mouth.

Every new Marine, even cooks and bakers and clerks, went to Infantry School to learn how to be a rifleman before going on to whatever other school might be his destination. The women, many of whom were cooks and bakers and clerks and pilots, also went to Infantry School. If you didn't know how to fight as a rifleman, the Marines didn't want you.

"Then you probably need a refresher course," Mackie said. "The first thing about perimeter duty is knowing what's in front of you, so you can recognize anything that doesn't belong in the middle of the night."

"Right, I remember." Horton looked at Mackie's profile. "Look at all the shapes out there. Watch them as night falls so you know what they look like in the dark, so a shadow doesn't have to move for you to know if it belongs or not."

"That's right. You're doing a good job so far. Or you would be, if you were looking outboard instead of at me."

"Ulp! I—I'm sorry, Corporal Mackie. It's just that it's been...." Flustered, Horton jerked his head to the front and tried to memorize the shapes that were turning into shadows.

"I know, it's just that it's been so long since Infantry School." Mackie looked away from the darkening landscape to his newest man. "That's why I'm giving you a refresher course. Now pay attention and do it right."

Two hours later, Mackie woke Orndoff to take the watch while he and Horton got some sleep. Two more hours, and Orndoff woke Cafferata. After Mackie and Horton had four hours sleep, Cafferata woke them for another watch.

Half an hour into their second watch, Horton tapped Mackie's shoulder, pointed, and whispered, "Does that look right?"

Mackie couldn't tell exactly where Horton pointed, but he'd seen the same shadow jitter. "Wake Cafferata and Orndoff," he whispered back. He toggled his helmet comm to the squad freq and notified everyone awake that something was making movement at his eleven o'clock, distance undetermined.

Cafferata and Orndoff took their positions at the firing aperture. They'd made less noise waking and moving into position than Horton had in moving to wake them.

A couple of minutes later, Sergeant Martin came on the squad freq. "My motion detector shows multiple movements, two hundred and fifty meters out. They're all across the squad's front and lapping onto the rest of the platoon."

Seconds later, Second Lieutenant Henry Commiskey, the platoon commander, spoke on the platoon's all-hands freq. "Everyone is reporting movement all around the firebase, we're surrounded. That also means they're in a circular firing squad formation. Stay low, and they'll be shooting each other. The Skipper is ordering illum. Don't fire until the lights go on. Acknowledge." The other platoon commanders gave the same order.

Then began the ritual: junior men reported to fire team leaders that they heard and understood the company commander's order, fire team leaders reported to squad leaders, squad leaders to platoon commanders, and back to the company commander. It didn't take many seconds for every man in the company to report up the chain of command that he had received and understood the order.

"They're closing slowly," Martin said on the squad freq. "Maybe they don't realize we know they're there."

"Stand by in five," Captain Carl Sitter, India Company's commanding officer, said on the all-hands freq.

Five seconds later, there was a series of muffled *booms* from the middle of the firebase. Just a couple of seconds later, sharper *bangs* sounded in the sky above, and brilliant light flooded the ground outside the perimeter, exposing hundreds of nightmare forms coming toward the wire.

"*Fire!*" Sitter shouted, and all around Marines began blasting away with rifles, machine guns, and grenade launchers.

The Dusters were caught off guard, unaware that the humans had detected them, so they didn't start moving instantly when the flares turned the pre-dawn night into a flickering noon-day brightness. That cost them casualties. The rate of casualties slackened when they began jinking and dodging, too fast for the Marines to take aim.

"Don't shoot where they are," Mackie shouted over the clatter of his men's firing, "shoot where they're going to be!" He saw the flash of a Duster twisting to change its direction and fired a three-round burst into the space he expected it to head. One bullet clipped the base of the Duster's tail and spun it around. He fired off another three, and the Duster staggered, and tumbled to the ground, dropping its weapon as it fell.

He rapidly shot bursts into spaces he thought Dusters were headed into, but usually missed. In his peripheral vision he saw his men firing three-round bursts the same as he was. Most of their bursts also missed, but a few hit. It didn't seem to have much impact on the numbers coming at the perimeter.

Mackie was vaguely aware of projectile hits on the bunker's face, but the Dusters' aim was far off because of their own rapid movement, and nearly all of their shots missed the bunkers altogether.

"Incoming!" Captain Sitter shouted on the all-hands freq.

Over the cacophony of fire from the Marines and Dusters, Mackie made out the whistle of artillery rounds hurtling toward the ground. "Down!" he shouted, and ducked below the lip of the firing aperture.

"Get down!" he shouted again, and grabbed Horton by the arm and jerked; Horton was still up and firing his rifle.

"What?" Horton looked confused.

"Incoming!" The word was drowned out by the sudden eruption of artillery rounds exploding beyond the perimeter. The noise was so great that the impacts of fragments slamming into the front and top of the bunker were felt rather than heard. Mackie was looking away from the barrage, and was able to see the blur of a chunk of jagged metal that flashed through the aperture, to impact against the bunker's rear wall.

The barrage stopped, bringing the bunker to a stunned silence. The noise had been so great that Mackie felt as though his ears were stuffed with cotton. He yawned wide and worked his jaw side to side to clear his hearing. His body felt like it had just gone several rounds with a boxer from a higher weight class. It took a lot of effort for him to force himself up to look out.

"Up!" he shouted when he saw outside. He threw his rifle into his shoulder and began firing again. Almost instantly, Cafferata was also up and firing. Orndoff took a few seconds to rouse himself and resume fighting. Horton remained curled on the bunker's flooring, his eyes wide and mouth gaping.

The Dusters had closed to less than a hundred meters when the artillery barrage began. The concussions had broken some of their bodies, and shrapnel had scythed through many others. But there were so many to begin with that there were still more of them than there were Marines inside the perimeter. And the closest were almost to the wire.

"Get up!" Mackie shouted, and kicked Horton in the ribs, not sure the new man had yet recovered enough that he could hear. He fired a burst at a Duster that was leaping at the wire.

Horton stirred and looked up vaguely.

"Get up!" Another kick. Another burst hit a leaping Duster.

Horton rolled onto his hands and knees and slowly pushed himself up.

"Your weapon, numbnuts! Where's your rifle?" He knocked a Duster down, but it landed on the wire.

Horton looked dumbly down and spotted his rifle. He bent to pick it up, then moved to his firing position and started putting out unaimed bursts.

The lumination flares that had preceded the barrage were dropping close to the ground and burning out. Another round of flares burst overhead. The fresh light showed Dusters throwing themselves onto the wire, pinioning themselves to it, turning their bodies into bridges for other Dusters to scamper across. As Mackie's hearing began to return he heard the fierce, manic *cawing* of the Dusters. He added his voice to all those crying out, "They're inside the wire!"

A Duster raced to the bunker and flattened itself next to the side of the aperture. It shoved the muzzle of its rifle through the opening and began jerking the trigger. Mackie let go of his rifle with one hand and grabbed the barrel of the Duster's with his other hand. He yanked hard and pulled the alien soldier to the front. Cafferata shot it, and his burst threw the thing away.

More Dusters crossed the wire and closed on the fronts of the bunkers. Most of those Dusters were killed quickly, although they managed to wound or kill some Marines. Worse trouble was caused by Dusters that raced around to the rear of the bunkers, where the entrances were.

"Hector, cover the door," Mackie snapped when he saw Dusters racing too far to the side to be coming at the front; he thought they must be going between the bunkers.

Cafferata turned just in time to hear a scrabbling at the bunker's entrance. He didn't wait, but started shooting at the entrance, trying to angle his shots to ricochet around the first corner. He was rewarded by a warbling caw followed by a thump. He sped to the entrance and poked the muzzle of his rifle into it and fired another burst. An anguished *caw* answered.

In front, Mackie saw bodies piling up in front of the bunker, and fewer Dusters coming at him.

A change in the tempo and echoes of firing in the firebase gave testimony to many Dusters attempting to enter the bunkers from their rears. The *caws* and *skrees* of Dusters rang throughout, as did the cries and shouts of many Marines. An occasional shriek told of human casualties.

Mackie was turning to see if Cafferata needed help at the entrance when a yelp next to him spun him back. Orndoff was falling back with a blade of some sort protruding from his chest. Mackie looked past him just in time to see Horton put a burst into the face of the Duster whose bayonet stabbed Orndoff.

"Are you okay, Hector?" he shouted.

"I'm good, honcho," Cafferata shouted back.

Mackie knelt at Orndoff's side. Orndoff was struggling to breathe with the weight of the weapon pressing on his chest. "Take it easy, Marine," Mackie said. "I've cut myself worse than that shaving."

He grasped the Duster rifle to keep it from flopping over and tearing up the Marine's chest. Orndoff gasped in pain from the movement. A quick look showed Mackie how to detach the bayonet. He disengaged it, and tossed the alien rifle away. Orndoff wasn't wearing his gear belt; none of them were. Mackie scrabbled for one and pulled the field dressing out of it. He packed it around the bayonet where it penetrated Orndoff's chest, pressing down onto the wound, sopping up the blood. He grabbed another dressing and added it, doubling the thickness to stop the bleeding. He tied the bandages off with a third dressing.

"Stay there and don't move," Mackie ordered. "Doc'll be here be here most ricky-tick to take care of you."

Orndoff looked at him wide-eyed, and gave a shallow nod.

"Now I gotta get back to work." Mackie gave Orndoff's shoulder a squeeze, and stood to resume fighting.

"How's it look?" he asked Horton. He could see for himself that almost all of the Dusters in sight to the front of the bunkers were down—which was good, as Horton just shrugged in reply. Many of the Dusters lay twisted in ways that couldn't be comfortable, much less natural. Only a few were moving, and none of them seemed to pose a threat. Not even the still-live Dusters who had given themselves up to be bridges over the wire.

"Kill anyone that looks like a threat, and let me know if they mount another charge," Mackie said, clapping Horton on the back. He turned toward the entrance. "How's it going, Hector?"

"It's quiet for now. At least they don't seem to be trying to come in anymore."

Mackie listened for sounds of battle outside his fire team's bunker. He could hear sporadic gunfire and some shouts from human lungs. There weren't many of the caws and shrieks of the Dusters. He toggled on his helmet comm and called Sergeant Martin.

"What's going on out there?" he asked when he got his squad leader. "It's quiet here now, but Orndoff has a chest wound and needs the doc."

"The reports are that most of the Dusters are down," Martin replied. "Hang tight until a corpsman can get to you. Do you have Orndoff stabilized?"

Mackie looked at his wounded man. Even though he was still grimacing, he seemed to be breathing more easily, and hardly any blood was flowing from around the edges of the field dressings. "I think so. He doesn't look like he's going into shock."

"Good. Keep him that way. Look sharp, the Dusters might decide to hit us with another surprise. Martin out."

"Keep me posted," Mackie said, but he knew Martin was no longer listening.

He joined Cafferata at the entrance and listened to the sporadic sounds of fighting elsewhere in the compound, but none close to their bunker. "Keep alert," he said, then went to the front to look out with Horton.

Mackie studied the bodies littering the ground, some broken and dead, others injured. "Any of them moving toward us?" he asked.

"Maybe. Could be. I don't know."

"You better know. If one of them has an explosive and gets close enough to chuck it in, we're screwed. Got it?"

"Y-Yes, Corporal."

"It's Mackie. Just Mackie out here."

"Right. Sorry about that."

"Don't be sorry, just do it." Mackie thought of something. "Keep watching." He scuttled to the section of flooring where his gear was and rooted through it. In a moment he was back with his shaving mirror. Holding it at an angle, he stuck it through the aperture and looked to see if it showed any Dusters laying against the bunker's wall where they couldn't be seen. There weren't any either under the aperture or at the sides of the front.

He realized he hadn't heard any shooting or *caws* since he'd left Cafferata's side. "Either of you hear anything out there?" he asked.

"I've got nothing," Cafferata answered.

"I don't hear anything," Horton said.

Lieutenant Commiskey came up on the platoon all-hands freq. "It seems the excitement is over. Each squad, put a fire team out to make a sweep through the platoon's area to make sure we don't have anybody faking it."

While Martin was assigning First fire team to join in the sweep, a welcome voice spoke up outside the bunker's entrance. "It's Doc Hayden. I hear you've got a patient for me."

Camp Zion, Aftermath of the battle

THANKS TO SHARP-EYED WATCHERS, MOTION DETECTORS, THE TIMELY USE OF IL-lumination, and close in artillery, India Company suffered a scant ten casualties, two of them killed, during the night attack. PFC Orndoff was the only injury in Third platoon's First squad.

The Dusters were nearly all killed or wounded. The wounded ones had already been gathered into a makeshift open-air dispensary where the company's corpsmen were tending their wounds. Not that they could do much for them other than bandage bleeding wounds and splint broken limbs. They couldn't use any medications to reduce pain or fend off infection, because they had no idea of how the aliens' systems would react to human medicine. Some of the Dusters didn't get any more than the most rudimentary wound coverings—the Corpsmen thought their injuries were so severe they had no chance of surviving more than a few hours without treatment by their own medical personnel, who would know better how to deal with their wounds.

"They aren't very good fighters, are they?" PFC Horton said in the cold light of dawn, looking at the bodies laying on the ground around and between the bunkers, bodies the Marines were gathering into stacks like cordwood. They were like nothing he had ever seen in life.

They were man-sized, bent at the hip almost parallel to the ground, balanced on powerful-looking thighs over spindly lower legs that ended in wickedly taloned feet. Their arms looked to be half the length of their legs, and held rifle-like weapons in long-fingered hands. Feathery crests rose above their heads, and ran down the length of their spines to a fan of feathers at the ends of their tails. Their heads jutted forward on the long necks he'd seen whipping side to side during the attack. They had long jaws, filled with rows of sharp, conical teeth. They were naked other than for leathery straps bearing pouches.

Corporal Mackie shook his head. "Don't fool yourself. They got slowed down by the wire, and the concussion of the artillery barrage must have disoriented them. Besides, they had a damn hard time trying to get to us in our bunkers. They're much better fighters than you think." He looked into someplace only he saw. "We're lucky they only killed two Marines this time. They've killed a lot more before." His head shot at Horton. "Who the hell do you think this firebase is named after? A Marine who was in this fire team and got killed by a Duster, that's who. So don't you say they aren't good fighters. You're dead fucking wrong. They can kill you just as dead as I can!"

Horton abruptly took a step back, shocked by the fury in Mackie's voice and eyes. "I—I'm sorry, C-Corporal M-Mackie. I—I didn't mean anything."

Mackie grunted and turned away. He didn't correct Horton on calling him by his rank instead of by just his name.

"Knock off the grab-assing, people!" Staff Sergeant Ambrosio Guillen, the platoon sergeant, bellowed. He and Second Lieutenant Commiskey were returning from a debriefing at the company headquarters. "Let's get this area policed up. We have a ton of bodies to bury."

Mackie cast a glare at Guillen, he wasn't grab-assing. He snapped at Horton, "This one," and picked up the taloned feet of a nearby Duster. He squeezed the ankles and twisted them hard enough to grind the bones together; if the alien was faking it would react to the pain. It didn't react.

Horton picked the alien up by its shoulders. Ever since he and his fire team leader had first picked up a Duster, he'd been surprised at how light they were compared to a human. "Hollow bones," Mackie had explained. "We think they're some kind of bird analogue."

They were fifteen meters from the nearest collection point. This alien joined the twelve that were already there, stacked two high.

Sergeant Martin came by and counted the baker's dozen. "Start a new stack with that one. The Skipper wants them stacked by the dozen, to make it easier to tally them." He looked around at the few bodies still on the blood-stained ground behind the bunkers. "Go forward and start a new stack with those bodies. I'll have Vittori's fire team finish up here."

"Right, honcho," Mackie said. He jerked his head at Horton and headed to the area between the bunkers and the wire perimeter. "Watch close, Hector," he said to Lance Corporal Cafferata as he passed their bunker. Cafferata sat on top of the bunker keeping watch over the land beyond. "You're just lucky Orndoff is out of it. If we were full strength, you'd be out here stacking Dusters along with me."

"Hey, sentry's dirty duty, bu they, somebody's got to do it."

"Keep that up, and I'll have you spell me and Horton all by your lonesome."

"Sure thing. Hey, any word yet on how Orndoff's doing?"

Mackie shook his head. "I haven't had a chance to check on him. I don't think Sergeant Martin has either. If Lieutenant Commiskey knows, he's not sharing."

Cafferata grimaced. Not being told how a wounded man was doing generally wasn't good news.

There were more bodies between the bunkers and the wire than there had been behind the bunkers—it had been a Duster slaughterhouse.

"Let's get started," Mackie told Horton. "We'll start with those three," he said, pointing at a trio of corpses that were already almost lined up.

Horton grabbed the shoulders of the nearest one and lifted. Then he looked to see why Mackie wasn't lifting the legs.

Mackie was standing immobile, looking beyond the wire. "We aren't going to be stacking those," he said softly.

Horton blanched when he looked to see what Mackie meant. There were bodies beyond the wire, bent and cast aside the same as the bodies inside it, and hung up on it. There were also bits and pieces of bodies, remnants of bodies that had been blown apart by the artillery barrage; they wouldn't stack.

Cafferata saw what Mackie was looking at. "We're going to need buckets to clean that up," he called.

"Buckets, yeah," Mackie said numbly. He bent to help Horton with the whole bodies inside the wire.

When the stacking of Duster dead was done, including the wounded who had been put aside in the makeshift dispensary and died of their wounds, there were more than three hundred of them. An additional fifty-eight were still alive and receiving rudimentary medical care. The bits and pieces of the Dusters blown apart by the artillery might have amounted to another fifty, or even more.

For centuries, the rule of thumb had been, attackers need to outnumber defenders by a margin of three to one in order to take a fortified position.

The Dusters had outnumbered the Marines at Camp Zion by nearly four to one.

"Damn," Mackie whispered when he heard the enemy count.

✪

Heavy equipment came in while the bodies and body parts were being collected. They dug trenches to bury the Dusters, and filled them in once the bodies and parts were deposited. The regimental chaplain said a few words over the grave site, in an attempt to invoke whatever god or gods the Dusters might or might not believe in.

Sick bay, Camp Zion

"Why did you leave the bayonet in him, Corporal?" asked Lieutenant Middleton Elliot, the battalion surgeon.

"Sir," Mackie answered, trying to keep "That's a dumb question" out of his voice and expression, "I didn't know what kind of damage had been done inside him. It's possible that the bayonet was keeping him from serious hemorrhage."

"I see they're making Marine junior NCOs smarter these days," the doctor said, nodding. "That was the right thing to do, even if it wasn't necessary. The bayonet jammed in PFC Orndoff's ribs, all that was cut was surface muscle. No internal organs, no important blood vessels. But if it had gone in two more inches, he could have been in serious trouble and you leaving the bayonet in might have been the only thing that kept him alive.

"Good job, Marine. Now get him out of my sick bay, I need the bed."

"Thank you, sir, I need him. You can have the bed." *You and that cute nurse I noticed looking at you when I came in,* he thought. To Orndoff, he said, "Come on, Harry. Let's get out of here."

"And just when I was getting comfortable."

First squad, third platoon's area

Neither of the killed Marines were from Third platoon; they were relieved that the platoon had only suffered three wounded, and that all were quickly returned to duty. In addition to Orndoff, Second squad's Lance Corporal James Burns and Third squad's Corporal Thomas Prendergast were wounded. Prendergast's wound was the worst of the three, his left humerus was broken—fortunately, it was a clean fracture. But he'd be on light duty for three or four weeks. He couldn't patrol, but he could stand sentry duty. Which was fine with the members of his fire team, because that meant they didn't have to patrol as often as they would have had his injury healed more quickly.

Prendergast notwithstanding, the rest of the Marines in the platoon had to go on patrols.

Seven kilometers southwest of Camp Zion

"What do you have, Mackie?" Sergeant Martin asked. He headed for his point fire team, which had stopped advancing.

"You tell me, Sergeant," Corporal Mackie answered. "It looks like a hell of a lot of Dusters were here recently."

Martin joined Mackie at the edge of an area cleared of underbrush, the first such they'd seen in the thin forest the squad had been patrolling through. Before examining the ground, he glanced about to see where Mackie's Marines were; they were set out in defensive positions, providing security.

"Vittori, take your fire team fifty meters up and set in," Martin ordered. "Button, watch our rear." He watched while the two fire teams moved into position. Satisfied that security was in place, he told Mackie, "Bring your men. Let's take a closer look." He made sure his helmet cam was running.

"Third fire team, up," Mackie called. "Go twenty or thirty meters in from us and look sharp," he said when they joined him and Martin. "We don't know if any Dusters are still in this area, or if they'll return." He looked at the squad leader.

"This looks like it might be a bivouac area," Martin said. "We're going in. Keep ahead of us. Twenty meter intervals."

"Aye aye," Lance Corporal Cafferata said. He and the two PFCs moved into the clearing.

The ground was barren except for slight traces of green where growth was starting to come back. Sunlight filtering through the treetops dappled the ground, making it more shaded than sunny. Martin examined the canopy and found it denser than he'd supposed, which could explain why this bivouac hadn't been spotted by a visual search. But an infrared search should have found it; it looked large enough to be the staging location for the entire force that had attacked Camp Zion three days earlier.

"Do you think these are scratches?" Mackie asked. "From their claws, I mean."

Martin nodded. "That's what it looks like to me." He took images of the scratches from multiple angles and heights.

"They cook their food." He recorded a rectangular scorch mark. "If this was a human site, I'd say this is where their kitchen was." Off to one side a muddy area bore circular gouges. "Dish washing," he hazarded.

A little farther and they found rows of two centimeter diameter holes, evenly spaced about a meter and a half apart side to side, three meters going deeper.

"Holes for tent posts maybe?" Mackie said.

Martin shrugged. "Could be. Or maybe they sleep on roosts. They are kind of bird-like. Let's see how many there are." He started giving orders immediately. "Cafferata, come here. Mackie, take your other men and find the far end of these holes. Count the rows. Cafferata, you go that way until you run out of holes. Count them, starting with that one." He pointed to the hole he wanted Cafferata to start counting on. "I'll go this way. Questions?"

"No," Mackie said. Cafferata shook his head.

"Let's do it." Martin stepped off

"Orndoff," Mackie said when he reached his men, "see the rows of holes? Count them, beginning with that one." He pointed at the first row beyond where Orndoff stood. "The first number is seventeen. Got it?"

"Start counting there, first number is seventeen. Got it."

"I'll take your flank. Move out."

It didn't take long to count the holes. Multiply the rows by the number in a row, and there were 576 holes. They also found three more scorched rectangles, each accompanied by a muddy area. More kitchens?

"All right," Martin said on the squad freq, "we either have 144 tents or 288 roosts, and four possible kitchens. Mackie, stay in place until Cafferata joins you. Then split in pairs and check the perimeter, see if you find any latrines."

Cafferata and Orndoff went one way, Mackie took Horton the other.

"Whew!" Horton exclaimed before they reached the corner.

"I smell it too," Mackie said. "It's like ammonia." He followed his nose to a stretch of disturbed dirt. There were a pair of holes at each end of it. Did the Dusters have a roost mounted over the latrine, like Humans used a platform with holes in it?

"Looks like they covered it over," Mackie said. "Let's go, this shit is burning my eyes."

"Mine too," Horton said.

They found three more along the side.

"We found four probable latrines," Mackie reported when they rejoined Martin.

"So did we, four of them," Cafferata said. "Real stinkers."

"What about tracks leading in?" Martin asked.

"Nothing like a beaten path, nothing that would indicate several hundred Dusters arriving in a formation. I did see some paths that looked like they'd been used recently."

"There was a bigger one that might be leading to Camp Zion," Cafferata said.

"Come with me," Martin said after a moment's thought. "I want to get vid of one of the latrines. And the bigger path you saw." That last was to Cafferata.

"We don't have to dig one up, do we?" Mackie asked.

"Not without orders from higher-higher. The science people might want to dig one up, though."

After getting vid of the supposed latrine, "Too bad we can't capture the smell," Martin observed. He called in a report describing what the squad had found, and sent the vids and other images he'd taken. His report concluded with, "It looks like they filtered in from multiple directions. There's no sign of whatever was in the postholes."

Captain Sitter took hardly any time to think before he ordered them to follow the bigger path, to see if it led to the Marine base. "I don't want just one squad to investigate the infiltration paths, that's a job for a larger unit, or for Force Recon."

The large path led to within half a kilometer of Camp Zion, where the Dusters appeared to disperse to take positions for their assault.

Troy Space, Partway From the Wormhole
to the Semi-Autonomous World Troy

AMPHIBIOUS READY GROUP 17 WASN'T DEAD; ON LIFE SUPPORT WOULD BE A more accurate descriptor of its condition. Five of the fifteen troop ships in the ARG had been destroyed by the Duster missile attack, as had two of the four support ships. Five of the other transports were injured—three would need to be towed to Troy orbit, the other two could limp in on their own. Only five of the transports remained whole after the attack.

Five troop ships whole, five injured, five destroyed. Nobody in the amphibious ready group found solace in the symmetry.

The fast attack carrier NAUS *Rear Admiral Isaac C. Kidd* was the only remaining warship of the detachment from Task Force 8 that had been deployed to escort ARG 17. Her space fighters had retrieved the surviving pilots of the SF6 Meteor interceptors that had died defending the ARG from the attacking missiles, and recovered the bodies of those pilots who hadn't.

Shuttles from the surviving troop ships were making their way from killed ship to wounded ship to killed ship seeking survivors. On every vessel there were some soldiers or crewmen who'd made it to stasis units in time. In a few cases, entire platoons remained intact. It took several days to locate all the survivors and transfer them to viable quarters on their wounded ship, or onto others that had space. Once everybody was rescued and bodies recovered, the remnants of ARG 17 and its escort would group into a rough formation and began the slow limp to Troy orbit, and the elevator ride planetside. The exception was the undamaged NAUS *Diamunde*, which filled with ready units and headed for Troy.

Company commander's office,
Alpha Troop, First of the Seventh Mounted Infantry,
NAUS Juno Beach

The amphibious assault ship *Juno Beach* had been sorely injured in the missile attack, and needed to spend months undergoing repairs in a shipyard before she could join another ARG. Still, she was able to make the short trip to Troy under her own power. Returning to the shipyards of Earth would require a tow from an uninjured ship.

Half of the troops who had embarked on the *Juno Beach* and survived the attack were still aboard her; the other survivors had been transferred to other ships that had made it through the one-sided battle. The units transferred included Alpha Troop, First of the Seventh Mounted Infantry, and the battalion's command group, which went to the Landing Platform, Shuttle, NAUS *Diamunde*.

Second Lieutenant Theodore W. Greig, commander of Second platoon, Alpha Troop, and his platoon sergeant, Sergeant First Class Alexander M. Quinn, stood in front of their company commander's desk. They weren't quite at attention.

"You didn't lose a single man?" Captain Henry C. Meyer asked incredulously.

"That's right, sir." A hint of pride was audible in Greig's voice. "No one was killed, not a single soldier of mine was even injured."

Meyer slowly shook his head. "Amazing," he said softly, and turned his head to look at the company's top dog, First Sergeant Powhatan Beaty.

Beaty's head dipped marginally in nod. "Second was the only platoon to come through intact, sir," he said. He bestowed a look of approval on Greig and Quinn.

"Lieutenant, Sergeant," Meyer said, turning back to them, "When we make planetfall, I'm going to rely heavily on you—at least until I get replacements for the other platoons' losses." He grimaced. Eight dead and seventeen wounded out of his 150 officers and men, before they could even make contact with the enemy. Before they could see them even. Well, at least most of his officers and men had made it to stasis units before the ship was holed and most of her atmosphere vented into space. He twisted his shoulders to loosen them from the tension that suddenly hit when he thought of his losses.

"The *Diamunde* is taking us to the geosync elevator station. Second platoon will be the first element of the battalion to make planetfall. Once there, you'll be under the command of the senior Army officer planetside.

The *Diamunde* will be in orbit around Troy before ship's dawn tomorrow. I need you to have your platoon at the debarcation station for transit to the elevator at 0530, ship's time. The enlisted mess will begin serving at 0430, so your platoon will have adequate time to eat before you board transfer shuttles. Personal items are to be stowed in containers with each man's name and army ID number. All weapons and field equipment will be carried into the shuttles by each man. That includes company-level crew-served weapons. Right. Did I mention Second platoon will be reinforced by a mixed weapons squad? Well, you are. Sergeant Gumperts is leading it, he'll join the two of you once he finishes organizing his squad.

"For the big picture, Troy has two continents, Shapland and Eastern Shapland." He shook his head. "Not real big on imaginative place names here. Anyway, the Army's area of operations is Shapland. The Marines are on Eastern Shapland. In addition to us, the NAU Forces headquarters is on Shapland, and some Navy fighter squadrons and a couple of Marine squadrons are there to provide close air support for us.

Questions?" he finished with a wry twist to his mouth. If he'd already told them everything he knew about the mission, he couldn't answer any questions.

"Yes, sir," Greig surprised his company commander. "What are the Marines doing? Do they have the situation under control?"

"The last I heard, and this isn't necessarily the latest intelligence, is that the Marines have beaten off enemy attacks and it's pretty quiet. They're just conducting mop-up operations." He gave the lieutenant a look that said, *Please don't have any more questions.*

"Thank you, sir."

"If that's all, you're dismissed."

Greig didn't exactly come to attention, but he did salute Meyer before turning about and leading Quinn out of the captain's small office.

"So what do you think, sir?" Quinn asked when they were far enough that Meyer couldn't overhear.

"If the Marines say all they're doing now is mopping up, it's probably fairly hot planetside."

Well deck, Landing Platform, Shuttle Diamunde

"Close it up," Bo'sun's Mate Thomas Gehegan called out. "Belly to back, back to belly. Keep 'em close and stay between the yellow lines!"

"Right, 'belly to back,'" Third squad's PFC Richard J. Gage said to PFC Nicholas Boquet, the man to his front in Second platoon's line. "Only a swabbie would want men to line up belly to back."

"Just make sure you keep your distance, Gage," Boquet said. "If I feel anything poking me, it better be your gear."

"What kind of gear you talking about?" PFC Jacob Sanford asked from his position behind Gage.

"The hard kind," Boquet said.

"There's hard and then there's hard," Sanford said with a laugh.

"Let's have some quiet in the line," Gehegan called out again. "Pay attention. Back to belly, belly to back, stay between the yellow lines."

"I still say only a swabbie would say that," Gage softly repeated. Boquet and Sanford laughed quietly.

Not all the soldiers were in spirits as high as Gage, Bouquet, and Sanford. They'd breakfasted on steak and eggs. Some in the troop had enough of a sense of history to know that steak and eggs was the traditional breakfast the Navy served to Marines and soldiers about to make a landing against an entrenched enemy.

"Knock off the chatter, troops," Staff Sergeant Albert O'Connor shouted.

There was little more chatter as Second platoon trooped single file between the yellow lines under the watchful eyes of several bo'sun's mates whose job it was to keep anybody from wandering off and getting lost among the plethora of orbit-to-surface and intra-orbit craft that filled the well deck.

"Tighten it up, troops," Sergeant First Class Quinn shouted when the platoon filed into an intra-orbital shuttle. Not that they needed to cram in; the shuttle could accommodate half a company, so there was plenty of elbow room for one reinforced platoon. Quinn's order was more force of habit than necessity.

The shuttle's hatch was closed and sealed when the last soldier was aboard, and it trundled to the sally port that was used when only one shuttle was launching, so that the entire well deck didn't need to be evacuated and then atmosphere pumped back in after the launch. The sally port was an airlock large enough to hold a single shuttle. Seal the sally port's hatch behind the shuttle, pump out the air, open the outer hatch, and a piston ejected the shuttle with enough force to propel it a hundred meters in a few seconds. At that safe distance, the coxswain piloting the shuttle would fire its engine and aim it at the elevator.

The-ship-to-elevator trip took half an hour. Once there, the shuttle docked at the elevator station and station crew sealed the egress tunnel to the shuttle's hatch. Bo'sun's mate James Byrnes "swam" through the egress tunnel to the hatch and opened it to enter the shuttle. Three more sailors followed him.

"Listen up, people," Byrnes said loudly enough to be heard throughout the shuttle. "By now you've probably noticed you're no longer under gravity. So to get you safely from here to the elevator, we're going to clip you to a guide line. I know you've all done this before, so I won't bore you with the standard safety lecture. Let's just get you clipped to the line and haul you aboard." Actually, he didn't know whether or not everybody in second platoon had transited from an intra-orbit shuttle to an elevator station—in fact, most of them hadn't. But he had orders to get them aboard as fast as possible because they were needed planetside.

Nobody suffered more than a minor bruise getting from their seats on the shuttle, to the egress tunnel, to the platform, to the elevator cabin, to their seats. The movement was counted as a major success.

Elevator to Troy

Gravity was restored in the station as soon as the shuttle disconnected and began its return to the *Diamunde*. It was only a quarter G, but even that small amount of pull was enough to let the soldiers know beyond doubt which way was "up" and which was "down." That prevented enough abdominal distress that nobody lost the hearty breakfast he'd eaten so recently. Second platoon wasn't in the station for long; an elevator cab was already docked and waiting for them. Still linked together, they were escorted into the cab and strapped into seats. Byrnes looked them over to make sure everybody was properly secured, then stood by the cab's entrance.

"Gravity will gradually increase as you approach planetside," he said, "until you'll be under a full G by the time you get there. When you disembark, good hunting." He essayed a salute before backing out of the cab and dogging its hatch. Only when the soldiers could no longer hear him he said softly, "Better you than me doing the hunting."

Nobody actually floated out of their seats as the cab plunged toward the surface of Troy, although several of Second platoon's soldiers later swore they were in free fall on the ride down. Lieutenant Greig took advantage of the period of inactivity to review the orders Captain Meyer had given him before his platoon left the *Juno Beach*.

On landing at the McKinzie Elevator Base, outside Troy's capital city of Millerton, the platoon would board the Marine vehicles waiting for them and be transported to a location two hundred and fifty kilometers northeast of the city where they would establish security for the battalion headquarters company, the first elements of which would follow when the *Diamunde* brought them. Over the ensuing two days, the rest of the First of the Seventh would reach the surface and join second platoon and the lead headquarters elements. In the meanwhile, a compliment from the Navy Construction Battalion would begin building a forward base for the battalion.

What he hadn't been told in that briefing was that a platoon from 10th Brigade's Mobile Intelligence company was also part of the initial complement, and would coordinate its activities with second platoon's. Greig had yet to meet First Lieutenant Archie Miller, the recon platoon's CO. The Mobile Intel platoon had already made planetfall via Navy shuttles, the same way the Marines had in the initial landing.

McKinzie Elevator Base

"Who's in command there?" a gruff voice shouted as Second platoon disgorged from the elevator cab.

A soldier detached himself from the group and headed toward the Marine who'd called. "I am. Lieutenant Greig. Who're you?"

"I'm Gunnery Sergeant Stewart, sir. I'm the man responsible for transporting you and your do- uh, sojers to where the squid CBs are building you a base."

If Greig noticed the "do-" he didn't acknowledge the "doggies" it implied, a slur on the Army.

But SFC Quinn, who joined his officer in time to hear Stewart name himself did. He gave the Marine a hostile glare.

Stewart looked blandly back at him.

"How many men you got, Mr. Greig? And crew served weapons?" Stewart asked, glancing toward the elevator base and noticing a machine gun.

"Fifty men, including Sergeant Quinn and myself. The weapons squad has one M-69, two M-40s, and two M-5Cs."

Stewart nodded sagely. "You'll probably need them. Especially the M-69." The M-69 "Scatterer" was a Gatling gun-type weapon, capable of firing two thousand rounds per minute. It had already been used to good effect by the Marines. "Right over there now," he pointed fifty meters away at a line of four skirted, armored vehicles. All of them spouted the barrel of a weapon, but two showed multiple barrels, some much bigger, "that's your transportation. Two Hogs and four Scooters. They're air cushioned, so the ride'll be smooth almost regardless of the terrain."

"I've ridden an amphib before, Sergeant," Greig said.

"Yeah, I imagine you have. But have your men?"

Greig nodded, conceding the point. "Only some of them."

"Now, fifty men you say? That includes your weapons crews?"

"Yes, Sarge. The weapons squad is thirteen men."

"Right. Split them up. I want half of them in one Scooter, the rest in another—the weapons take a lot of space. Your platoon has three squads?" Without waiting for an answer, he continued, "Put one and a half squads in each of the Scooters. Put your platoon sergeant and radioman with half of your weapons squad in the rear Hog. You and the rest of your weapons ride up front with me. That'll give just about everybody room to stretch out a bit. The normal load for Scooters and Hogs is more than that.

Got it?"

"Got it, Sarge."

"With all due respect, Sir, it's Gunny, not 'Sarge'."

Midway Between Millerton and
the Forward Base Under Construction

"WHAT WAS THAT?" SECOND LIEUTENANT GREIG YELPED WHEN THE HOG HE was in jolted violently.

"I'd say we just got hit by something," Gunny Stewart said calmly as he reached for the comm link to the convoy commander's compartment and listened as the lieutenant in it gave orders to the vehicles. He could also hear the commander of the lead Hog, the one he and Greig were riding. What he heard gave him warning to grab a handhold to steady himself as the armored vehicle began jinking and jerking violently in evasive maneuvers.

The Hog shuddered as its thirty-millimeter main gun spat a burst of explosive rounds. A lighter tinkling testified that the Hog's fifty-caliber guns were also spraying the surrounding area. He faintly heard firing from the other vehicles in the convoy.

Grieg didn't have the same warning Stewart had, and was thrown from his web seating when the Hog began its violent maneuvering. The gunnery sergeant reached out an arm to grab Greig's jacket collar and jerk him back onto his seat.

"Strap in and hold on, Lieutenant," he said.

"Th-thanks."

Reverberating pings and thuds told of enemy fire hitting the Hog, but nothing penetrated the vehicle's armor—yet.

"Do you have comm with your people?" Stewart had to shout to be heard above the bangs and rattles of incoming and outgoing fire, and the roaring of the maneuvering Hog's engine.

"I ran a comm check as soon as we boarded," Greig shouted back.

"That was then. If you still have comm, tell them we're under attack. But hold tight, we'll get them out of this." He continued listening, unable to see outside—the armored vehicles had no windows or periscopes in the troop cabin. The vehicles had periscopes for the vehicle commanders and drivers, and the Hogs for the gunners, but that was all the visibility anybody had with the hatches closed.

Crew Cabin, Hog 1-3-B

"Damn, but they're fast!" shouted Corporal Donald L. Truesdale as he swiveled his quad-fifty, spraying fifty-caliber rounds at the side of the hill the aliens were scrambling down. The jinking and jerking of the Hog's evasive maneuvers constantly threw his aim off, and most of his bursts went high or wide or plowed into the dirt in front of the aliens.

"Fire shorter bursts, Truesdale," Staff Sergeant William E. Shuck, the vehicle commander, ordered.

"Git me more ammo," Sergeant Phillip Gaughn called to the loader, Lance Corporal Fernando L. Garcia.

"It's in your bin," Garcia shouted back; the automatic-filler bin next to the thirty-millimeter main gun was filled almost to the top with rounds. At Gaughn's current rate of fire, it would be a few more minutes before Garcia needed to top it off.

"Run 'em over?" the driver, Sergeant James I. Poynter shouted at Shuck.

Shuck looked through his periscope and saw, behind a thin screen of slender trees, a knot of about a dozen Dusters fifty meters ahead and slightly to the side of the Hog. Some of the Dusters were firing rifle-like weapons, others were assembling what looked like a crew served weapon that might be big enough to do damage to the Marine armored vehicles.

"Smash 'em!" Shuck snapped.

"Yahoo!" Poynter bellowed. He stomped on the accelerator and yanked the steering yoke to the left, aiming straight at the cluster of aliens, who looked up, startled at the sudden roar coming at them.

The aliens started to scramble out of the way when the Hog was ten meters away, but not all of them made it. Four or five got sucked under the air cushioned vehicle and were shredded by the gravel and debris being flung about by the powerful fans that lifted the Hog off the ground. So did the big weapon they were mounting.

"Turn about," Shuck ordered, and Poynter twisted the yoke, spinning the Hog around on its axis. "Head for those small boulders!" he said when he saw an area covered with stones up to the size of a soccer ball. "Squat on them."

"Aye aye," Poyter shouted gleefully. He sped the Hog to the small field of boulders. There, he vectored the fans to blow straight down and applied enough power for them to lift the Hog an extra dozen centimeters.

Large rocks and small boulders sprayed out in all directions from under the vehicle. Many of them slammed into Dusters unable to dodge them, tearing off limbs, tails, heads, plowing holes through bodies.

"What's happening?" Greig shouted. He let go of a handhold with one hand to grab Stewart's arm to get his attention and shouted his question again.

"It sounds like the Dusters are getting slaughtered," Stewart shouted back.

Moments later the only sounds were the roars of the vehicles' engines and the blasting of their weapons; there wasn't any more incoming fire from the Duster ambush. The convoy didn't stop to deal with the Duster casualties.

"What about the enemy bodies?" Greig asked. "Should we just leave them there like that? Shouldn't we collect their weapons and check the bodies for documents?"

"Let 'em police up after themselves," Stewart said. "Besides, if we unass from these vehicles, any of them still able to shoot will get some of us. And they never seem to have documents. Even if we could read their chicken scratching."

Advance Firebase One, Under Construction

The scene that greeted Greig and Sergeant First Class Quinn when they dismounted from the armored Hogs was one of controlled chaos. Thick lines of dirt berms were piled man-high on the west side of the construction area, opposite the direction the convoy had come from. Ferrocrete cladding had been laid on some of the berms, and a machine was busily laying ferrocrete on another section of dirt berm. Other machines were piling more sections of earthen berm, yet more were digging holes. In the already-finished sections it looked like finishing touches were being put on the entrances to bunkers that were built into the berm. Men in dirty uniforms bustled about, supervising the machines delivering materials from one location to another, or supervising other men. There were the tops of a few more bunkers inboard from the berm. A large tent stood in the middle of the complex. A spindly tower sprouting antennas, with rotating dishes near its top—Greig identified them as radar, infrared, and other detection devices—was twenty meters to one side of the large tent. A more substantial looking tower topped by a basket with a man in it was an equal distance on the other side of the tent. A spike rose from the side of the basket, flying the flag of the North American Union. In all, it looked like the base when finished would cover more than twenty acres.

Greig found the site surprisingly quiet despite all the activity.

"You must be Greig," a middling-big man said, extending a hand to shake. His uniform was as dirty as everybody else's. Given his age, probably mid-fifties; Greig would have taken him for a chief petty officer had it not been for the gold oak leaves on his collar points. "Welcome to Firebase Anonymous."

"Yes, sir," Greig said. He started to salute, then extended his hand to shake.

Stewart made the introductions. "Mr. Greig, this is Lieutenant Commander William Harrison. He's the engineer in charge of building this base for you."

"Pleased to meet you, sir. Anonymous?"

Harrison grinned. "I don't know how you do it in the Army, but in the Navy and Marines, we name our forward bases after heroes, usually dead ones. We don't have either yet, so it's up to you to name this place. So unless you brought a name with you, we call this place Firebase Anonymous One."

"Ah, yes, sir. I'm glad to hear that. I mean, no heroes or dead."

"We've been here for five days," Harrison said, clamping a hand on Greig's shoulder to lead him toward a finished section of berm. "And this is all we've had time to accomplish so far. But now that you're here, I can take my people off security duty and put them to work constructing, and the pace will pick up dramatically. I see that Chief Cronin has your people well in hand. He'll see to getting them settled in and chowed down." He waved a hand at the tent. "That's our temporary mess hall. One table is designated as officers' and chiefs' mess. You and your platoon sergeant will join my top people and me for meals—allowing for who's on duty."

Looking back at his platoon, Greig saw a burly man standing next to SFC Quinn and gesturing, evidently giving information and instructions. Looking around more, he asked, "What about quarters? Where are they?"

"We spent a couple of days roughing it, bedding down on the ground. Since then we've taken to sleeping in the bunkers. Except for the ammo bunkers, that could be damn dangerous. We're still roughing it, the cots we were promised haven't been delivered yet." He shrugged, as though cots were irrelevant. "Defensive positions right now are more important than quarters, so we're concentrating on the berm and fighting positions. Plus ammo bunkers, of course."

They reached a finished section of berm and Harrison ducked into a bunker, drawing Greig along with him. The entryway had an open blast door on the outside, closely followed by two ninety-degree turns, and another blast door, also open, on the inside. An aperture, wide enough to allow three men to fire rifles through it at the same time—or one rifleman plus a machine gun—was in the center of the wall facing outward. Against each side wall, an open bin with dividers served as lockers for the bunker's occupants. A thin mattress lay on top of each of the lockers. A second bunk was half a meter above the lower. The floor sloped toward a corner of the back wall, with a sump hole at the lowest point.

"A grenade sump?" Greig asked.

"You got it. So far the Dusters haven't used grenades, or any other hand-throwable explosives that we've heard of. But you never know. Better to be safe.

"Now, look out here." Harrison guided Greig to the aperture.

Greig stooped slightly to see through the opening in the front of the bunker. He saw scorched ground stretching three hundred meters to a line of scraggly trees, the face of a thin forest. Small boulders, none larger than an athletic ball, speckled the barren ground.

"The day before we got here," Harrison said, "the Marines bombed a square kilometer with Dragon's Breath."

Greig whistled. Dragon's Breath was a fiery weapon so horrendous it was banned for use against people. It was, however, still used sometimes to clear ground, sometimes even enemy-held cropland, although that use was generally frowned upon, especially if there was a civilian population that might starve from loss of the crops.

"Nobody's going to get close to Firebase Anonymous without us knowing they're on their way.

Just then Harrison's comm squawked at him, "Incoming from the west, fifteen klicks."

"Let's see what that's about," Harrison said, heading for the bunker's exit. Outside, he headed at a brisk pace for a bunker that barely showed above ground level. "Command post," he said over his shoulder to Greig, who was scrambling to catch up.

The CP bunker was easily twice the size of the fighting bunker Greig had just seen. A long table along one wall held workstations, not all of which Greig immediately recognized—he thought some of them must have construction or engineering functions that he wasn't familiar with. A man and two women were bent over three of the stations.

"What'cha got for me?" Harrison asked, leaning in to look over the shoulder of one of the techs.

"Three aircraft," she answered. "Unfamiliar design. But they look human."

"Defense?"

"Only one AA is operational," said another tech. "It's locked onto the nearest aircraft."

"They've started orbiting, sir," the first tech said.

"Comm, any contact?" Harrison asked the third tech.

"Not on any Navy or Marine freq. I'm trying Army now." Seconds later, "Bingo."

"Put it up."

"Aye-aye." She touched something and a voice came out of a speaker.

"...ee Bee base, this is NAUA Mike India Papa dot Nine Bravo, orbiting twelve klicks from your location. Do you hear me? Come on, guys. I know you see me, you've got a lock on my lead aircraft."

Harrison picked up a mike. "Mike India Papa, this is Charlie Bravo Actual. Where the hell'd you come from?"

"Charlie Bravo Actual, been doing our job—reconnoitering. What do you think?"

"Advance to be recognized, Mike India Papa Bravo." Harrison put the mike back down. "I've seen the Dusters and heard their voices. No way one of them could speak good human. Were you expecting a Mobile Intel platoon?"

"Yeah, but I thought they'd follow us on the ground, or already be here when we arrived."

✪

Fifteen minutes later three P-43 Eagles, bristling with sensor antennas and weapons, were settled in the middle of the compound and the twenty enlisted members of the First platoon of the 9th Infantry Division's mobile intelligence company were forming up in front of their aircraft.

A tall soldier with blackened lieutenant's bars on the collars of a cruddy shirt walked to where Harrison and Greig stood in front of the CP bunker. "Sir, I'm First Lieutenant Archie Miller," he said, waving a casual salute at Harrison. "I'm in nominal charge of that band of reprobates you see behind me. We're First platoon, 9th Mobile Intel Company."

"And I'm Lieutenant Commander Bill Harrison. I'm in charge of building this here base. Until it's finished and I turn it over to the Army,

I own it. That makes me your landlord. This," he jerked a thumb at Greig, "is Second Lieutenant Ted Greig. He's base personnel, responsible for security here, and for running patrols out there. You and yours are TAD here." Temporary Additional Duty, on loan, not permanent personnel. Harrison gave a wry smile at his men being labeled as TAD. "That sort of makes him your superior officer, even though you outrank him."

"That so?" Miller stuck a hand out for Greig to shake. "Glad to meet'cha, Louie."

Greig took Miller's hand, and didn't flinch at Miller's crushing grip. He knew his hand would be sore later, but he wasn't going to give the MI officer the satisfaction.

"So, Bossman, Whaddya want us to do first?" He gave Greig's hand a final squeeze before releasing it.

"How about a report on what you found? While you're doing that," he looked at Harrison, "I imagine the commander can have someone show your people where to stow their things."

"Chief Cronin's taking care of that right now." Harrison nodded in the direction of the MI enlisted men, where Chief Petty Officer Cronin was already taking them in hand. He sniffed. "While he's at it, I'm sure he'll also introduce them to the shower point. If you've been out there snooping and pooping, I expect they'd like to sluice off the accumulated crud. After that, it'll be chow call for you and yours.

"In the meantime, let's get you settled in. You can begin briefing Mr. Greig while you're getting your gear stowed and yourself cleaned up."

✪

Lieutenant Commander Harrison billeted First Lieutenant Miller and his platoon sergeant, Master Sergeant James H. Bronson, in a half-finished bunker, then pointed the direction to the officers' and chiefs' shower point. It was smaller and more centrally located than the enlisted shower, but was otherwise the same: a canvas-walled enclosure with water fed from a fuel drum set above it on a scaffold. While Miller was stowing his gear, Lieutenant Greig got ready for his own shower; he hadn't had a chance to clean since the transfer from the *Juno Beach*. He was finished and dressed by the time Miller arrived.

When both were clean and in fresh uniforms, Miller accompanied Greig to the mess tent. Some of the Mobile Intelligence troops were filtering in after having showered themselves, as was a squad of Greig's platoon. Unlike their officers, the enlisted men didn't sit together, but stayed with their own. In the manner of enlisted men of all armies, they didn't sit close to the officers.

The first thing Miller told Greig was, "We're tied into the satellite net. Everything we found and recorded got uploaded to the Navy intel people as we got it. Now it's your turn to find out." Harrison joined them as he began giving his briefing.

"We flew around for two days," Miller said between chews of his ham steak. "Every couple of klicks one of our birds would make a stop-and-go touchdown. Sometimes a team would drop out." He gave Greig a penetrating look. "You understand why we made a lot of touch-and-goes without letting anybody out, don't you?"

Greig nodded. "If the Dusters were observing your flights, they wouldn't know whether or not you were letting a patrol out. That's a basic tactic for reconnaissance teams."

"Good. Maybe you're not as dumb as most Leg LTs."

"Careful there, Lieutenant. Mounted Infantry is a lot smarter and tougher than Legs."

Miller grinned, and washed down a mouthful of reconstituted mashed potatoes with a drink of strong Navy coffee. "I know that, Ted. Just wanted to make sure you do." He stuck out a hand. "Call me Archie."

Greig took the hand and shook; Miller's grip wasn't as tight as the first time. "Sure thing, Archie. We're on the same team here. So what did you find?"

Miller sighed. "We found a lot of they-wuz-here. We searched in the vicinity of every town, village, farm, or other homestead, as well as a bunch of other likely hiding locations. Almost everywhere we looked, we found signs of Dusters having been there but nary a Duster to be spotted." He grimaced. "We've got what, less than a division and a half left from the entire VII Corps? Plus the Marines who made planetfall first? Worse, most of what's left of VII Corps still hasn't made planetfall. If I can extrapolate continent-wide from what we found, they've got us outnumbered by at least four-to-one, probably more—and that's not until the rest of the corps gets here. We're good fighters, but they know where we are, and we can't even make an educated guess as to where they are. That's tough odds."

Harrison interjected, "What I hear from Task Force 8 is, they aren't having much more luck than planetside assets are in locating the Dusters."

Greig swallowed. "The Navy and Marines have ground attack aircraft, that should go a long way toward evening the odds."

"The same thing applies. They know where our airfields are, we don't know where they are. They could knock out a lot of our aircraft on the ground. Bang, there goes that advantage."

"Navy has limited assets for orbit-to-ground fire support," Harrison said. "So we can't look for much help from that direction."

"You're just a feast of good cheer, aren't you?"

"I'm only telling it the way I see it. Did you get the full briefing about them?" Miller asked.

"If I didn't, I wouldn't know it," Greig answered. "What do you know that maybe I don't?"

"In our interstellar explorations, we've found evidence of seventeen other sentient civilizations. All of them had been destroyed, much like what happened to the colony here. Thinking is, these Dusters are the same bunch that did in those others."

Greig gasped. "I knew there had been a few, but I had no idea it was that many. Seventeen?"

"Seventeen." Miller lowered his voice to where Greig and Harrison had to strain to hear him. "That's what has me quaking in my boots."

Camp Puller, Headquarters of NAU Forces, Troy,
near Millerton, Shapland,
Semi-Autonomous World Troy
Office of Lieutenant General Bauer

"Sir," Captain William Upshur said, standing in the doorway of Lieutenant General Bauer's small office, "Navy has sent us the reports from the Army Mounted Infantry platoon. I have it along with an abstract G-2 prepared for you."

Bauer looked up and held out his hand for the flimsy and the crystal his aide offered. "Thanks, Bill. Did Colonel Neville say anything about it?"

"No, sir. He said it's self explanatory."

"I'll let you know if I need anything more."

"Yes, sir." Dismissed, Upshur returned to the outer office.

Bauer skimmed the flimsy as he slipped the crystal into his comp. The flimsy provided a brief description, little more than a table of contents, of the MI's report. The crystal proved to be of great interest; it included visuals of Duster presence and the destruction they'd wrought on human settlements and structures, as well as maps showing where the MI platoon had scouted. They'd covered a considerable area.

"Sir," Upshur reappeared in Bauer's doorway.

"Yes, Bill?"

"I have a follow up report from India Three/One. One of their patrols found what appears to be the Duster's staging location for their assault on Camp Zion. It's got some interesting images."

"Show me. And have someone get me some coffee, please."

"Aye aye, sir." Upshur handed Bauer another crystal before returning to the outer office to get a cup of coffee for his commanding general.

Bauer studied the report from I/3/1's patrol and compared it with the MI report. After a couple of minutes' contemplation, he ordered, "Have General Porter assemble my primary staff and their seconds, if you please. Army, too. If he's here, I'd like General Purvis to attend as well. And link in Admiral Avery."

Of course, what a lieutenant general pleases, he gets.

Briefing room, NAU Forces, Troy HQ

"A-ten-Hut!" Brigadier General David Porter, the acting NAU Chief of Staff barked as Bauer strode into the room. The assembled generals and colonels broke off their conversations and stood.

"Seats!" Bauer said, as he reached the podium in the back of the room. There was a minor clatter as the staff heads and their seconds resumed their seats. He looked at the vid connection that showed Rear Admiral Avery, attending remotely from his office on the NAUS *Durango*, Task Force 8's flagship.

Bauer acknowledged Avery with a nod. "Admiral."

"General," Avery said back after a few seconds delay for the greetings to go to orbit and back.

Bauer looked out at his staff. "I had Colonel Neville prepare materials on recent findings by both Marines and Army reconnaissance patrols for each of you to study. The Dusters appear to have vanished. I don't believe for a moment that they've all been wiped out. And they certainly haven't quit Troy, we would have seen them leave, and the Navy would have attacked their shipping.

They're still here, most likely preparing a counter-attack. We need to find out where they are hiding, and neutralize them. To that end, I want patrolling, both ground and aerial, stepped up.

"When the Dusters launched their missile attack on ARG 17 they did it from underground installations on Minnie Mouse. When they counter-attacked us in Jordan, they entered structures from the basements, which they had reached via previously undetected caves and tunnels. I think it's likely, particularly in light of their evident absence from the surface, that they're hiding underground. So our main focus will be on locating caves and tunnel systems. Admiral Avery will use his orbital resources to locate gravitational anomalies. We will coordinate with Navy on that, and investigate whatever they find.

Brigadier General Shoup will be the center man in this. I want preliminary plans tomorrow early afternoon.

Questions?"

Major General Julius Stahel stood up; the commander of the 9th Infantry Division was the ranking Army officer present. "Sir?"

"Yes, General."

"Your orders include the Army, don't they?"

"Absolutely, General. The Army units, whether they are planetside or still in space, are integral parts of NAU Forces, Troy. I want your staff who have reached planetside, and the surviving staff of your 10th Brigade who are here, to work with my staffs. As units of VII Corps reach planetside, the Marine elements on Shapland will relocate to Eastern Shapland. General, this is your area." Bauer looked at the few ranking Army officers who had managed thus far to reach Troy. "Do what you can with what you've got. General Shoup will include you in his plans the same as he will the 1st Marine Division and 2nd Marine Air Wing."

"Thank you, sir."

"If there are no more questions, you've got work to do. Get it done."

There was a minor clatter of chairs as the assembled officers stood while Bauer stepped off the small stage and marched out of the briefing room.

Briefing room, NAU Forces, Troy HQ, the next day

"Gentlemen," Bauer said to the Marine and Army division commanders, the commanding general of the 2nd Marine Air Wing, the operations officer of the 1st MCF, and the Navy Construction regiment commander. "We have preliminary reports from the increasing number of Marine and Army patrols that have been prowling about since yesterday. While most of our initial contacts with the enemy were in cities, towns, and other human settlements, it appears that they have abandoned built-up areas in favor of more remote locations, albeit in proximity to human settled locations. We are going to take the battle to them, not wait in cities and towns for them to come to us.

"To that end, I want the divisions to establish platoon and company-size firebases throughout your respective areas of operation, from which you will conduct aggressive patrolling. 2nd Marine Air Wing will position squadrons in locations where its aircraft can give rapid support to the ground elements—General Bearss, the MAW will be reinforced by three Navy Kestrel squadrons and a Navy Search and Rescue squadron.

"Captain Rooks, I know that you and your construction regiment will do a stellar job of building defensible firebases, bearing in mind that our foe is fond of attacking *en masse*, in the alien version of human wave attacks. Except that we can't assume that the leading waves will be either well defined or armed with dummy weapons as have some human forces in the past.

"The Navy, meanwhile, will continue its search for enemy bases and gravitational anomalies that could indicate underground installations.

"A salient point to keep in mind is that the human population is no longer here. We can hope that some day they will return, or that other humans will repopulate Troy. With that in mind, destruction of the infrastructure should be kept to a minimum when possible. Otherwise, the entire planet of Troy is a free fire zone.

"Again, Brugadier General Shoup will be your main contact person to coordinate your activities.

"Questions?"

Nobody had any. The commander's intent was clear.

"You know what to do. Good hunting, gentlemen."

Dismissed, the commanders took their leave, leaving Bauer alone with his operations chief, Brigadier General Shoup, and his aide, Captain Upshur.

"See what you can do about pulling Whiskey companies out of every regiment or higher," Bauer said. "I have a dreadful feeling that we're going to need them."

A "whiskey company" was a unit consisting of cooks, bakers, clerks, mechanics, and other non-trigger-pullers, for the purpose of providing replacements to trigger-puller units when their casualties reduced their ability to function.

Near Jordan, Eastern Shapland,
Semi-Autonomous World Troy

"Keep your eyes open, Horton," Corporal John Mackie called to his newest man. Despite having been in combat, PFC William Horton still wasn't used to the frequently short sleep hours infantrymen had.

"I'm awake," Horton called back. "Just blinking, that's all."

"Blink faster. You almost walked into that bush." Mackie shook his head. Horton required closer supervision than Mackie'd had to give the others thanks to his lack of experience. *It's a good thing Orndoff's wound was minor,* Mackie thought, *or he'd still be on light duty and I'd only have one man I could rely on.*

The close supervision was especially needed now; India Company had been on the move almost constantly with little chance for sleep for six days. Everyone was drowsy, everybody was having trouble staying awake even while walking. Mackie was glad he was acting fire team leader because his extra responsibilities, the need to pay attention to his men, helped him stay awake.

"Sorry, Mackie," Horton mumbled. *How the hell did he see me?* he wondered. He glanced down at himself; the Marines' utility uniform had a camouflage pattern that tricked the eye into sliding right past it, even here where the foliage was closer to grey and dark blue than it was to the green he was used to back on Earth. He looked toward where he'd heard Mackie's voice, but it took several seconds for his fire team leader to register in his vision. He shook his head. *At least he's not calling me "new guy."*

For his part, Mackie divided his attention between keeping an eye on his three men and searching his surroundings, looking for any sign of the alien enemy.

The Marines were investigating gravitational anomalies the Navy had discovered, anomalies that might or might not indicate the presence of underground spaces where the Dusters were hiding. But the Marines had had no contact with the Dusters since they'd beaten off attacks two weeks earlier. That was when Duster forces surged out of concealed underground bunkers and caverns to attack the Marines from inside their perimeters, and even inside buildings the Marines were occupying.

Third platoon was negotiating an area of scrubland. Sparsely-leafed, tree-like growths spread spindly branches over the shrub-like bushes that seldom reached chest high on a man and grew every place sunlight reached the ground.

"Watch your dress, people," Sergeant James Martin shouted, "keep it staggered." The constant refrain of squad leaders supervising their Marines on the move. First and Third squads were on line in an inverted "V" formation, with Second squad on line fifty meters to their rear, ready to move toward whatever squad might need assistance. A two-machinegun squad was in the middle of the delta formation.

On the squad level, the Marines were using ordinary voice communications, shouting orders, questions, and answers. If there were Dusters in the area, they probably knew the Marines were there. It was almost impossible for anyone to move about silently in this terrain, so there was no need to keep quiet. On platoon level and higher, the Marines were spread far enough that radio comm was necessary.

"Look alive, people," Second Lieutenant Henry Commiskey's voice came over the platoon's comm into every helmet. "We're just about on top of that anomaly. If anybody's home, they might..."

A sudden rattle of gunfire and a cacophany of shrill *caws* and *skrees* cut off the rest of what the platoon commander was saying.

"First squad, hit the deck!" Martin shouted. "They're to our left!"

"Orndoff, Horton, do you see anything?" Mackie called. He involuntarily ducked from the projectiles he heard cracking overhead.

"Only bushes and bees," Orndoff called back.

"Nothing," Horton answered. He sounded excited, his voice rose sharply on the one word.

Mackie didn't see where the fire was coming from, either. The bushes of the ground cover were just thick enough to block the Marines' view of anything more than fifty meters distant. "Fire at the bases of the bushes," he ordered. "Move your shots around." He made sure his rifle's selector switch was set to burst, and began putting three round bursts into the bases of the nearest bushes. A quick glance to his sides showed his men doing the same. All around, he heard other fire team leaders shouting commands at their men, and the shouted replies. Fire from the Marines grew in volume.

"Where are they, honcho?" Mackie called to Martin on the squad radio net. "We're firing blind here."

"When I find out, you'll be the first to know," Martin answered. "Keep doing what you're doing."

Commiskey spoke into the platoon comm: "Everybody, keep low! They're all around us. Like a circular firing squad. Maybe they'll shoot each other!" His voice cracked.

"Yeah, sure," Mackie muttered. A spray of leaves pattered his head and back, clipped off a branch above him by a too-close burst of alien fire. "Unless they're standing full up, they're firing too high to hit each other." He grinned grimly. "Too high to hit us, either."

"Heads up, First squad," Martin shouted into his comm. "My motion detector says they're coming at us. Two hundred and closing. Watch for movement, then fire waist high." Even though the Dusters massed about the same as a human, they carried their torsos almost parallel to the ground, so a waist-high shot would hit a Duster head on.

The machine guns began firing twenty-round bursts side to side over the heads of the riflemen, scything through the tops of the bushes.

Shrill *caws* and shrieks ripped through the foliage, dopplered as the aliens closed the distance.

Then Commiskey gave a command that had seldom been heard in centuries, "Fix bayonets!"

In far fewer seconds than it would have taken humans to cover the distance, the Dusters appeared, jinking and dodging side to side within fifty meters of the Marines who began firing at the attackers who were moving too rapidly for anyone to aim at. Instead of the disciplined fire on which the Marines had long prided themselves, it was spray and pray: throw out enough bullets and some are bound to find a target.

In an instant, Mackie saw that the aliens were crossing each other's paths. He picked a spot and began firing at one. The first shots missed the Duster he sighted on, but hit another that jinked through the same small area. He managed to knock down two more before the Dusters closed with the Marines.

Mackie jumped to his feet, too focused on the nearest Duster to see what was happening to his sides. If he'd spared any attention, he'd have seen that the rest of the squad had also surged upright to meet the aliens with the blades attached to the muzzles of their rifles.

Here, the Marines had a slight advantage over their much faster opponents; their arms and rifles were longer than the Dusters'; a human could skewer one of them before it got inside its own reach.

But there were three coming directly at Mackie.

He pivoted sharply to his right and swung the butt of his rifle low at the head of the right-most Duster. The alien was moving too fast, but its neck followed its head into the path of Mackie's rifle butt. The Marine felt a satisfying *crack* of breaking bones. The Duster he'd struck was tossed aside, into the feet of the middle of the trio, sending that one tumbling. The third skidded to a stop and spun toward Mackie, stretching its head on its long neck to bite at him. Mackie stepped back to get out of the way of the toothed beak, and tripped on an exposed root. That saved him, as the Duster tripped by the first one had regained its feet and was lunging with its weapon at the Marine from his side, and its thrust went over him.

Mackie turned his fall into a backward somersault to increase his distance from the one coming from his front. The two Dusters collided in the space he'd just occupied, and staggered, dazed from the impact. Mackie leaped to his feet and plunged his bayonet into the side of the nearer alien. The third *cawed* loudly and kicked with one of its taloned feet before the Marine could wrench his bayonet free. Claws ripped at Mackie, tearing through his shirt and gouging his rib muscles. He let go of his rifle and, grabbing the alien's leg, yanked with all his strength.

The Duster let out a shriek and tried to wrest its leg from Mackie's grip, but only succeeded in throwing itself off balance. Mackie wrenched the leg upward, twisting the knee joint far enough to disjoint it. The alien let out a shrill cry, and thudded to the ground when Mackie let go of its leg.

With all three of his opponents down, Mackie took a few seconds to look around for his men.

On his right, Orndoff had a Duster by its head and was spinning it around. To his left, Horton was stomping a downed alien. Farther away Cafferata was swinging the butt of his rifle at another's head and neck. All three Marines had red staining their uniforms, but Mackie couldn't tell if the red was the blood of humans, or the slightly different red of the aliens' blood. Beyond his men, he saw other Marines grappling with Dusters, some against more than one. Approaching shouts sounded like more Marines were on their way to aid First squad.

He didn't have time to analyze the situation; another Duster was almost on him, its bayoneted rifle probing straight at him at groin level. And Mackie's was still stuck in the ribs of one that he'd already fought. Mackie bounded upward, legs spread. Not high, but enough to clear the rifle, which went between his thighs. He came down on the alien's forearms, his belly slammed into the Duster's beak, jamming its head back on its long neck. The impact hurt, but Mackie didn't have time to consider what injury he might have suffered. His hands reflexively snapped up, under the alien's jaw, knocking its head back. The thing began to fall forward from its momentum, but Mackie's body blocked its motion, and his weight bore its front down. Mackie swiveled, swinging his left leg up and over to disengage from his foe. With one hand he grasped the alien's weapon, and with the other slugged it in the side of the face. In an instant, he had the unfamiliar rifle in his hands, and used it like a club to knock the Duster down and pummel its head into the ground.

The Duster that had Mackie's bayonet sticking out of its side was still alive, writhing in agony, flopping the Marine's rifle side to side. Mackie stomped on its neck as he bent to grab his rifle. The alien spasmed. Mackie got a good grip on his rifle, twisted, yanked, pulled it free.

Crouching, he looked around for another enemy to fight. While he'd been engaged, Second squad and some of the machine gunners had arrived to reinforce First squad. Dead and wounded Dusters littered the ground around the Marines. Some of the Marines were down as well. But Mackie couldn't take it all in right away; he was faint from loss of blood and collapsed.

✪

"It's about time you woke up, Mackie."

Mackie turned his head toward the side and saw Hospitalman Third Class David E. Hayden kneeling next to him where he lay on the ground.

"Hey..." Corporal Mackie started, then had to work some saliva into his mouth and swallow. "Hey, Doc, what are you doing there?"

"Patching you up, what do you think?"

"Patching...?" Mackie started to pat his belly and ribs, but flinched at the pain and stopped.

"Don't worry," Hayden said. "You'll live. And you'll be back to full duty before Sergeant Martin decides to give your fire team to Cafferata."

"How about Orndoff and Horton? They're mine, I need to know."

"Horton's wounded about as bad as you. Orndoff wasn't as dumb, he barely got scratched."

Mackie nodded, satisfied; all of the Marines he was responsible for were alive. That was important. "But we won?" he asked.

"The standard definition of victory is whoever holds the ground when the shooting stops is the winner. We're still here, the Dusters aren't. So, yeah, we won."

Mackie looked around and saw spindly-branched trees with bushes growing where sunlight reached the ground. "This is where we fought?"

"Yeah. We're waiting for transportation back to Jordan. Before you ask, I don't know when it'll get here."

Mackie fell back, and grimaced at the pain that lanced through his rib wounds from the impact.

"Now rest easy," Hayden said, patting Mackie's shoulder. "I'll check on you later." The corpsman stood and continued his rounds.

Mackie's eyelids suddenly felt heavy. He closed them, thinking *Doc must have slapped me with a sedative.* In seconds, he was sound asleep.

✪

Orndoff was there when Mackie woke up again. This time he recognized the ground cover he was laying on, keeping him off the dirt, weeds, and pebbles.

"How ya feeling, honcho?" Orndoff asked.

"I've been better. How're you?"

Orndoff shrugged. "A damn sight better'n you." He raised his left arm to display the field dressing wrapped around it. "Just a scratch. Nothing serious."

"That's your second wound." Mackie shook his head. "How's Horton? Doc didn't tell me much."

"He got a leg wound, a bad one. A Duster kicked him hard, gouged deep into his thigh. He damn near bled out before I got a tourniquet on him. Doc's pumping him full of plasma and whole blood." He took a deep breath, nodded. "He'll pull through all right."

"And the rest of the squad?"

"Pretty much everybody got hurt." Orndoff looked unfocused into the distance. "I heard someone say the platoon had better'n fifty percent casualties, with most of 'em in First squad."

"How many dead?" Mackie choked on the word.

Orndoff shook his head. "Lieutenant Commiskey made us stay in our squads and fire teams when the Dusters broke and ran. I haven't been able to get around to see how anybody else is doing. Staff Sergeant Guillen chased me back when I tried. Told me my ass was his if I didn't stick with you." He shrugged. "That's why my pretty face was the first thing you saw when you came to."

"How's Martin?"

"Dinged. Worse than me, not as bad as you."

"Where's Horton?"

Orndoff pointed with his chin. "On your other side. Doc's keeping him under until he's sure he's got enough blood in him." He cocked his head. "Sounds like transport's on its way."

Mackie listened and heard the drone of approaching air-cushioned vehicles. In minutes, five "Eighters" hove into sight. They were air cushioned, amphibious vehicles, each capable of carrying a reinforced rifle platoon. Four were enough to carry an entire company, three if they squeezed in. But the casualties required more space, so regiment had sent five.

"All right, people, let's get the wounded aboard first," Captain Carl Sitter's voice came over the company freq.

"Platoon sergeants," First Sergeant Robert G. Robinson followed up, "you know your platoon's assignments. Get it done."

Platoon sergeants barked orders over their platoon freqs. Squad and fire team leaders raised their voices, repeating the platoon sergeants' orders. There weren't as many raised voices as there should have been; too many of India Company's squad leaders and fire team leaders were casualties. Still, the boarding of the casualties, followed by the able, went smoothly enough, and quickly. It wasn't long before India Company was on its way back to Jordan.

Field Hospital, Jordan, Eastern Shapland,
Semi-Autonomous World Troy

On the second day after its fire fight against the Dusters, India Company held a formation. They formed up outside the battalion's field hospital rather than on the battalion parade ground, because several of the wounded, even though out of intensive care, were still bed-ridden. Lieutenant Colonel Ray Davis, the battalion commander, spoke first.

"Marines, I know you suffered in close combat against the Dusters. Some of you are still suffering. Some, absent comrades, will suffer no more. But I assure you, the Dusters suffered more than you did. They left more of their own dead in Third platoon's area alone than India Company had Marines in the entire engagement. Their losses were horrendous. Whatever their unit strength was to begin with, they are no longer capable of functioning as a unit of that size. India, Three/One, however, is.

"But you won't have to. India Company is going into battalion reserve until your wounds are healed, and your absent comrades are replaced and integrated into the company.

"Thanks to you, we now know the location of a major Duster underground base and how to identify their entrances. The 6th Marines are in the process of reducing the base you found.

"Marines, you did an outstanding job. In this action you acquitted yourselves in the highest tradition of the Marine Corps, and you will again and again. Every time the Dusters have come up against you, they have been severely bloodied and thrown back with devastating losses. Ultimate victory will be yours."

Davis bowed his head for a moment, then raised it high and said forcefully, in a pride-filled voice, "3rd Battalion, 1st Marines has a long and proud history. You carry on in the best tradition of that history. Three/One is the best battalion in the Marine Corps, and I am proud and humbled to be your commander.

"Now, many of you received wounds in this recent action. For some of you it was a second wound suffered against the Dusters. I wish I had the Purple Hearts medals to award to you now, but we will have to wait until medals come from Earth. But I do have the printed citations, and your company commander will hand them out to you in an appropriate ceremony.

"Marines, I salute you." He raised his right hand in a salute.

"COMP-ney, a-ten-SHUN!" battalion Sergeant Major Harry L. Hulbert bellowed.

Every one standing snapped to attention. The bed-ridden did as well as they could.

"PRE-sent ARMS!" Hulbert called out, and everyone who could saluted, and held his salute.

Davis looked over the company before cutting his salute and about-facing to march away.

Hulbert let the battalion commander get twenty meters away before shouting, "OR-der ARMS!" the command for the Marines to cut their salutes. He saluted the company commander, Captain Carl Sitter, then followed the colonel.

Sitter waited for Davis and Hulbert to reach their vehicle and leave before facing his company. "Platoons, report absent comrades."

First Lieutenant Christian F. Schilt saluted Sitter and sounded off. "Sir, First platoon, three absent comrades."

Second Lieutenant Herman H. Hanneken then reported, "Sir, Second platoon, five absent comrades."

Second Lieutenant Commiskey reported, "Sir, Third platoon, seven absent comrades."

Finally, First Lieutenant Ralph Talbot reported, "Sir, weapons platoon, three absent comrades."

Twenty-five "absent comrades." Nearly one out of seven members of the company. Far too many, far too heavy a loss. But not all of the twenty-five had been killed. A few, pitifully few, were too badly wounded to be returned to full duty in the forseeable future, if ever. Twenty-five billets in the company to fill.

"The platoons need to be reorganized and some Marines will be promoted to give you rank commensurate with your positions. Some replacements, but only fifteen or so, not more than twenty, will come from the division's shore party and various headquarters units. When they arrive and are assigned, you will need to integrate them as quickly as possible.

Platoon commanders and platoon sergeants, I want your recommendations for reorganization and promotions in two hours.

Gunnery Sergeant, the company is yours."

Gunnery Sergeant Charles F. Hoffman stepped forward and saluted. "Sir, the company is mine. Aye aye, sir." He watched while Sitter led the company's officers and first sergeant away, then about faced.

"Platoon sergeants," he ordered, "when I dismiss you, take your platoons and keep them together, ready to reassemble." He looked from one end of the formation to the other, noting without expression how many of the Marines were laying on beds or leaning on crutches instead of standing at attention, then said, *"COMP-ney, dis-MISSED!"*

✪

The company was reassembled in less than an hour. The platoon commanders and sergeants had already decided how to reorganize their platoons, and which of their Marines needed promotions, so most of that hour had been taken up with getting approval from Lieutenant Colonel Davis and the promotion warrants printed.

Captain Sitter held a brief ceremony to award the Purple Heart citations to the wounded Marines, followed by the promotions.

The first replacements arrived the next day.

7

Force Recon compound, Headquarters,
NAU Forces, Troy, near Millerton

THE NAVY IN ORBIT SEARCHED THE SURFACE OF TROY FOR GRAVITATIONAL ANOMalies which could indicate the presence of caves or tunnel systems that the Dusters were believed to use to hide in and to move about undetected. Infrequently, when the Navy found such an anomaly, the Navy also found Dusters on the surface. On those few instances a Marine or Army battalion was sent to do battle. More often, there was no sign of the aliens visible on the surface. On those occasions, Marine Force Recon was sent to investigate, to discover whether or not the aliens were using the caves or tunnels. Usually, they didn't find any sign of Dusters.

But they always had to check. Just in case.

"Attention on deck!" Gunnery Sergeant Ernest A. Janson bellowed.

"At ease, Marines!" Captain Walter Newell Hill, commanding officer, First platoon, First Force Recon Company boomed as he strode into the company classroom where two squads waited. First Lieutenant George H. Cannon, First section commander, accompanied him.

The ten Marines of Third and Fourth squads resumed their seats in the two rows of folding chairs near the small stage that Captain Hill jumped on to.

"We have a mission," Hill began.

No shit, most of the enlisted men thought, but none said out loud. *There's no other reason we would be here now.*

"The Navy found has another anomaly with no visible sign of Dusters on the surface."

Which is what we are for, most of them thought. *To find out if any bad guys are there.*

"Here is the satellite view of the area of the anomaly." Hill pressed a button on the lectern he stood next to, and a screen behind him lit up with an overhead view of several square kilometers of scrubland. "This is the area of the anomaly." A dashed line appeared overlaying the landscape. A narrow, many-doglegged section appeared on the south side, with several alcoves of various sizes sticking off its sides. The farther it went, the larger the alcoves became. It terminated in what must be a large cavern, or amphitheater. Three short legs led off the cavern to the northwest in different directions,

"N-1 suspects those legs are entrances to a cave-tunnel complex. Your mission is to determine whether they are indeed entrances, and whether there is any sign of Dusters using them. You are not to enter the tunnels, if that is in fact what they are. You are to avoid contact with the enemy if they prove to be there. Remember, your mission is to snoop and poop and gather intelligence, not to fight.

"Transportation into and out of the area will be provided by Eagles from MMH-628, cover will be provided by AH-5 Cobras, from MAH-115.

"Third squad, your call sign is 'Raider,' Fourth squad is 'CAP.' Control is 'Big Two.'

"Are there any questions? If not, your platoon sergeant will provide you with maps, detectors, water, rations, and anything else the mission requires.

"Good hunting." He stepped off the stage and headed for the classroom exit.

"Ah-ten-HUT!" Jenson bellowed, and the ten Marines of the two Force Recon squads stood and came to relaxed positions of attention.

Cannon followed the company commander. As he passed his men he said just loudly enough for them to hear, "Go get 'em, tigers!"

Jenson waited until the officers were gone, then stepped to the front of the stage and waved a come-here gesture. "Gather around," he said. The ten joined him. "Here's your maps. Test them now." He handed each squad leader what looked like a thin roll of fabric.

The squad leaders accepted them, unrolled them, snapped them to rigidity, and pressed various controls that appeared on the edge of each.

"Full power," Third squad's Staff Sergeant William J. Bordelon said.

"Full power," Sergeant Joseph R. Julian of Fourth squad said.

They pressed other controls and each pad displayed a matte map of the Force Recon area, centered on them. More controls enlarged the area shown, or gave a tighter view. Another brought up blue dots and rectangles, showing the location of people and vehicles.

"My map seems to be working fine," Bordelon said.

"Mine too," Julian said.

"You will go in here and here," Janson said, pressing buttons that brought up an X on each map. "These are your primary extraction points." He brought up a Z on each map.

"Here's motion and scent," Jenson said, handing over detectors. "We'll test them outside. I'll issue water and rations later."

The squads spent the next two hours studying their maps and making their plan of maneuver.

Later, fully equipped, they gathered at the compound's vertical takeoff and landing pad where two T-43 Eagles waited for them.

Captain Hill and First Lieutenant Cannon joined them. The officers looked them over.

"If there are any Dusters where you're going," Hill said, "they'll have a damn hard time seeing you."

"Yes, Sir," Bordelon said, not necessarily believing the company commander. He and the other Marines going on this mission knew what had happened to the First platoon of Second Force Recon Company before VII Corps was assembled and left Earth to retake Troy. The Force Recon field uniform was patterned in such a way as to make the eye slide past it, rendering the wearer nearly invisible to the naked eye. The Dusters had almost wiped out the entire platoon, so they knew the aliens must have some way of seeing them no matter how nearly invisible they were to human eyes. But they weren't about to gainsay their company commander, so neither Bordelon nor any of the others said anything other than, "Yes, Sir," when he said the Dusters wouldn't be able to see them.

"Good hunting, Marines," Hill said. He and Cannon shook each of their hands before they boarded the aircraft.

Scrubland, fifty kilometers from Jordan,
Eastern Shapland

The Eagles flew zigzag routes, touching down frequently on high grounds and hollows, until the Marines jumped off five kilometers from the anomaly; Third squad to its east, Fourth to its west. The Eagles made several more touch-and-goes away from the anomaly before turning back to their squadrons' airfields. The multiple touchdowns were to prevent watchers from knowing exactly where the squads were dropped off.

"Get ready, we're approaching your drop point," a voice buzzed in Staff Sergeant Bordelon's headset.

Bordeon took off the headset and hung it on a hook in the cabin. That was the signal for the squad to prepare to jump. He turned on his shoulder-mounted camera and looked to see that his men did as well.

Where Third squad dropped off was the sunny side of a defile. Knee-high bushes grew among the rocks and small boulders that speckled the ground, evidence of an ancient rock slide. Spindly trees popped up, mostly in the bottom of the defile. Fourth squad came down in a north-south oriented defile, with ground less rocky. Bushes here frequently rose to waist high, and trees were more frequent and not as spindly, although none of the Marines would characterize them as shade trees. In both areas, insectoids flitted and buzzed around the bushes once the interruption of the Eagle and disgorgement of the Marines had settled. Avians swooped among the insectoids, seeking a meal. High above, other avians glided on rising thermals. Occasionally one dove at a swooper, and sometimes caught its own dinner.

Bordelon looked all around, moving his torso so the camera picked up all directions.

Third squad went to ground on the shady side of its defile, a hundred meters from where they'd exited the Eagle. They formed a five-pointed star, with their feet touching in the middle. Lance Corporal Kraus, the best shot in the squad, carried its only rifle. The others were armed with sidearms; Force Recon's job was intelligence gathering, they believed that their mission was a failure if they got into a fire fight, so they went lightly armed.

They waited, watching for anybody coming to investigate the touchdown of the aircraft.

After a half hour's wait without seeing or hearing any sign of someone coming to investigate, Staff Sergeant Bordelon checked his map to verify that the squad was where it expected to be. The Marines were in the right place. He got onto his comm and sent a two word message: "Raider, moving," then tapped Corporal Stein and pointed. He didn't get an answer to his message, and hadn't expected one.

Stein rose to his feet and started along the defile. Bordelon followed, then came Lance Corporals Kraus and Roan. Sergeant Vaughn brought up the rear.

Stein followed the defile for a kilometer before stopping and looking back to his squad leader for instruction.

Bordelon pointed to the left, where the top of the defile had crumbled into a V-shaped notch. Stein headed for the notch, stepping carefully so as to not dislodge any of the stones on the slope. He stopped just below the notch and eased to the side before cautiously rising up to where he could see through it. Seeing no threat on the land beyond, he darted through the notch, keeping bent low enough to not show above the notch's side and dropped twenty meters beyond it. The other four Marines followed rapidly, all staying below the top of the notch. They took the same five-point circle they had when they first went to ground.

This time they only waited and watched for fifteen minutes before Bordelon signaled Stein to move out again.

They went bent low on a tangent to their objective, keeping out of the sightline of anyone who might have come straight out of the suspected tunnel entrance. The ground here was less rocky than in the defile, and more trees grew, providing limited concealment from potential hostile viewers. Along the way they zigged and zagged, sometimes heading more directly toward their objective, sometimes away from it. Moving slowly and never straight, it took three hours to get within three hundred meters of the possible tunnel mouth. The ground steadily rose.

Again, they went to ground in a five-point star. Bordelon deployed his motion and scent detectors for the first time. He spoke into his comm, "Raider in place." Again, he expected no reply, and didn't get one.

The motion detector was set to show only movement of something half the size of a man or larger, so the flitting insectoids and swooping birds didn't register on it. For the half hour they waited, neither did anything else. The scent detector didn't note any wafting chemicals that would indicate the possible nearby presence of a Duster.

Bordelon kicked into the cluster of feet in the center of the star—the signa thers and no farther. It was the first word any of them had said out loud except for Bordeon's comm messages since they boarded the Eagles back at the Force Recon compound.

Everyone stopped and went to a knee, looking in different directions. Except for Bordelon, who went to Vaughn's side. There, crossing Vaughn's path left rear to right front, were the distinctive taloned footprints of several Dusters.

Bordelon followed the tracks with his eyes—they went directly to the so-far unseen location of the suspected tunnel mouth. He signaled Vaughn to come with him. Along the way they gathered Roan. When they reached Kraus, Bordelon signaled Stein to join them. All five lowered to a knee and put their heads together.

"Tracks, leading there," Bordelon said softly, and pointed where they led. "We go. Be ready."

While the squad began an oblique approach to the suspected entrance, the squad leader sent another terse message, "Sign found. Investigating."

The tracks disappeared into a meter-wide gouge in the sloping ground. Bordelon stopped his squad and advanced alone, with his detectors held before him. The motion detector didn't register anything, but the display of the scent detector started jumping as soon as he extended it toward the opening. Carefully, he continued up the slope to where he could lie above the entrance. He stretched both detectors to aim into the tunnel. The motion detector didn't register anything but the scent was strong.

Found 'em! he thought, and shot a thumbs up at his men. Back on his feet, stepping softly with the scent detector extended, he walked along the ground in the direction of the tunnel, and onto the roofs of some of the side caverns shown in the Navy scans. He was looking for scents rising from ventilaiton shafts. He thought there must be some, but either there weren't any or the shafts had baffles that absorbed scents.

Deciding that further search would be futile, he returned to his squad. A few meters from the tunnel entrance, he pulled what appeared to be a large pebble out of his pocket and dropped it on the ground. The pebble wasn't as innocent as it looked. When activated by a given radio signal, it would radiate a pulse, that guided on, allowing Marines to home directly on it, and to the tunnel entrance.

He pointed the direction for Corporal Stein and sent another message as the squad began its movement, "Raider leaving objective. Success."

It took Third squad two hours to reach its extraction point, where they waited twenty minutes for an Eagle to respond to Bordelon's signal that they were there.

Force Recon compound,
Headquarters NAU Forces Troy

Fourth squad returned to base nearly an hour after Third; they'd had to investigate three possible tunnel or cave entrances.

Captain Hall delayed the debriefing of Third squad until Fourth squad returned. When both squads were assembled in the company classroom, he handed the debriefing to First Lieutenant Robert M. Hanson, First Force Recon Company's S-2—intelligence—officer.

Staff Sergeant Bordelon went first. Hanson's eyes glowed at the finding of strong Duster scent emanating from the cave entrance.

Captain Hall grinned a predatory grin. Lieutenant Cannon looked at Third squad with obvious approval. They eagerly watched the vids the Marines had taken, especially of the tracks leading to the tunnel's entrance. They were mildly disappointed that Bordelon hadn't found any ventilation shafts.

Then it was Third squad's turn.

"Sirs," Sergeant Julian began, "The landscape on the northwest of the subject area isn't as rocky as what Staff Sergeant Bordelon described in his sector. It's still scrub forest, but with more trees and fewer bushes.

"We found no sign of Dusters until we approached the suspected entrances. There were a few footsteps, but not from as many individuals as Third squad discovered." The vids he showed made that clear. "These entrances, it's pretty clear, are smaller than the one to the south. My best guess is only one of these entrances is in use, and that simply as a way into open air when Dusters feel the need to get out of the cave." He shrugged. "At least that's what I'd think if the enemy was human instead of alien. One of the other two gave no detectable scent, it probably wasn't broken all the way through."

He had more to say, but nothing of significance. Neither did any of his squad mates, they thought he had covered everything they'd discovered.

"Outstanding, Marines," Captain Hall said at the end of the debriefing. "I'm sure whatever unit is sent to clear out that nest will find your intelligence immensely valuable.

"That is all. Gunny Janson, take charge. After they've showered and changed uniforms, you may sound the liberty call." He left the classroom with the other officers in tow.

"You heard the man," Janson said when the officers were gone. "Get yourselves cleaned up and take off on liberty. Base liberty, of course."

The ten Marines headed for their quarters and a shower. Liberty call didn't mean much, there wasn't really anywhere to go.

The next day the two squad leaders met with the officers and platoon sergeants of Company I, Third Battalion, First Marines to plan the company's approach to the cave-tunnel complex. The following day, the two squads went out again, to prepare to guide India Company to the cave-tunnel complex—and to assure that the Dusters were still there.

Ward 3, Field Hospital 4, near Pikestown,
West Shapland

"Up and at 'em, Mackie. The doctor tells me he needs this bed."

Corporal John Mackie, dressed in a hospital gown and thin robe, looked up from the book he was reading to see his squad leader, Sergeant James Martin standing at the foot of his hospital bed. Then he looked around the ward where eight of the twelve beds were already empty, and back at his squad leader. "Sure he does, Sergeant Martin. What do you think he's going to do with it?"

"He's a doctor," Martin answered, stepping around the bed to Mackie's side and lowering his voice. "How do I know what he's got planned? Maybe he's got something on with one of the nurses and needs a horizontal surface. Have you *seen* them, the nurses? Some of them are pretty choice." He looked toward the nurses' station, beyond one end of the ward. The station was the pivot point for this ward and two others. The fourth side opened into a corridor that led to the main entrance of the field hospital.

Mackie snorted. "No shit, I've seen them. What do you think I've been doing here? Can't spend all of my time sleeping and reading."

Martin laughed at that. "If almost anybody else in the squad said that I'd think he was joking. But you actually read a lot." He clapped Mackie's shoulder. "How's your gut?"

Mackie patted his abdomen. "I've got a scar, but that's about it. I heard you got wounded, too. How are you doing?"

"I'm a Marine sergeant. I heal faster than mere corporals."

"Yeah, sure. But you're okay?"

"I was released a couple of days ago. You're the last man from First squad who hasn't returned to duty yet. Even Horton's back, and his leg was hurt worse than your tummy."

"Then let's go." Mackie stood and opened the slender locker that stood next to the head of his bed. It held two field uniforms, his pack, and gear harness. The pack was empty and nothing hung on the harness. In seconds, he had his miniscule collection of toiletries swept from the bedside stand into a carrying case, which he put in the pack along with his book and library crystal. Another minute and he was out of the hospital gown and in uniform.

"Follow me," Martin said, and stepped out, toward the nursing station and the exit. Mackie fell in a pace to his left and rear.

"Corporal Mackie," the nurse at the station, a lieutenant junior grade, said sternly, "I don't want to see you back here. Understand?"

"Yes, ma'am, I understand." Mackie said with a grin at her as he passed.

She smiled at the "ma'am," as she was only a couple of years older than he was.

Out of her hearing Mackie said to Martin, "The Navy sure makes good nurses."

"Oh, yeah, the best." Martin agreed, remembering a night back in Riverside when he'd met an off duty nurse, and the night had turned into a weekend.

Firebase Zion, near Jordan,
West Shapland

Firebase Zion was a barren place, as such advance positions usually were. The vegetation had been removed inside the base's combat-wire perimeter, and fields of fire had been cleared some four hundred meters beyond the wire, making a rough circle nearly a kilometer in diameter of denuded ground. Holes, the beginnings of bunkers, had been dug a few meters inside the wire, with narrow zigzag trenches connecting them. Inboard from the bunkers were square tents, each capable of housing six men. Most of them had their sides rolled up, exposing cots that stood on plasteel pallets. A discarded packing crate squatted by each cot. A larger tent more or less centered in the compound served as kitchen and mess hall. A road cut through the field of fire from the north and terminated in a gate wide enough to admit an Eighter in the wire fence.

The Eighter that transported the now-recovered casualties from the hospital to the firebase rolled through the opened gate and pulled up in front of the command bunker, an unfinished hole with a roof that did little more than provide shade. Captain Carl Sitter heard the vehicle coming and stepped into the open as the Marines were jumping out of the vehicle. The platoon sergeants had also heard the Eighter coming and headed for the CP, where they stood off to the side.

"Detail, fall in at attention!" Gunnery Sergeant Robert Robinson ordered.

In seconds, the seven Marines who'd just been released from the hospital and the four squad leaders who escorted them on the Eighter were in line facing their company commander.

"Welcome back, Marines," Sitter said. "I'm very glad to see you. Not only because you are well again, but because the company needs you." He paused to look each of them in the eye. "There are still Dusters out there, and indications are they plan to hit us again.

Before they do, we have work to do. We need to finish making this firebase a strong defensive position, and we have to go out there," he gestured toward the landscape beyond the perimeter of the firebase, "and locate and neutralize any Dusters that are still in the area, break up any assembly points they're making."

He turned to face Robinson. "Gunnery Sergeant, the detachment is yours."

"Aye aye, sir." Robinson didn't salute, not here where an enemy sniper might be watching for such a sign. As soon as Sitter ducked into the CP bunker, Robinson turned to the platoon sergeants. "Take your Marines to your areas and get them settled in. But do it quickly. You have your orders, brief your men and get ready.

"Do it."

Staff Sergeant Guillen pointed a finger at Martin and Mackie and crooked it in a "follow me" gesture. The two stepped out briskly to join their platoon sergeant who was already heading for Third platoon's part of the perimeter.

"We haven't had any contact since you got hit," Guillen said, looking at Mackie, when they caught up. "But we keep finding signs of them being out there."

"What kind of signs, Staff Sergeant?" Mackie asked. He and Martin hadn't discussed what was happening on the trip from the hospital, other than who the new men were and how they were fitting in.

"Fresh scratch marks in the ground, like from claws. Fresh scat. The kinds of thing that we'd think were made by a bear, or a big cat on a different world." He shook his head. "But nobody's seen a big predator here. Or any kind of animal much bigger than a middle size dog."

Martin listened as intently as Mackie did to the explanation; he hadn't heard any of that during the two days he'd been back. But then, Third platoon hadn't put out any patrols during that time.

"Has there been a lot of sign?" Mackie asked.

"Not much. Just enough to make me pretty sure there are still Dusters in the area, just like the Skipper said. And they aren't staying underground."

When they reached the squad area, Guillen told Martin, "Get him settled in, then take him to Sergeant Adams for his weapons and other gear." That was the end of talking about what they'd seen on patrols.

"Aye aye," Martin said. To Mackie, "Right here, all the comforts of home."

The comforts of home didn't amount to much. They consisted of a pair of two-man tents with their sides raised for ventilation, and a couple of boards laid across two stacks of sandbags at a tabletop-height for a man sitting on the ground. A field-expedient stove squatted a few meters from one end of the table and a water-dispensing camel was an equal distance from the other.

"We don't get the squad tents?" Mackie asked when he saw the tent he was assigned to.

Martin shook his head. "Squad leaders and up."

Then they were with Mackie's men.

Mackie was pleased with himself because he remembered his new man and was able to greet him by name."How's everything going, Horton? How's your leg? Any problems fitting in? Everybody treating you all right?"

"No, Corporal," PFC Horton answered. "Ah, I mean, yes, Mackie." He stood from where he'd been lounging in the shade of one of the tents and shifted foot-to-foot.

Mackie knuckled Horton's shoulder. "You mean you've got problems fitting in, and everybody's treating you like shit?"

Horton flushed. "N-No, Mackie. I mean, I mean..."

Mackie laughed. "I know what you mean, Horton. Relax. I'm I'm easy to get along with, just busting your chops a bit. Cafferata's the one you have to worry about."

"Say what?" yelped Lance Corporal Cafferata, who'd been sitting cross-legged in the other tent's shade.

"I didn't stutter, Hector. New guys have to watch out for you. Every one of them, and all the time." To Horton in a conspiratorial tone, "You should have seen him when he was in Second fire team and Porter joined us. Hector rode him mercilessly. The Skipper had to threaten him with a court martial to make him stop. At that, poor Porter almost got locked up in a psych ward."

"You're so full of it, John," Cafferata snorted.

"That's 'Corporal John' to you, Lance Corporal."

"That's enough you two," Martin finally interjected with a chuckle. "Mackie, let's go to Sergeant Adams, get your weapons and gear."

"Good to see you, Orndoff." Mackie waved at the other man in his fire team as he started off with the squad leader. "How's the arm?"

"Welcome back, Honcho," Orndoff said, and returned the wave, showing that his wounded arm was fully recovered.

The company supply room was another roughly dug and covered bunker in the central area of the firebase. Unlike the command bunker, the supply bunker could be locked to prevent theft. Sergeant Adams was in it, shifting containers about to find the ones belonging to the just-returned Marines. He already had their weapons stacked by the entrance.

"Sergeant Adams, I've got Mackie here," Martin said when they reached the entrance.

"And I'm getting everything ready," Adams shouted from the depths of the bunker. "Just a sec." In a moment he was at the entrance, dusting his hands against each other.

"Mackie, Mackie, Mackie. Corporal. Right. I think this one is yours. Check the serial number." Adams snatched an M23 rifle from the rifle rack, glanced quickly at its serial number, then handed it to Mackie. While Mackie verified that it was the right rifle, Adams laid out magazines, a bayonet, a water camelback, and a first aid kit. "Put these on your belt," Adams said, and turned to make a pile of body armor. "We finally got armor, would have prevented a lot of wounds." He glanced at Mackie's midsection. Helmet with integral comm, night vision glasses, foul weather gear, field bedding, and other miscellany. He even tossed in an extra pair of boots. Finally he handed Mackie a pad and said, "Sign these."

Mackie looked at the weapons and gear he was given, compared them to the listings, one for the rifle and one for everything else, and signed.

As Mackie and Martin turned to leave, the supply sergeant called after them, "I don't want to hear any shit about combat losses. You got that, Mackie?"

"You hear that, Sergeant Martin?" Mackie said loudly enough for Adams to hear. "Sergeant Adams says I have to stay out of combat."

"Sergeant Adams isn't your squad leader, Mackie," Martin said. "I am. I say that when the shooting starts, you head into it."

"You're the boss."

"Damn skippy, I am."

In front of the India Company CP

"At ease," Captain Sitter ordered, and his men relaxed their stance. Most of the Marines of the company were in formation in front of him. Only the few on perimeter duty, watching the surrounding landscape for approaching enemy, weren't present.

"We have just returned from a briefing on the current situation," Sitter said after a moment. "Here is our mission for today.

"We are going out to check out another anomaly the Navy found. The Navy didn't see any positive signs of Dusters, just an anomaly that probably indicates the presence of underground spaces. So Force Recon went in. They found entrances to a tunnel or cave system, and indications of Duster activity going in and out. They couldn't tell if the Dusters are still in there or if they vacated recently. Our job is to find out if the Dusters are still there and kill any alien bastards that we find.

"The Force Recon squads that went there yesterday will meet us at our drop off points and guide us to the entrances.

"Are there any questions?" That was a question not normally asked of an entire company.

"Yes, sir," somebody from Second platoon called out.

Sitter looked at him. "Ask."

"If the Dusters are at this anomaly, how many can we expect to find?"

"I don't know. Nobody knows. For that matter, if the Navy knows how many Dusters might be there, they haven't told us."

Sitter ignored the *sotto voce*, "Typical squids, not telling the Marines what we need to know."

The captain's gaze swept the company, but nobody else seemed about to ask anything. He said, "If that's everything, platoon sergeants, take your platoons. Officers, with me. Dismissed!" He about faced and marched into the CP bunker. Only after the company's officers followed him did the platoon sergeants move their Marines back to their areas.

✪

"Third platoon, on me!" shouted Second Lieutenant Commiskey as he neared the platoon's area following the officers' meeting in the company CP. "Gather around, semi-circle."

In moments, forty-six of the platoon's Marines stood in an arch to the front of their platoon commander; the platoon sergeant and right guide flanked the officer.

"Listen up!" Commiskey said. "This anomaly is in the same area where we fought them the last time. This time we will thoroughly search what might be a tunnel complex at the anomaly. Yes, I know, the 6th Marines cleaned up after our fight. But they didn't go underground. Third platoon will go into the tunnels, if any are there. Second platoon will set security outside the complex, they'll be the anvil on which our hammer hits the Dusters. We will kill or capture any Dusters we find, and destroy any equipment or supplies. On leaving, we will collapse the tunnel system. First platoon will be company reserve.

"Our order of march will be First squad, me, one gun team, Second squad, Staff Sergeant Guillen, the other gun team, Sergeant Binder, Third squad.

"We move out in thirty. Squad leaders will issue ammunition and tunnel visions—your regular night vision glasses probably won't do enough in the tunnels.

"Questions?"

There were, but "Why do we have to do this?" wasn't an acceptable question, so nobody asked anything.

Camp Zion, near Jordan,
Eastern Shapland

"What do you think, Mackie?" Lance Corporal Cafferata asked as the two Marines lounged on top of their bunker, waiting for the orders to move out. First squad's other two fire team leaders sat leaning against the bunker's front.

"I think a lot of things, Hector," Corporal Mackie replied. "What do you want to know?"

Cafferata made a face. "You know. The only damn thing we need to know about. Are the Dusters in the cave we're going to? What are they doing there? Or did they leave, have we beaten them? Have they shot their wad?"

Mackie mulled over the questions for a moment before answering. During the pause, Corporals Vittori and Button pulled away from the bunker's front and looked up at the junior fire team leader to hear what he'd say.

"The last one first," Mackie finally said. "I don't think they've shot their wad. If we start thinking we beat them, things could go very badly for us the next time we run into them. As for your other questions, how the hell do I know? I don't have a pipeline into G-2 or N-2. And they sure as shit aren't telling me what they know." He shrugged. "What I think beyond that is, we need to stay sharp and be ready to do some serious ass-whomping on the Dusters." He shuddered. "Especially if we meet them in caves."

Cafferata screwed up his eyes and peered hard at the trees. He muttered under his breath.

"What's that?" Mackie asked. "I couldn't make it out."

"I said something like I don't understand why some people don't just give up when they know they're facing Marines."

"Dusters aren't people, they're aliens. That's why."

"You think about these things, Mackie," said Sergeant Martin from the back of the bunker. "That's why I keep you around."

Mackie and Cafferata spun about, bringing their rifles to bear at the unexpected voice. In front of the bunker, Vittori and Button ducked down and grabbed their rifles, ready to fire around the bunker's corners.

"Goddam it, Sergeant Martin!" Mackie shouted when he saw the squad leader. "You've got to stop sneaking up on us like that."

"I keep telling you, you need to have three-sixty awareness. Remember the house on Sugar Cover Place? You don't know that the Dusters can't come up inside the bunkers and hit you from behind when you're sitting like this.

"Now get your fire team leaders ready. It's time for us to go spelunking."

For the first time, First squad's fire team leaders became aware of the other squad leaders, the platoon sergeants, and Gunnery Sergeant Hoffman yelling for the company to assemble.

Scrubland, near Jordan, Eastern Shapland,
Semi-Autonomous World Troy

A squadron of T-43 Eagles airlifted India Company's First and Third platoons six kilometers from the main entrance of the cave-tunnel complex that First Force Recon's Third squad had confirmed was a Duster location. Second platoon was dropped seven klicks from the rear entrance to serve as a blocking force if any Dusters tried to escape that way. They also had a squad of sappers, who would endeavor to blow the tunnel mouths once the platoons going in through the main enterance made contact with the aliens, thereby preventing the Dusters from using them as bolt holes. Divisions of

AV16 C Kestrels rotated in a holding orbit five minutes flight from the cave-tunnel complex, in case India Company found itself in a fight on the surface.

A nearly invisible Marine stood up from the scrub and walked to the company command unit.

"Captain Sitter," Staff Sergeant Bordelon said, greeting the company commander.

"Staff Sergeant," Sitter said.

"We got close enough to the tunnel mouth to pick up strong scents, sir. I went over the top with my sniffer, and didn't find any ventilation holes. Still, I have no doubt the Dusters are still there."

"What about the rear entrance?" Sitter asked.

"The bolt hole is the same as before. Individual tracks coming and going from one mouth, no scents from another. The third still seems unused."

"Outstanding. Let's go dust some aliens."

"Aye aye, sir." Bordelon turned from Sitter and signaled his squad. The other four Force Recon Marines stood from where they'd been effectively invisible, and started heading along the route they'd already planned. Bordelon took his place as the second man in the short column.

"Third platoon, follow our guides," Sitter ordered on his comm.

Third platoon hastened to get close enough for their point to easily make out the hard-to-see trailing Force Recon Marine. Sitter came with the company's heavy machine gun and mortar section. First platoon brought up the rear. They went slow and easy, and took three hours to cover the six kilometers. They moved as silently as they could, but two hundred men can't move as quietly as five, so they were much noisier than the earlier recon patrol had been.

Not that there were any Duster observation posts or patrols out to hear them.

Outside the cave-tunnel complex

Captain Sitter went with First platoon and had Third platoon station fire teams along the way to relay messages from the depths to the weapons platoon and sappers left on the surface.

Lieutenant Commiskey listened to the company command circuit on his helmet comm, said an "Aye aye" acknowledgement, then toggled his comm to the platoon freq.

"Listen up, Third platoon." he said. "The company's in place. We're going in. Sergeant Martin, move out."

"Aye aye," Martin answered on his comm. Using naked voice he said, "You heard the man, Vittori, go."

"Roger," Corporal Joseph Vittori said. "Harvey, lead off. I'm right behind you."

PFC Harry Harvey didn't say anything, he just ducked into the opening in front of him, and started into the tunnel. It went down at a steep angle and quickly dropped below the level of the flat ground above, where it turned sharply, cutting off most the light that filtered in from the outside, Then turned again, plunging the tunnel into darkness deep enough that normal night-vision glasses couldn't penetrate. Harvey slid his "tunnel vision" goggles over his eyes. Vittori followed about two meters behind, and likewise slid his tunnel vision goggles into place. The rest of First fire team trailed him, with each man putting on his goggles as he turned the corner. Then came Martin and Third fire team.

Mackie wanted to be next after Martin, but knew that he had to be in a position to control his men, so he put Horton behind the squad leader and positioned himself in front of Cafferata. Orndoff connected with Second fire team.

The tunnel had a flat floor and smooth sides. Even though it was almost wide enough for two men to walk side by side, the ceiling was so low that the Marines had to walk slightly hunched over. There were no lights, at least none that were on. The tunnel vision goggles didn't show colors, but the walls shimmered with a slight gloss. The gloss didn't translate into a slickness to the touch. Mackie wondered, not for the first time, whether the Dusters had some form of echo-location or other sense that allowed them to "see" in reduced or non-existent light.

About fifty meters in, the smoothness of the wall on the right was broken by a doorway. Martin reported it to Commiskey, who came forward while Martin set security.

"What do you think, Sergeant?" Commiskey asked after he examined the door.

A lever-like handle was recessed into one side of the door. Other than that, there was no visible slot or other knob that looked like a locking device. The top of the door was low enough that a man would have to bend almost double to go through it.

Martin shook his head. "Doesn't look like there's anything important in there. But then, we don't know how they secure things."

"So the only thing to do is take a look."

"That's right, sir. So if you'll step back—"

"A good commander never asks his men to do something he won't do himself. *You* step back, Sergeant."

Martin gave Commiskey a penetrating look, then made a curt nod and said, "First fire team, move forward twenty meters. Third, move forward and follow us in." To Commiskey, "I'm with you, Lieutenant." He pressed his back against the wall to the side of the door opposite the handle.

Commiskey faced the wall next to the door and reached for the handle. It didn't move when he pressed down on it. He lifted, and the door popped open into the space beyond it.

Martin was ready, and dove through the open doorway. He rolled away from it and came up in a crouch, pointing his rifle into the chamber; his eyes swept the room, the muzzle of his rifle tracked with his eyes. He saw Commiskey follow him the same way on the other side of the door. The officer held his handgun ready.

"Mackie," Martin shouted, "get in here!"

In seconds, Mackie and his men were spreading out inside the room.

To the Marines, it was a modest-size room, no more than fifteen meters deep, less than that in width, about double the height of the tunnel outside it. Pillars dotted the chamber, holding up cross beams that supported the ceiling. It looked to have been a storeroom, although whatever had been stored in it was now gone, leaving only a few racks and some shelving. It only took a minute to check behind the pillars to make sure nothing was hiding there. They didn't take the time to check the walls for hidden doors.

Commiskey reported the room to Captain Sitter, then told Martin, "The Skipper's going to have the sappers prepare it to blow on our way out," Commiskey said. "Let's continue."

In a moment, First squad was back in the tunnel, heading deeper into the complex. Every fifty to a hundred meters they found another room on one side of the tunnel or the other. The chambers varied in size from the smallish first one to the size of a small auditorium. Six rooms were as empty as the first one. The sappers prepared each of their entrances to blow once the Marines passed on their way out.

The seventh, compared to the other six, was mid-sized. And that wasn't the only difference.

Forty pairs of bowl-shaped objects—the Marines could only compare them to nests—were spaced through the chamber. One nest in each pair was larger, large enough to act as a bed for a Duster. The other, much smaller, was divided into segments; perhaps the Duster equivalent of a locker.

There was a long moment of silence before Mackie broke it. "I suddenly have an image of Dusters hunkering down on these things, with their heads tucked under a wing."

"Just like nesting birds," Martin said.

"Or dinosaurs," Mackie said softly.

All of First squad filtered into the... "It's a squadbay!" Cafferata exclaimed.

"Damn," somebody muttered, his voice muffled by the material of the nests.

"Look at the spacing," Mackie said.

"What about it?" Vittori asked.

"They're far enough apart that a Duster can stand next to one and his tail won't overlap any of the others."

"I do believe you're right," Martin said when he looked at the distance between nests.

"This is just like the Cretaceous nesting colonies paleontologists found back in the twentieth century."

"Mackie," Corporal Button said, wandering among the nests, searching, "sometimes I think you read too much. If you put that effort into being a Marine, you'll make Commandant one day."

Mackie snorted. Before he could make any other reply, Commiskey entered the squadbay.

"How recently was this occupied?" he wanted to know.

"Are they warm-blooded?" Martin asked.

"Don't know."

Martin removed a glove and bent over to feel the middle of a nest. "If they are, it's been long enough for the bedding to drop to room temperature. If not..." His camouflaged shrug went mostly unseen.

"Has anybody seen anything of interest in here," Commiskey asked, "other than these nest-things? No hidden doors? Nothing?"

Nobody spoke up.

"All right then, let's move out. We need to go through this whole complex until we find the Dusters. Time's wasting."

"Mackie, you know so damn much about the Dusters," Martin said, "third fire team has point. Lead the way."

"Got it," Mackie said. "Orndoff, point."

Orndoff grunted, and led the way out of the apparent squadbay and turned deeper into the tunnel.

An hour into the tunnel complex

The tunnel had long since stopped being straight lines and ninety-degree turns, with a ceiling constantly low enough that a man had to stoop to avoid banging his head. Neither were the walls and floor as uniform as they had been for the first few hundred meters. The floors and walls of the rooms became more uneven, and showed signs of having been worked to even them out a bit. And it always went down. Sometimes the slope was barely perceptible, occasionally it was acute.

"It looks like they cut a tunnel into an existing cave network," Corporal Mackie observed over the squad freq.

"No shit, Sherlock," Sergeant Martin said sardonically. "Just keep looking for bad guys."

There were more empty rooms, and chambers that showed signs of occupancy. There was no way the Marines could tell how recently the chambers had been occupied; perhaps their denizens had all been killed during the earlier fights. That was something everyone could hope for. It wasn't something that many believed.

"Got a big one here," Mackie said when he followed PFC Orndoff into a huge, oval-shaped chamber, maybe two hundred meters deep and nearly as wide at its widest point. Its back wall sloped away from the entrance in two terraces. Very little of the chamber had been worked; a few stalagmites jutted up from rubble on the floor, which looked as though it was in the process of being cleared. Stalactites hung from overhead. The walls were drapperied with flowstone. It was more properly called a cavern.

"Damn, I wish tunnel vision let us see colors," Corporal Vittori said when he entered the chamber. "I'll bet this place is gor—"

A bullet hit him square in the chest, knocking him backward.

"Down!" Mackie shouted at the same time as Martin. The eight Marines other than Vittori who were in the chamber dove for the floor and took cover behind stalagmites, some stubs, some still standing. They threw their rifles into their shoulders and began blasting into the depths of the cavern.

Martin didn't shoot, he looked for where the fire was coming from. He couldn't see the Dusters themselves because they were too well hidden, but he could see their muzzle flashes above the upper terrace.

"First fire team," he shouted, his voice rising over the cacophony of echoing gunfire; the *cracks* of bullets zinging past, the *pings* of ricocheting and shattering slugs. "Upper terrace, ten o'clock high to twelve. I think there are four in that area. Second fire team, noon to two. Third fire team, some of them are below the upper terrace. Look for their muzzle flashes."

The Marines' fire evened out, became more regular and more disciplined. Sparks thrown by bullets impacting stone showed where bullets were striking, hitting ever closer to the muzzle flashes of the Dusters' weapons.

Only once he saw that his men were hitting near where he knew the enemy had positions did Martin finally call, "Vittori, sound off!"

"Here," Vittori croaked.

"Are you okay?"

"Hurts, but—" Vittori paused while a cough blasted through his body. "—but I'll live." He gasped, but his body armor had stopped the bullet.

"See to it that you do, Marine." Martin looked to see where his men's rounds were hitting. He didn't need to adjust anybody's fire.

During the few seconds Martin took to give his men orders and check on Vittori, Lieutenant Commiskey darted into the cavern and dove for cover behind a thick stalagmite stump. He quickly assessed the situation, and ordered over the platoon freq, "Adriance, get your squad in here! Intersperse with First squad! First gun, let Third squad get in, then move in to lay down covering fire, right to left. The bad guys're mostly high."

"Third squad, move!" Sergeant Adriance shouted. "Keep low. Move, move, move! Spread out, spread out!"

There was more shouting and crashing of pounding boots as second squad scrambled into the chamber, and thuds as diving bodies hit the room's floor.

"Fancy meeting you here," Adriance said when he hit the deck next to Mackie. "Where are they?"

"They're on the upper terrace. Watch my tracers, they'll guide you." Mackie switched his rifle to short bursts and cranked off a couple.

"Got it," Adriance said. "Glowen," he shouted at his First fire team leader, who was to his right, "See where my bullets are going?"

"That's an affirmative," Corporal Glowen shouted back. "First fire team, put them where I'm hitting." He started pouring short bursts into the same area.

Mackie snorted. "We gotta stop meeting like this, Harry," he said between trigger pulls. "It could get dangerous."

Adriance's response was drowned out by the sudden staccato of the machine gun firing over their heads.

A few meters to Mackie's left, Commiskey got out his infrared scope and began scanning above the terrace—he had to ignore flashes from the speeding projectiles. *There!* He saw a greenish glow, the heat thrown off by bodies. "Gun, look for my mark! Five meters to the right of where you're hitting now."

"Ready," Corporal Andrew Tomlin called back.

Commiskey sighted on the infrared glow and pressed the button on the side of his scope that sent a brief pulse of laser light at the green. He saw red through the scope; the gun saw white in tunnel vision. Almost instantly, a long burst of machine gun fire blanketed the marked area. Fire from there ceased.

Martin had followed the verbal exchanges and the shifting of fire. "Third fire team," he said on his squad freq, "shift your fire to your right."

Mackie repeated the order to his men, even though they'd already heard it. "We're shifting right," he told Adriance.

"Got it." Adriance told his First fire team to also shift their aim to the right. Then he looked to see what the rest of his squad was doing.

The fire of two squads and a machine gun reverberating and echoing off the walls of the cavern was deafening, so much so that the Marines couldn't hear the Dusters' return fire. The sparks and flashes of ricocheting bullets added to a sense of visual confusion, as did bits of stone chipped off the flowstone and other rocky structures.

Suddenly, with a crash so loud it stunned the Marines in the cavern, a large section of ceiling above the rear wall collapsed onto the top terrace and avalanched down the rear wall. Dust billowed out, obscuring everything in its path. All shooting stopped.

Mackie gasped for breath; he felt like he'd been kicked in the chest and his lungs needed to be restarted. His ears rang so loudly he didn't think he could hear anything. He shook his head to clear it, blinked rapidly and repeatedly. He fish-mouthed, trying to squeak out sounds that might be words. His eyes finally focused on the mountain of dust and debris coming toward him, and he knew in a flash the danger the Marines were in.

"Pull back!" he croaked into his comm. He hawked to clear his throat and managed more clarity, "Pull back!" He slapped Adriance on the shoulder and jerked a thumb back, giving him the same message.

Adriance nodded, he was already on his comm odering his squad out of the cavern.

Dimly, Mackie heard indistinct sounds coming over his helmet comm; he thought it was Commiskey and Martin ordering everybody out. Looking to his flanks, he could barely make out the forms of Marines withdrawing. He scuttled to his right, then to his left to make sure his men were getting out. He was turning to exit himself when he bumped into Martin, who was checking that his squad was moving out.

"Third fire team, on the move," he managed to say. He used hand signals to repeat the message in case Martin's ears were still too numb to hear him.

Back in the tunnel, Commiskey moved Third squad back the way they'd come, where it would be out of the way of the Marines coming out of the cavern. He quickly considered what to do next.

Captain Sitter came forward to see what was happening. He thought the only viable option was a withdrawal. It was likely the tunnel would get blocked here, and he didn't know of any way out other than the way they'd come in—or farther forward.

"Pull back," Commiskey ordered, both over his comm and with hand signals. The Marines reversed their order of march and began heading out.

Corporal Vittori was the only casualty—unless loss of hearing and a few nicks and scrapes from flying rock chips counted—but was able to walk unaided.

Rumbles and crashes of more roof collapses followed the Marines as they withdrew. A few well-placed explosive charges collapsed tunnel sections and chamber entrances behind them. Pausing only to cover the sappers as they set off the charges they'd earlier set in rooms off the tunnel, it took less time for the platoon to reach open air than it had to reach the cavern where they'd had the fight.

Outside, the Marines gathered at a safe distance and watched dust and tiny rock chips billowing out of the tunnel, while constantly looking at their surroundings, watching for Dusters.

Outside

The sappers with Second platoon had blown the rear entrances as soon as they felt through the rocks the fire fight in the unfinished cavern. As soon as the Marines who had gone in were all out, Sitter had the sappers blow the main entrance.

The company stayed in place until the next day, in case any Dusters managed to get out. None did. Neither did other Dusters come to investigate. After twenty-four hours of waiting, a squadron of Eagles came to carry India Company back to its roost.

Advance Firebase One, under construction

THE DAY AFTER ALPHA COMPANY'S SECOND PLATOON SHOWED UP, THE FIREBASE was even more active than when the mobile infantrymen arrived. The soldiers immediately took over all security duties, and all of the engineers of the CB company set to on the base's construction.

First Lieutenant Miller, nominally subordinate to Second Lieutenant Greig, simply said he was taking his platoon out for a longer range patrol than the infantrymen could go on. The Mobile Intel platoon boarded their P-43 Eagles and took off.

Greig put two of his squads on perimeter duty.

"Sergeant O'Connor," he said to his Third squad leader, looking beyond the wire at the landscape rather than at the sergeant, "I want you to take your squad out a klick and a half, and do a circumnavigation of the firebase. Take a GPS, a map, and a motion detector. Go out the south gate and come back the same way."

Staff Sergeant Albert O'Connor looked to the south gate and the three hundred meters of scorched ground from it to the surrounding forest. "I sure wish we had our Growlers," he said. Growler, the M-117 armored vehicle used primarily by Mobile Infantry units.

"So do I, Sergeant. But we don't. That's why I only want you to go a klick and a half."

O'Connor nodded. He didn't like it, but he understood.

"Go slow and easy. I don't want you blundering into a Duster unit."

"You and me both, LT."

"Keep your eyes open for any sign of Duster activity. The Marines are still conducting mop-up operations and making kills, so we know they're still out there." Greig chewed on his lip for a moment. "We just don't know where. Try to avoid contact if you do see any Dusters. But I want you to be fully armed, five hundred rounds per man, so in case you can't avoid contact you can properly defend yourselves."

"Right, LT. Avoid if possible, kill the sonsabitches if we have to." He shook his head. "I wish we had body armor."

Greig hung his head and didn't answer that. Then, "Equip every man with a medkit and four liters of water. No rations, you won't be gone that long. Be back in three and a half, four hours.

"Run a comm check now. Run another when you reach the trees, and another at a klick and a half. Your call sign is Rover one."

"Wilco." O'Connor turned away and put on his helmet. "Third squad, comm check. Sound off." In two minutes all three of his fire team leaders responded, and he'd heard the men answering the fire team leaders call for a comm check.

While he was doing that, Greig walked off a hundred meters. "Rover one, Two Actual. Comm check. Over."

"Two Actual, Rover one. I hear you five-by. Three's comm check is successful. Over."

"Two Actual out."

The two looked at each other across the length of a football pitch, satisfied that they had communications at this distance. O'Connor headed for his platoon commander to get the extra equipment he would need for the patrol.

"Third squad, on me," O'Connor called when he reached his squad area, laden with ammunition and other gear.

In a moment his nine men stood before him in a tight group. Briefly, he told them what they were going to do, and dismissed them to get their weapons. When they reassembled, he had them fill their camelbacks with four liters of water. He gave their rifles a quick check and issued each of them what they needed to get up to the required five hundred rounds.

Satisfied, he gave the order to move out. "Sergeant Gasson, you've got point. South gate. Move fifty meters into the trees, stop, and set in a semicircle defense."

"Allen, move out," Sergeant Richard Gasson ordered his most experienced pointman.

Corporal Abner Allen spat to the side and headed for the south gate.

In the forest

Three hundred meters later, the squad moved under the trees. The ground at the edge of the forest was speckled with fast growing weeds and tiny saplings, growing in profusion now that more light was reaching the ground after the destruction of the trees in the burned area. Fifty meters in, half a dozen or more different varieties of tree were fairly close to each other and the cover was much thicker, dimming the light. Some of them grew arrow-straight with thinnish trunks, others were gnarly with thicker boles. Some lacked branches until they were close to ten meters tall, others began branching as close as a meter above the ground. At least one variety had buttress roots. The canopy gave almost total cover, nearly blanking out direct sunlight. Less undergrowth grew under the trees.

"Hold up," O'Connor ordered. "Positions."

The nine soldiers quickly moved into a semicircle and lowered themselves to the ground, facing outward with their rifles at their shoulders, ready to fight.

O'Connor looked around, and his lips twisted in something that wasn't quite a grimace. The forest was denser than he'd expected, and he wasn't comfortable in all these trees—it was entirely too possible for a foe to come close without being detected. If there'd been avians flitting about, sounding their cries and singing their songs, they could present an advantage to the soldiers. They'd likely go quiet if a large group of animals, think aliens or human, began moving through. Even the insectoids made precious little noise scrambling over and through the detritus. The flying insectoids left them alone; O'Connor suspected they'd already tried to dine off the Sea Bees and decided humans weren't to their taste.

Well, they'd really have to pussyfoot to walk quietly—there was too much detritus cruching and crackling under foot. He'd been disappointed by how much noise his men made moving through the forest. Still, it could be worse. After all, he had the motion detector. When he swept it in a circle it didn't show anything larger than a squirrel moving in the trees. He wondered what kind of animal was the Troy analog of squirrels. Or if the colonists had imported squirrels. Nonetheless, it felt spooky.

Time for the comm check.

"Two Actual, this is Rover one," he said into his helmet comm. "Comm check. How do you hear me? Over."

It was only a few seconds before Lieutenant Greig's voice came back. "Rover one, this is Two Actual. I hear you five by. You me? Over."

"Two Actual, Rover one. Five by. Over."

"Sitrep. Over."

O'Connor took a deep breath. How could he describe how the forest felt? He decided on just the basic facts. "Two Actual, Rover one. The trees are dense, less than ten meters between trunks, mostly about five meters, often closer. There's a lot of noisy ground cover that makes silent movement difficult if not impossible. Motion detector shows nothing bigger than a mid-size rodent nearby. Over."

"Rover one, continue your mission. Two Actual out."

O'Connor kept his face blank. It didn't sound like he'd gotten any of his misgivings across to the LT. Not that he'd made any real attempt to do so.

"Third squad, get up. Move out, same order as before." He checked his GPS and pointed the direction for Allen.

Allen spat to the side and started walking. His eyes pierced every shadow, looked at every possible hiding place, checked for booby-trap triggers. The muzzle of his rifle was in constant motion, always pointing where his eyes looked.

O'Connor called for another halt twelve hundred meters deeper into the forest and made his second comm check. He was surprised that, despite the trees between his current location and the firebase, that Greig's voice came through as clearly as it had when he made his first check. He finished his sitrep with, "We're going widershins."

After signing off, he called to the pointman. "Allen, go left."

Allen spat to the side and did as he was instructed.

"Widershins?" Sergeant Gasson asked.

O'Connor shrugged. "It's remotely possible that the Dusters are listening to our comm and able to break our encryption. If they understand English, maybe they know that counter-clockwise means go to the left. Widershins is archaic enough that they'll probably have no idea what it means. And, you'll note, I didn't say we were turning. A listener might think it's a code name for a location."

Gasson gave his squad leader a speculative look. "Smart. I guess that's why you make the big bucks."

"You got that right. Except for the big bucks."

O'Connor frequently checked his GPS, and corrected Allen's route when necessary to keep him going in a circle.

About three kilometers around the circle

Corporal Allen, on point, froze in place and lowered himself to one knee. He lifted his head and turned his face side to side. From behind, he looked like he was trying to locate the direction of a smell. Sergeant O'Connor padded to his side and squatted.

"Tell me," he said.

"Something. Maybe ammonia. There." He swung the muzzle of his rifle in an arc of about twenty degrees to his right front.

"How far?"

"Can't tell. Faint."

O'Connor sniffed. He wasn't sure, but he might have picked up a hint of ammonia in the air. "Not close," he murmured.

Allen shook his head, agreeing that it was not close.

"Let's check it out," O'Connor said. He turned to Sergeant Gasson, who had come up to find out why they'd stopped. "Allen and I are going to check it. You take the squad."

"Right. Be careful."

"I didn't last long enough to become a staff sergeant by being careless." To Allen, "Let's go."

The corporal led the way, stepping carefully to avoid making noise as much as possible, sniffing all they way. O'Connor watched sharply for any visible sign of Dusters.

"Getting stronger," Allen whispered after they'd gone a hundred meters deeper into the forest.

O'Connor nodded, he smelled it more sharply now as well. They slowed their pace, flowing from shadow to shadow, from the cover of one tree bole to another.

A casual *cooing* brought them up short.

Allen stretched his arm back and held up a finger at O'Connor, signaling *wait a minute*, then lowered himself to his knees and elbows to crawl forward. He only went ten meters before stopping and going flat to the ground. Moving slowly, he shifted his rifle to his shoulder and took aim.

Don't shoot unless you're spotted, O'Connor thought at Allen. *Please, don't shoot!* He had no way of knowing how many Dusters were nearby, but he was sure there had to be more of them than his squad had soldiers.

Allen watched carefully, and didn't pull the trigger. After a couple of minutes, he started easing backward until he reached O'Connor. He didn't speak, but signaled with a head nod for the two of them to withdraw farther. O'Connor nodded understanding and began a reverse elbows-and-knees crawl.

When they had gone beyond the point where they'd first heard the coo, Allen stopped.

"It's a latrine," he whispered with his lips near O'Connor's ear. "A Duster was relieving itself." He shook his head, marveling at what he'd seen. "It's a strange arrangement. There are two sticks poking up at each end of a short trench, with two poles going from one end to the other. The Duster is perched on the poles, one foot on each. It looked like it had a cloaca, with black-streaked white shit coming out of a slit."

O'Connor nodded, and signaled for them to go around the latrine. They went crouched low. It wasn't long before they saw the edge of a forest encampment. Leafy, tent-like structures were laid out in rows. Thin whisps of smoke rose from what the humans thought must be cook fires. The leafy overhead was just as thick as any other place O'Connor had seen—maybe even thicker. He wondered if the added denseness would block the infrared signals from live animals from getting out, whether the Mobile Intel platoon could spot this encampment from the air.

Some Dusters went about in purposeful-looking marches. Others lounged near the presumed tents, doing things to their weapons and gear. Cleaning them? Probably. O'Connor took images, 2-D and vid both, of the encampment, and used his GPS to record its location.

It wasn't possible to get an accurate estimate of the number of Dusters in the encampment, the two weren't at a good angle to see deep into it; the nearer tent-things obstructed their view. Still, going by the sounds of *cooing*, and *gobbling*, and the occasional *caw*, he estimated that there were the equivalent of a human battalion of the aliens in the camp. He thought they must feel very secure that they didn't have security out. Or had he and Allen lucked out and simply slipped between observation posts?

After a few minutes O'Connor decided they had gotten all the intelligence they could and were risking discovery. He signaled Allen and they withdrew. The first thing he did when they rejoined the squad was call in a report on what they'd found.

Lieutenant Greig didn't take time to look at the images before saying, "Continue your circuit. But be very careful. Now we know they're nearby."

"You got that right," O'Connor said, ignoring proper radio procedure.

"Two three," Greig said, "I'll be in touch with any change in orders. Until then, continue your mission. Over"

"Two Actual, two three. Roger, wilco. Over."

"Two Actual, out."

O'Connor signaled for the squad to gather close. "Keep watching outboard," he cautioned his men when they did. "Listen up, and listen good. There's a Duster camp less than half a klick in that direction." He pointed. "We are going to continue on our assigned route. I don't know if the Dusters have any patrols moving that could intercept us. When we move out, be as quiet as you can, be the most alert you've ever been in your life. We might have to fight our way back to the firebase.

"Same order of march. Five meter intervals. Move out."

Allen didn't hesitate. He spat to the side—away from the direction of the Duster camp—and began walking in the direction in which O'Connor pointed.

In a minute, eleven very tense soldiers were continuing their circuit.

★

Lieutenant Greig was nervous about having the squad continue on the same route knowing that the aliens were so close, but they needed the intelligence. He notified the CB boss, Lieutenant Commander Harrison, of the discovery, and sent a report to Captain Meyer, who was still high above on the elevator station.

"Get that Mobile Intel platoon back to reinforce you," Meyer said when he found out that the MI platoon was out on its own. "At least one other platoon from the battalion is planetside. I'll ask to have them diverted to your location. Alpha Six Actual, out."

"Roger," Greig said to himself. Another platoon. Great. Even if he got the MI platoon back and got another platoon from the battalion, they weren't nearly enough to fight off so many Dusters. He knew from his briefings that nobody, Army or Marines, had artillery in place to support this firebase. The only fire assets that could be called on was a Marine AV 16C squadron. Maybe Meyer would ask Battalion to request that Brigade ask the Marines to sortie. The best would be for the Marines to strike the Duster camp before the aliens made a move.

But he couldn't ask for that in the open. Not as long as the possibility, no matter how remote, existed that the aliens could intercept and understand human transmissions. All he could do was make sure his men were ready to account well for themselves if the time came.

Not for the first time, he wished the Army had its own fast-flyers and didn't have to rely on the Marines and the Navy. The Army's aircraft were transports of various kinds, and the slow moving aircraft that provided support for the ground forces.

★

Allen stopped and knelt, looking at something on the ground.

Gasson joined him. "What'cha got?"

Allen pointed at marks that crossed their route. They resembled the tracks of a large bird, or perhaps lizard, with long claws. They were moving in a direction that would, if continued in a straight line, pass half a kilometer southwest of the firebase.

"I'll tell O'Connor," Gasson said. Allen didn't answer, just peered into the surrounding forest.

In a moment the squad leader had joined them. "How many are there?" he asked when he saw the tracks. Allen shook his head. "Could be lots hidden under the leaves."

"So maybe a fire team, but it could be a battalion?"

Allen shook his head again. "Not a battalion. Maybe fire team, maybe company." He shrugged.

O'Connor didn't ask any more questions, just took images and transmitted them to Greig. He listened to the lieutenant's answer, then ordered, "Follow that track."

Allen spat to the side and changed direction to follow the tracks.

Tension mounted as the men of the squad realized they were trailing an unknown number of Dusters. The tension would have been greater if they hadn't known they were getting closer to their firebase and help.

Broken circuit, tangental to Advance Firebase One

"Keep it staggered," Staff Sergeant O'Connor called to his squad. They were moving away from where he and Corporal Allen had observed the Duster camp, so he wasn't as concerned about maintaining quiet. "Let's not all get taken out by one burst." Ever since the mid-nineteenth-century development of the Gatling gun, infantry officers and non-commissioned officers have been concerned about the possibility of their men being wiped out by a head-on burst of automatic fire, and constantly told them not to stand directly behind one another. That, of course, did not apply on the parade ground where officers can indulge in their fantasies of commanding troops in the tactics of the Napoleonic Wars. So O'Connor admonished his squad to keep it staggered, and not walk directly one behind the other.

He himself wanted to be staggered more than the others to get the least obstructed view to the front. But they were still in the forest, and he couldn't see very far ahead even if he did walk farther to the side. Better to rely on Allen to spot trouble ahead before that trouble spotted the squad. O'Connor wasn't enough of a tracker to tell how old the tracks they were following were. They could have been less than an hour, or they could have been several hours old. But not so old that if whoever left them had set in an ambush, as they would have likely left the ambush position by now.

O'Connor thought walking into an ambush was a greater possibility than catching up with whoever they were trailing and being spotted by their rear guard before Allen spotted them.

He saw that the light was increasing ahead of the squad indicating that they were nearing the edge of the cleared area around the firebase when Allen stopped, lowered himself to a knee and looked back. O'Connor followed Gasson to the pointman.

Wordlessly, Allen pointed; the tracks he'd been following split, some continued straight, some bent to the right.

O'Connor looked in both directions but didn't see anything to tell him what the Dusters were up to. He called Greig, requesting instructions.

It took the better part of a minute for Greig to provide any. "Go left half a klick and then come directly in."

After acknowledging the new orders, O'Connor turned to Allen. "Stay far enough inside the trees to be behind someone lining up for an assault, but close enough to see into the open. When we get out, head straight for the main gate at a brisk walk. Got it?"

Allen nodded, spat to the side, and moved out on the new route. They didn't encounter anyone or any problems in the half-klick movement through the trees, then turned toward the firebase.

They were in the open, still more than a hundred meters from the firebase's wire, when shrill cries from the edge of the forest shattered the quiet of the day, and heavy fire began coming at them.

"Run!" O'Connor shouted, and began sprinting toward the open gate. The caws and shrieks behind him rapidly grew in volume, and the bullets whizzing and zinging past them felt closer.

"Third squad, *down!*" Lieutenant Greig shouted over the platoon freq.

O'Connor repeated the order. He dove to the ground and twisted around to face the forest. He began firing at Dusters, hundreds of them who boiled out of the forest, racing, jinking and jiving in a chaotic mass, at his squad. "Everybody, fire!" he shouted. To his sides, he heard the fire team leaders turning their men to face fire on the Dusters.

Then with a *r-i-i-i-p-p!* the M-69 Scatterer opened up, raining bullets over the heads of the soldiers of Third squad. One of the M-5C machine guns joined the Scatterer, and the two M-40 mortars began lobbing their bombs into the mass of Dusters. The rifles of a squad added to the death flying at the Dusters. Blood spurted and geysered from hit Dusters, feathers flew, and chunks of flesh and bone were flung about.

But there were so many of the aliens that it seemed to O'Connor that the monstrous casualties they were taking hardly seemed to dent their numbers. Already in the few seconds since O'Connor had first heard the cries of the Dusters they had halved the distance from the forest's edge to the humans. And there seemed to be as many as there were to begin with.

"Kill them!" O'Connor bellowed, firing as fast as he could at the charging enemy. The mass of Dusters was so dense that nearly half of his unaimed bullets found a target, and many of the hit Dusters tumbled to the ground. His men were striking almost as often as he did. He could see that the Dusters' speed was so great that they would have caught his squad if the men had kept running instead of stopping to allow the platoon's weapons squad to fire over them. He looked at the rapidly closing enemy and realized his only satisfaction now would be how many Dusters died with him and his men in the next few minutes.

"What's wrong with you?" he screamed, when he realized the mortar had stopped firing.

Before the words were fully out of his mouth a blur flashed through his field of view. He was buffeted, almost rolled over by the shock wave that accompanied the most deafening *boom* he'd ever heard.

Marine air had come!

The first strike was by two AV 16C Kestrels, which used the shockwave from their sonic boom to break up the Duster mass and cause casualties.

O'Connor raised his head and saw far greater disruption among the Dusters than at first. The aliens' chaotic movement was intended to confuse their enemy; this chaos was Dusters staggering about in confusion and disorientation, and tripping over their comrades who'd been injured by the sonic concussion.

A second pair of Kestrels swooped down at subsonic speed, firing their weapons along the long axis of the mass of Dusters. Blood, feathers, flesh, and bone fountained into the air. He realized that the aliens were no longer shooting at his men, and the rest of Second platoon had stopped firing.

"Third squad, on your feet!" he shouted. "Head for the gate." He looked around to make sure everyone heard and was obeying his order, and saw two limping soldiers being assisted by others. Before he could make a satisfied grunt about his men taking care of each other without being told to, he noticed an unmoving lump.

"Ah, shit." He sprinted to the downed soldier and found PFC George Buchanan staring lifelessly in a puddle of blood; an enemy projectile had hit him where his neck and shoulder met. O'Connor suspected the shot had hit Buchanan's heart, killing him instantly. He hoped it was instantaneous, that the soldier hadn't suffered.

He quickly glanced toward the Dusters. Noticeably fewer of them were milling about now, and none were charging or firing, not even at the Marine aircraft that were coming in for another strike. Those who could were staggering toward the cover of the trees. He hoisted Buchanan over his shoulders in a fireman's carry. No help for it, he carried his own rifle in his free hand but left Buchanan's to be retrieved later.

Speeding toward the gate, he almost felt like cheering when he heard the Marines' continuing fire on the Dusters.

Aftermath

They held a brief memorial service for PFC Buchanan, the first member of Alpha Troop to die in action.

"Brief" was all they had time for. Brigadier General Rufus Saxon, 10th Brigade's commander, and the battalion commander, Lieutenant Colonel Douglas Hapeman, flew in as soon as the battle was over to assess the situation.

"You need to get this cleaned up, Lieutenant," Saxon said to Greig as the three strode through the chewed up ground where the Marine

Kestrels had slaughtered so many Dusters. "These bodies are going to start stinking something fierce in a very few hours. You don't have any heavy equipment to dig a trench-grave, so you're going to have to burn them. Put your boys to work gathering the bodies in one spot. I'll get you enough fuel to bonfire them. Got it?"

Greig had hoped Saxon would send in some engineers with equipment to dig a trench and bulldoze the corpses into it, but that wasn't to be. "Yes, sir," was all he could say.

Saxon gave him a look. "I know you'd rather do it with heavy equipment. That'd be faster, certainly, but after the action you just had, and losing your first soldier, I think your boys need something other than their loss to keep their minds occupied."

"Yes, sir, the general is right," Greig said. He wanted to say something very different, something that would get a mere second lieutenant in deep trouble if he said it to a brigadier general. So he simply said, "Yes, sir, the general is right."

Saxon gave the field of carnage a long, penetrating look. "The Marines estimate that between their air and your ground fire, we killed about a quarter of the Dusters that attacked. What's your assessment of their casualties?"

"Sir, a quarter sounds about right," Greig said.

"You must have been hit by something more than a regiment."

"At the time, it looked more like a divsion, sir."

Saxon barked a curt laugh. "And you only lost one man." He grinned fiercely. "These beasts may have made a quick hash of the colonial guard that was here when they first attacked, but now they're up against professionals. They don't have a chance."

"Begging the general's pardon, sir, but they pretty much wiped out a Force Recon platoon. That sounds pretty tough to me." Greig swallowed at his own temerity; it didn't do for a second lieutenant to gainsay a brigadier general.

Saxon barked another laugh, and clapped a hand on Greig's shoulder. "Force Recon. Marines," he said dismissively.

Greig stayed quiet. Unlike many officers in the Army, he held the fighting ability of the Marines in high regard.

Soon after, Saxon said, "Carry on" and headed for his aircraft.

"I'll get you some protective gear," Hapeman told Greig, wrinkling his nose at the smell that was already beginning to rise from the scattered corpses and body parts. He followed Saxon.

Graves detail

"This is bullshit, Mr. Greig," Sergeant First Class Quinn groused.

Second Lieutenant Greig shook his head without saying anything. He agreed with his platoon sergeant, but couldn't complain to the sergeant about the inadequacy of the protective gear that the battalion commander had provided them with. The breathing filters cut down on the mounting stench of decomposition, and the long-cuffed disposable gloves kept the men's hands off the alien flesh and bones, but did nothing to keep them from trodding in the offal, or prevent anything from splashing on their uniforms, or any exposed skin.

"We should have full-cover hazard suits," Quinn continued.

"Should, would, could," Greig said impatiently. "That won't get us anywhere. We'll make do with what we have. Do you understand me, Sergeant?"

"Ah, yeah, sure, uh, sir. We do what we can with what we got." Then in a low voice that might not even reach Greig's ears, "And hope none'a them creatures got anything that can kill us from simple contact."

But his words did carry.

"Sarge, if the Dusters were carrying any pathogens that could harm us, I'm sure the Navy scientists would have told us."

"I'm sure." To himself Quinn added, *They would'a told our brass, but would the brass have passed the word to us?*

All but a few soldiers assigned to picket duty to watch for another attack were set to clearing the field of corpses and body parts. The area was extensive enough that they didn't make one big pile, but made several, more than fifty meters apart. It took almost an entire day to assemble the piles. Then they were doused with fuel and set ablaze.

"Goddam!" Sergeant Gasson complained. "The fire stinks almost worse than the bodies did when we were collecting them."

"Could be worse," Staff Sergeant O'Connor said calmly. "We're upwind from the fires." He nodded toward the forest beyond the burning piles. "The wind is blowing the stink away from us, into the forest. If the rest of the Dusters, the ones that got away, are still in there, if they didn't go far, far away, how do you think they feel smelling their buddies burning like that?"

Gasson chewed on his lip, looking beyond the flames. After a long moment he said, "Yeah."

Advance Firebase One

"Heads up!" Corporal Allen shouted as he grabbed his rifle and fired a shot toward the smoke-shrouded treeline.

"What's up?" Sergeant Gasson called.

"Dusters!" Allen shouted again and fired another round.

"Back, get back to the line!" Staff Sergeant O'Connor bellowed to his squad. They were gathering and burning corpses of the Dusters who had fallen outside the wire- and spike-studded trench.

Lieutenant Greig and SFC Quinn took up the cry, even though neither of them had seen any Dusters through the smoke from the burning alien corpses.

"To your positions!" Greig ordered on his all-hands freq.

It took little more than a minute for the graves detail to pick up their weapons and make it back through the opening in the wire wire stacked pyramid-like, four rolls high, over the board-bridge over the trench, and scramble into their defensive positions.

Greig picked up his infra scope and looked into the slowly thinning cloud of smoke. "Damn," he swore under his breath. In infra he saw Dusters jinking and darting toward the firebase. "They're coming," he said into the all-hands freq. "Wait for my order." *Where the hell is that Mobile Intel platoon?* He'd contacted them more than an hour ago and told them to come back, that he needed them at the firebase because the Dusters were here. He lowered the scope and peered at the slowly thinning smoke, scanning from side to side. Then he dimly saw hunched over shapes flitting through the smoke he shouted, *"Fire!"* Hundreds more shapes quickly became visible close behind.

All the weapons of the reinforced platoon opened up. The CBs had also taken up weapons and added their fire to the soldiers'. The answering *caws* of the Dusters couldn't be heard over the din of the outgoing gunfire—but the *cracks* of the Dusters' fire *could* be heard, and the *thuds* from the impacts of their bullets as random shots struck the faces of the bunkers. Some of the flitting forms fell or tumbled under the withering fire from Second platoon and the CBs. Then the Dusters started dashing through the smoke, darting here and there, going sideways more than forward, but always closing the distance to the wire. Dusters flipped, flopped, crashed to the ground. Some of them got up again and resumed their charge, although most of the fallen either stayed down or began crawling between the burning pyres, back toward the trees. But most of them kept coming.

The first dozen Dusters to reach the wire flung themselves onto it and writhed, bleeding from multiple punctures, pinning their bodies tighter and tighter to it until they couldn't move any more. Their shrill *caws* and agonized shrieks sent chills through some of the soldiers and inspired them to shoot at the pinioned aliens, to kill them, to put them out of their misery, to still their cries of pain.

"Ignore the ones on the wire," Greig commanded. "Shoot the ones still coming!"

The next dozen Dusters to reach the wire clambered up the bodies of their comrades already there and threw their own bodies onto the top tier of wire, pinning themselves to it, adding their *caws* and shrieks to the cacophony. The third wave scrambled over the first two and dove onto the downslope of the wire, completing a bridge over it that the following aliens used to cross the obstacle unharmed.

The first of the Dusters who crossed the wire on the living bridges jumped into the studded trench and collapsed when spikes impaled their feet. Screaming in agony, they fell onto more spikes. The initial

Dusters had intentionally sacrificed themselves to make bridges, but none of them knew about the spikes in the shallow trench until their feet got impaled. The first to reach the shallow trench became unintended bridges over the spikes.

Hundreds thudded across their fallen mates, driving them deeper onto the spikes, snapping their bones, killing them. Those hundreds raced across the remaining killing ground at the bunkers that continued to blast death at them. More and more Dusters fell to the fire from the soldiers and CBs. And still they came on, shrieking *caws* and shrill battle cries.

In their bunker, Gasson and Allen kept up a steady fire of three-round bursts at the charging Dusters. PFCs Charles F. Sancrainte and Denis Buckley joined them at the embrasure, firing at the charging aliens. The zigging and zagging of the attackers made it impossible to properly aim at them, but their sheer numbers made accurate aim unnecessary. If you picked a spot and kept shooting at it, sooner rather than later a darting, dodging body would cross through that space at the same time a bullet did, and a Duster would bite the dust.

But the Dusters weren't jinking directly at the fronts of the bunkers, mostly they angled and re-angled to the spaces between bunkers, to get between and behind them, where they knew the entrances were. As many as fell in the open ground between the wire and the studded trench, even more made it between the bunkers to attack them from the rear.

"Allen, cover the rear!" Gasson shouted.

The corporal scooted to the dog-legged entrance of the bunker and lay prone with his chest and shoulders in the tunnel section that emptied into it. He pointed his rifle around the corner just in time to see a Duster's head poke around from the outer section. He pulled the trigger of his rifle, sending three rounds at the beaked head. The alien was fast and jerked back just in time for Allen's shot to miss. The Duster stuck its rifle around the corner and let off a long burst, but its projectiles went high. Allen fired another burst, hitting the weapon and knocking it out of the alien's hands. The shriek that came told Allen he must have hit the Duster's hand or wrist as well as its weapon. Scrabbling noises said the wounded alien was backing out. or was being dragged out of the way.

Excited chittering came from outside, and a dark object crashed into the tunnel, and caromed around the corner to roll toward Allen.

"Grenade!" he shouted, and scooted back and flattened against the side of the bunker next to the entrance.

The grenade exploded with a deafening roar before it reached the corner to the final leg. Shrapnel ripped into the tunnel walls, but none entered the bunker itself.

Instantly, Allen went prone, shoving his chest and shoulders back into the tunnel, rifle first. The muzzle slammed into the beak of a Duster who was already reaching the inner bend. Allen pulled his rifle back far enough to get off a burst, and the Duster's head exploded from the impact of three bullets hitting from only a couple of centimeters distance. Allen pushed his rifle around the corner and quickly cranked off three more three-round bursts. Screams answered him, along with fire from alien weapons. He heard the movement of bodies withdrawing, and waited a few seconds before taking a quick look around the corner. He saw the twitching corpse of the first one he'd killed, and the sprawled body of another halfway around the next corner.

After waiting a few more seconds before looking again, he saw the second body being dragged back. He scrambled over the body of the first one to the corner onto the one being dragged and stuck his rifle around it to fire another three bursts. A scream met his fire, and the tension he'd felt in the body of the Duster he was on fell away; whoever had been pulling it was out of the fight. He fired again, but didn't hear any cry or other sound to indicate he'd hit another Duster. He scrambled back.

While Allen had been fighting off the Dusters trying to enter the bunker, Gasson and the rest of the fire team were at the embrasure, still shooting at the charging aliens, but not hitting as many as before—most of the surviving enemy had reached the area between the bunkers where they were safe from the continuing fire.

But not all had reached that momentary safety. One, shrieking madly, zigging and zagging manically, reached the bunker and jammed its weapon into the embrasure. It fired a burst into the face and chest of Sancrainte, making him Second platoon's second fatality. Gasson and Buckley each fired two bursts into the alien, killing it and tossing its blood-spewing corpse away to land in a broken heap.

And then there were no more Dusters in front of the bunkers.

"Buckley, stay, guard," Gasson snapped. He spun about and in three steps went prone, on top of Allen, to peer around the corner. Seeing only the two Duster corpses, he scooted back and off Allen.

"Let's get these things out of the way," he said.

Allen put his rifle down and reached around the corner with both hands to grasp the Duster by its upper arms. He pulled it none too gently as he crawled backward into the bunker. As soon as he had the body far enough, Gasson reached over him to grab the Duster and unceremoniously yank it the rest of the way in, where he flung it into a corner.

As soon as the first body was out of the way, Allen took up his rifle again and crawled to the second body. "Cover me," he said over his shoulder. A quick glance showed Gasson on one knee, aiming his rifle past him. Allen reached the body and pulled it by the arms, just as he had the other. It was tight, but he squeezed past Gasson who had tucked himself into the angle of the corner and kept aiming down the short length of the tunnel. In the bunker he tossed the body onto the other, and took a quick look through the embrasure at the vacant landscape visible through it.

"Stay sharp, Buckley," he said, clapping the PFC's shoulder. "When they figure out we've got them blocked at the entrance they might come around front again."

"Sure thing, Corporal," Buckley said, glancing nervously at Sancrainte's body where it lay on the pallet the dead soldier had used as a bed.

Allen scrambled back to Gasson, who was waiting for him inside the entrance tunnel.

"I'm bigger than you," Gasson said, "so I'll go first. At the entrance you either kneel over me, or lay on me. Between us, we can cover almost a hundred and eighty degrees. Got it?"

"Got it, Sarge. Any time you're ready."

Without another word, Gasson scooted into the long leg of the tunnel and fired around the next corner before looking down it. When he did he saw sky and ground and running, scaled legs that ended in taloned feet. And some crumpled bodies, a couple of which he thought must have been Dusters Allen had killed.

He bent himself around the corner far enough to see farther to the sides of the entrance, about a ninety degree field of vision. Almost immediately he saw a Duster looking in his direction and skittering toward him. He snapped off two quick bursts and was satisfied to see the Duster drop his weapon as he fell face down. He put another burst into the Duster when he saw it scrabbling toward its rifle.

Then Allen was leaning over him and looking farther out.

"Damn, but there's a shitload of 'em," the corporal said, putting his rifle to his shoulder and cranking off a few three-round bursts.

Gasson skooched forward until he could see almost a one-hundred-and-eighty-degree arc. "They've got no discipline! They're just running around."

"If they slowed down so's we could hit 'em, this'd be a goddamn turkey shoot!" Ignoring the fact that the Dusters weren't slowing down, that they were running as fast, firing as wildly, and jinking as unpredictably as during their charge, he began putting bursts out at randomly selected targets. Beneath him, Gasson did the same. They fired again and again, and some of their bursts hit.

But not all of the Dusters were as undisciplined as the ones the two soldiers were shooting at.

"They're on top of the bunker!" Buckley twisted around and shouted the warning at the entrance. If he could have, he would have squeezed through the embrasure to shoot at the aliens he heard on top of the bunker. But the opening was too narrow, he could barely sitck his head through it, and then only if he first removed his helmet.

"Look up!" Buckley shouted.

But Gasson and Allen couldn't hear Buckley's shouts over the din of firing, their own and the Dusters'. Allen was leaning out, completely exposing his head and shoulders, when a burst from above slammed into him and knocked him onto Gasson, driving the fire team leader flat. Two Dusters dropped off the top of the bunker and fired under Allen, into Gasson. With the two soldiers out of the way, the two Dusters darted into the entry tunnel determined to kill its last defender.

Unfortunately for them, Buckley had heard the shooting at the mouth of the tunnel, and its sudden cessation, and knew what it had to mean. He was ready when the Dusters came in, and—in the tunnel that was too narrow for them to jink—killed both of the attackers.

Buckley waited, dry-mouthed, for more Dusters to appear, either through the tunnel or outside the embrasure.

Command post, Advance Firebase One

Lieutenant Greig watched appalled as the Dusters overran his platoon's defenses, and the positions manned by the CBs. He knew his men had slaughtered many, many of the attackers before they reached the line of bunkers. But there were so damn *many* of the alien soldiers that it was only a matter of time, and not a very long time, before they completely wiped out the small human force. He'd put in a request for Marine air support, but was told none was immediately available, that all the Marine Kestrels and Eagles were on other missions, but the first available would be sortied to his aid.

At least his men had acquitted themselves well.

Then the manic running about of the Dusters took on a different tone, and many of them looked to the sky beyond the perimeter.

Greig grabbed his glasses and looked where the Dusters were looking. There! Coming fast, were four aircraft. They were still too far away for him to make out, but whatever kind they were they were going to save his platoon and the CBs!

The Dusters started to break and run. Only a few at first, but more and more as they saw the first ones fleeing. Soon, before the aircraft reached close enough to the firebase to lay effective air-to-ground fire on them, the Dusters were in full rout, being pursued by fire from the defenders. By the time the first aliens reached the trees, the aircraft were above them, raining fire. They were MH 15 Alphonses—the MI platoon had finally arrived!

The Butcher's Bill

Second platoon, Alpha Company, First of the Seventh Mounted Infantry had lost eight men killed and another seven wounded badly enough to require evacuation to a field hospital—or even to orbital facilities. Close to half of the platoon required replacements. And from where were they going to come? The CBs had lost seven, dead or severely wounded. Where were their replacements going to come from?

Lieutenant Greig decided then that the Troy operation was even more of a royal cockup than he'd already thought—which, after the beating that ARG 17 had taken upon arrival in the Troy system, was saying a lot.

What next?? the lieutenant wanted to know. But there was nobody who could—or would—tell him.

VMA 214, Marine Corps Aviation Facility, near Jordan,

Lieutenant General Bauer wanted combat air close to Jordan, because there had been so much Duster activity in the area. Major General Hiram I. Bearss, Commanding General of Marine Air Wing 2, selected an area that was many square kilometers of level ground. The Dusters were known for using cave and tunnel complexes as staging areas and to move about undetected. The Navy in orbit was still conducting its search for gravitational anomalies and hadn't covered all the Jordan region, but Myers concluded that a level landscape wouldn't have caves or tunnels. Myers tasked Marine Air Group 14 with establishing an expeditionary air field and assigning a ground-attack squadron to it.

The air facility was quickly constructed and Marine Attack Squadron 214 assigned to operate out of the newly established MCAF Jordan. Except for one mission flown by a four-aircraft division in support of the Army's Alpha Troop, First of the Seventh Mounted Infantry, life was quiet for the first week and a half that VMA 214 was at Jordan, with nothing more than routine patrols looking for possible Duster movement. So no one was unduly concerned about the airfield not having any security beyond its own personnel, most of whom were occupied with maintaining and operating the squadron's AV16C Kestrel attack aircraft.

★

"Ah, shit!" Gunnery Sergeant Robert G. Robinson swore from his position supervising the control tower. He got on the horn to the ready room. "Sir, better scramble," he said when Major John L. Smith, VMA 214's executive officer and the senior pilot in the ready room, answered his call. "Got a shitload of Dusters coming our way. On foot, from the east." Before Smith could ask for details, he continued, "Maybe six hundred of 'em, hard to tell, the way they're jinking. I don't see anything but small arms, but who knows what kind a shit they got outta sight." *Where the hell did they come from?* he wondered. *Ain't supposed to be no goddam tunnels or caves nowhere around here*

While Robinson was reporting, a *whooga whooga* alarm began sounding throughout the MCAF. On the ground, he saw pilots racing from the ready room to the flight line where a dozen AV16C Kestrels were lined up with their canopies standing open. Ground crew bustled around the aircraft, checking their armament and fuel levels, pulling the safeties on their missiles, pulling the chocks that kept them from moving when buffeted by gusts of wind. Half a dozen additional pilots ran from the mess and the barracks to the ready room to prepare themselves to fly. More ground crew trundled six more Kestrels from the hangars alongside the taxiway and began checking their ordnance and topping off their fuel tanks, preparatory to moving them onto the flight line.

And the speeding alien soldiers were fast closing on the runway.

"Tower, have them launch when ready," Lieutenant Colonel Merritt Edson, the squadron commander, snapped on his comm—he was one of the pilots running from quarters to the ready room.

"Aye aye, Skipper," Robinson replied. "Yo, who's ready to go?" he asked on the squadron freq.

"I am," Captain Jefferson J. DeBlanc was the first to answer.

"Then fly away little birdie. Next?" As the pilots answered their readiness, Robinson sent them off, until five were airborne and diving, guns blazing, at the Dusters.

But five Kestrels were all that made it into the sky before the aliens reached the runway to block the aircraft lining up to take off, and shooting at them from close range.

The next Kestrel, sixth in line, attempted to take off into the charging Dusters. It didn't have enough speed when it lifted, and tumbled into the end of the runway, bursting into a flaming ball.

Captain Henry T. Elrod, the next in line, fired his guns into the charging enemy, and tried to take off through the hole his cannon rounds made in the mass of Dusters. But the hole filled in before he reached it, and three of the aliens got sucked into his Kestrel's engines. The aircraft spun about uncontrollably with its guns still firing. The cannon fire knocked out two more Kestrels that were taxiing toward the runway.

First Lieutenant Kenneth A. Walsh was starting to turn onto the runway when he saw Elrod spin and fire at the Kestrels coming behind him. Almost instinctively, he twisted his stick in the opposite direction, pointing his aircraft away from the Dusters. He checked his rear-view and saw the nearest aliens were a hundred meters distant. He put on his wheel locks and air brakes, then hit his afterburner, sending exhaust flame gouting nearly two hundred meters rearward. Fifty or more Dusters were immolated by the torch-like flame. He released his locks and brakes, and sped the wrong way, going with the wind rather into it. Cutting the afterburner, he spun about to face the Dusters from half a kilometer distance. No other aircraft had turned onto the runway; Dusters were flooding off it to surround the Kestrels and mob the ground crews. But many were still on the runway. Walsh began firing his guns and launching his missiles at them.

Walsh saw explosions on the taxiway, and fireballs bloomed where three of the Kestrels waiting to turn onto the runway maneuvered—making it obvious that some of the Dusters had carried demolitions.

In the tower, Robinson looked on aghast as the aircraft of VMA 214 were destroyed on the ground, and as the ground-crew Marines were being shot down or torn apart by the vicious claws of the Dusters. He patted his hip where he should have been carrying a holstered sidearm, but no weapon was there. Neither were the two controllers with him armed. *Shit,* he swore, *why don't we have a grunt company for security?* But he knew why—and saw just how wrong the decision had been.

"Marines," he said to his controllers, "I hope to shit you remember your hand-to-hand combat training, because I believe we're about to be in a fight."

Rapid footsteps on the stairs leading to the control room gave proof to his words.

Robinson and the two controllers managed to kill four of the Dusters before they were overwhelmed.

✪

"Now what do we do?" First Lieutenant James E. Swett asked as he circled over the air facility and the aircraft burning on it. Dusters still milled about on the ground, but Swett's plane, like the other four airborne Kestrels, was out of ordnance.

"We roll them, then head for Puller," Major Smith answered. "On me, echelon left!" The Kestrels lined up, angling back to Smith's left. They followed their XO down to thirty meters above the ground, and flashed past the enemy soldiers at just below mach speed, knocking them down with the concussion of their passage. Some Dusters were injured or even killed by debris thrown up by the zooming aircraft. A few were thrown bodily into burning hulks and burned to death. All suffered injuries from the concussion.

Then, running low on fuel, the five surviving aircraft of VMA 214 headed for Camp Puller, outside Millerton.

Camp Zion, near Jordan

"Third Platoon, saddle up!" Second Lieutenant Commiskey shouted as he scrambled out of the company headquarters bunker.

"Move, move, move, move, move!" Staff Sergeant Guillen bellowed, following Commiskey out of the bunker."

"What's happening, Honcho?" Corporal Mackie shouted, buckling on his harness and running out of his fire team's bunker, rifle slung over his shoulder, helmet perched on his head.

"When I find out, you'll be the first to know," Sergeant Martin shouted back. He held his rifle and helmet in one hand and his harness in the other. He was rapidly striding to the open area behind the platoon's section of perimeter, where the Marines would soon assemble. "First squad, get your asses out here!" he roared

The Marines of Third platoon were boiling out of their bunkers, strapping on gear, checking the action of their weapons, patting pouches to make sure they were fully armed and had everything else they were sure they'd soon need. As they lined up in formation the squad leaders quickly went along their lines, inspecting their men, double checking that they had all their gear and ammunition.

"'Toon, A-ten-HUT!" Guillen bellowed as he ran to face the formation. He looked to the side where he saw Commiskey racing to the platoon, then beyond where he saw three armored Scooters and a Hog warming up.

Commiskey took his position before his men. "Third platoon, the Air Facility is under attack, and we're going to relieve them. Vehicles are readying for us now." He turned to Guillen. "Platoon Sergeant, is the platoon ready?"

Guillen looked at the squad leaders. "Inspected and ready," they said, almost in unison.

"Where's guns?" Commiskey asked, noticing that the machine gun squad that often accompanied Third platoon wasn't there.

"Coming up, sir," Sergeant Matej Kocak shouted. His voice was accompanied by the jangling of weapons and unsecured gear.

Commiskey looked and saw the seven men of the gun squad running to join the platoon. He nodded approval.

"Platoon Sergeant, move the platoon to the vehicles."

"Aye aye, sir." Guillen snapped the orders that got the platoon, with its attached gun squad, marching in formation to the Hog and the Scooters that were now turned face away from the platoon and lowering their ramps to allow the Marines to board them. HM3 David E. Hadyen with his medkit, clambered aboard.

In little more than another minute, the armored vehicles closed up and sped out of the Marine firebase.

MCAF Jordan

The airfield had been put together so rapidly it only had a few sections of barrier fencing around it, allowing the vehicles to roar in unimpeded. They stopped near a Kestrel that hunkered alone, half a kilometer from the control tower and the burned and smoking hulks of other aircraft.

"What happened here?" Commiskey asked the pilot who stood in his Kestrel's open cockpit.

"First Lieutenant Walsh, sir," the dazed-looking pilot answered. "We got flat mobbed by Dusters." He shook his head. "I think they're all gone now."

"Where are the rest of your people?"

Walsh waved a hand at the devastation visible in the middle distance. "I'm not sure anybody's left."

"Hang tight, Lieutenant," Commiskey said. "We'll check it out." He told the armored vehicle platoon commander to advance on line to a hundred meters from the nearest smoking hulk.

Wind blew lightly across the runway when the Marines raced off the Scooters and Hog, and formed up on line, the smell of scorched metal and electronics and charred flesh wafting up at them.

"Advance at a trot," Commiskey ordered. "Stagger it and watch your dress."

The Marines of Third platoon stepped up their pace and a minute later, with bodies clearly in view, they slowed to a walk. There were Duster bodies, some bloodied, some charred. The human bodies were all blood smeared. The charred remains were immediately recognized as alien because even in death, the Dusters were bent at the hip, their thighs bulged, and their faces jutted in muzzles over elongated necks. A shift in the breeze sent the odor of burnt fuel at the Marines, but the smell wasn't strong enough to disguise the stench of dead flesh.

"Check for live ones," Commiskey ordered.

"Is anybody alive?" Guillen bellowed. But nobody answered.

"Hey, this one's breathing!" Corporal Mackie shouted, bending over a Marine laying prone, with blood pooled next to his hip. "Corpsman up!"

Doc Hayden pounded up and dropped to his knees next to the wounded Marine and visually examined him. "Are you awake, can you hear me?"

The Marine moved his lips, trying to say something, but his voice was far too faint for Hayden to have any hope of understanding him.

"Stay with me, Marine. I'm gonna patch you up. You'll be running around before you know it." Having seen no injury, and only the blood by the wounded man's hip, Hayden carefully slipped his hands under the casualty to find the exact location of the wound and feel for others. Satisfied, he said to Mackie, "Help me roll him over. You do his shoulders. Nice and easy, we don't want to aggravate his wounds."

"Right. Say when." Mackie took a grip on the wounded Marine's shoulders and waited for Hayden to say when to move.

The corpsman carefully took hold both above and below where he'd felt the wound and nodded at Mackie. "Now."

The Marine groaned when they moved him, but didn't cry out. Working rapidly, Hayden used scissors to cut the casualty's uniform away from the wound and packed a dressing into it, even though the bleeding had slowed enough that there was only a small amount still seeping. He didn't see any other wounds.

"That's going to take some cleaning," Hayden said, mostly to himself. "It's a good thing you landed on your belly the way you did," he told the Marine. "It shouldn't have, but the way you lay applied enough pressure to allow the blood to start coagulating."

He got a stasis bag from his medkit. "Give me a hand with this." Together, Hayden and Mackie put the Marine, whose name they didn't know, into the stasis bag, which would hold him in a state of virtual suspended animation until he could be moved to a hospital for treatment.

While Hayden was working on the hip-wounded Marine, Guillen supervised other members of the platoon in locating other still-living casualties and assembling them near the corpsman.

There had been nearly two hundred and fifty members of VMA 214 on the ground at MCAF Jordan when the Dusters attacked. Only seven of them survived the one-sided fight.

Marine Corps Aviation Facility Jordan, Eastern Shapland

FIVE OF VMA 214'S SEVEN SURVIVORS WERE IN STASIS BAGS. DOC HAYDEN had doped up the two least badly injured. The seven were loaded onto one of the Scooters, a lightly armed but heavily armored amphibious vehicle, which Lieutenant Commiskey dispatched back to Camp Zion. The more-heavily armed Hog amphib went along as escort.

"Secure that facility," Captain Sitter told Commiskey. "A division of Eagles is on its way to your location. When it arrives, battalion wants you to track the Dusters that attacked MCAF Jordan. Find out where they went, but do not engage. You are a recon in force. Understood?"

Commiskey acknowledged the order, although he didn't like it. If he had to run a reconnaissance, he'd prefer to do it with only a fire team rather than with a full platoon. Four or five men could move much more stealthily than the forty of a platoon, would be much less likely to be detected, and were less likely to get into a fight against heavy odds.

When the P-43 Eagles arrived one landed while the other three orbited.

"You Commiskey? I'm Captain Fleming, MMH 628. Me and my birds are here to assist you," said the gangly pilot who disembarked from the P-43 that landed. He stuck out his hand to shake. Looking around at the carnage he continued, "I understand there's a combat engineer detachment on its way to clean up this mess. Now, what do you have in mind for me an' my birds to do?"

"Good to meet you, Captain," Commiskey said, now that Fleming had stopped talking long enough for him to speak. "You can see what the Dusters did here. Our intelligence is that several hundred of them headed west after this fire fight." He almost choked on the last two words. What had happened on the ground here was far too one-sided to be called a fight.

Fleming nodded vigorously. "I saw the raw vid of it from the fast flyers. It looked like four, maybe five hundred of the things took off after the Kestrels rolled them."

"We're following them. I want you to scout for us."

Fleming cocked an eyebrow. "You got what here, one platoon? You plan on taking on four, maybe five hundred Dusters with only one platoon?"

"No, sir, not at all," Commiskey said with a vigorous shake of his head. "My orders are to conduct a reconnaissance in force. My platoon's job is to find out where they went, not to fight them."

"Uh-huh. A whole platoon for a recon patrol." It was obvious that Fleming had the same misgivings about the mission that Commiskey did. "Well, we'll be a lot of help. The Dusters'll hear us coming before they spot you. With any luck, or skill—I'd rather it was skill you know—we'll spot them in time to tell you where they are so you don't get into a fight you can't win."

"Sir," Corporal John Pruitt, the platoon's communications man, interrupted them, "just got a call. Two Hogs and a Scooter are on their way. They're three klicks out."

"That'll give you what," Fleming asked, looking around to see the armored assets already on the airfield, "three Scooters and two Hogs? Here's hoping you don't need the fire power, but it's a damn good thing you got it if you need it." He looked skyward. "I think I'll go up now and start scouting. We'll look a klick or two to your front when you move out, and frequently sweep your flanks. Sound good to you?"

"Yes it does, Captain. Thank you."

"My call sign is Farsight," Fleming said, "yours is Nearsight."

"You're Farsight, I'm Nearsight. Got it."

Fleming gave a wry smile. "If you hear me using the call sign 'Classroom,' that's me talkin' to my squadron operations."

A moment later, Fleming's Eagle was airborne.

Commiskey still wasn't happy about the recon in force, but the four Eagles and two Hogs made the recon seem less suicidal.

He told Guillen how he wanted the platoon organized into the armored vehicles when the rest of them arrived.

Twenty-seven kilometers west of MCAF Jordan

Farsight One, currently flying about two-and-a-half klicks ahead of the ground patrol, suddenly shot sharply up and twisted to the left, heading back in the direction of the armored vehicles. Flashes of brilliant light shot up from inside the trees at the space the aircraft had just vacated, and tried to track the bird as it jinked, twisted, and bobbed up and down in evasive action. In seconds the other three Eagles dove to treetop level and headed toward the area Farsight One had been flying over when it lofted. The three aircraft began firing their guns and rockets into the area the flashes had come from. Farsight One dropped low and spun about to join the other Eagle in their attack. After a moment's firing, the four Eagles backed, spun, and withdrew at speed.

Few of the Marines of Third platoon were in positions to see what was happening in the sky. Commiskey, on a periscope, was one of the few.

"Farsight, this is Nearsight," Commiskey said on the ground-air freq. "What's happening? Over."

"Nearsight, Farsight," Fleming's voice came back, "lots of bad guys moving on foot in your direction. We slowed them down and probably weakened them a bit. But there's still a lot more of them than there are of you. I advise you to hit reverse. Over."

"Far, Near. You say on foot. They don't have vehicles? Over."

"Nearsight, Farsight, they've got gun carts, you might have seen them taking pot shots at me. I didn't see any troop vehicles. But those suckers run fast. Over."

Yes, the Dusters were very fast on their feet, much faster than a human could run. But were they faster than the Marines' armored vehicles? Commiskey didn't think so.

"Far, Near, you said 'lots.' How many is 'lots'? Over."

"Nearsight, Farsight, I didn't have time to take a count, and the trees obstructed my view. But I'd say half a battalion. Could be more."

Half a battalion. Half the size of a Marine battalion could be the four or five hundred that fled from the air facility. Far too many for Commiskey's platoon of Marines to take on, even with the added fire power of the armored vehicles. And the Dusters had antiaircraft weapons. Did they also have antiarmor, or could their AA be used against armor? Commiskey remembered from his studies of history that AA artillery was sometimes used very effectively against armor.

Before Commiskey could respond to the size of the approaching enemy force, Fleming said, "We're making another run on them. I'll let you know what else we learn about their strength. Out."

Commiskey ordered the armored vehicles to halt and get on line facing toward the Dusters, to give maximum firepower if the aliens came at them.

The four aircraft maneuvered at low altitude to strike the Dusters from different directions, crossing them in a narrow "X" to hit the widest possible number. Commiskey watched through the periscope.

The first two Eagles flashed toward each other on parallel courses, firing their guns and launching rockets as they flew. The Dusters' return fire was late, and missed by wide margins. The second two followed quickly, cutting across the path of the first pair. This time the AA artillery was ready, and began firing even before the two birds were overhead.

Farsight Three was hit, and pirouetted like a top before staggering away, trailing smoke, in the direction of the air facility. An explosion erupted in the trees, large enough to rock the Scooters, still several hundred meters distant.

The remaining two aircraft orbited to the rear of Third platoon's vehicles.

"Nearsight, Farsight," Fleming said after a moment. "If you're going back, you may have to pick up Farsight Three. I'm not sure he can make it all the way. Can you do it? Over."

"Farsight, Nearsight. I will if possible." *If we're still alive,* was what he meant.

"Nearsight, Farsight, we need to rearm, so we're disengaging now. Good hunting. See you soon. Out."

"Right," Commiskey said to himself. He got on the comm to Captain Sitter to ask for instructions.

"Dismount," he ordered after he got orders from the company commander. "On line between the vehicles."

✪

"What is this happy horseshit?" Mackie demanded as he shuffled his men into line along with the rest of the squad between two of the Scooters. "There's bad guys up ahead, and we don't have any cover here."

"You got trees for cover, Mackie," Martin snapped. "You're a Marine non-commissioned officer, now act like one and knock off the bitching."

Mackie flinched, like he'd just been slapped in the face. But he knew Martin was right; as a corporal and a fire team leader, he had to set the example for his men. Complaining the way he just had was a bad example; it could have a negative effect on his men's morale.

"Sorry," Mackie said. "So what are we doing, honcho?"

Martin held up a finger, signaling for quiet. Commiskey's voice came over the all-hands freq.

"Listen up," the platoon commander said. "The airedales say there are at least four hundred Dusters a third of a klick to our front, and coming this way. It could be the same ones that made the mess at the MCAF. The airedales put a hurting on them, but couldn't stop them. I talked to the Skipper. When the Dusters get inside two hundred meters, we're going to hit them with everything we've got, then mount up and get the hell out of Dodge. Wait for my signal before you fire.

"Does everybody understand?"

"You got that?" Mackie asked his men. All three replied in the affirmative, and he reported to Martin that Third fire team was ready.

Seconds later, the roar of an Eagle's rotors sounded above the platoon. Mackie looked up and saw one hovering several hundred meters up and slightly ahead of the platoon's line. A moment later, two more joined it and they began raining fire into the forest beyond the platoon's front.

Then came the order:

"Fire, fire, fire!"

The command was repeated by Guillen, Sergeant Binder, and the squad leaders.

Mackie screamed, *"Fire, fire, fire!"* at his men.

Along the line, forty-two rifles, two sidearms, two machine guns, and the cannons and guns of three Scooters and two Hogs blasted death into the forest.

Shrieks and *caws* and *skrees* cut faintly through the sounds of gunfire from the depths of the forest. Immediately, fire came back at the Marines. But it was wild, unaimed—point and jerk fire—most of which went too high to be any danger.

After thirty seconds of blazing fire, Commiskey shouted on the all-hands, "Mount up, mount up!" and the Marines of Third platoon jumped up and scrambled to reboard the armored vehicles.

"By squads!" Guillen bellowed.

"By fire teams!" the squad leaders shouted.

"Cafferata, Orndoff, Horton, with me!" Mackie cried, looking side to side to make sure his men were with him.

In the air, Eagle Two got hit, and spun toward the rear, dropping rapidly. The fire from the remaining two converged on one location, and an explosion erupted where their impacts joined—they killed the Duster weapon that had wounded Eagle Two.

"There they are!" Orndoff shrilled as he reached the rear of the Scooter right behind Horton, and scrambled aboard.

Mackie, standing slightly aside to follow his men, looked into the forest and saw the maniacally skittering Dusters coming through the trees. He grabbed Cafferata's arm and almost threw him aboard before jumping in himself. He turned around to give Martin a hand just in time to see the squad leader struck in the chest by a shot from a Duster's rifle. Martin fell backward, but Mackie managed to grasp his wrist and pulled him forward, into the Scooter.

Corporal Vittori, now the senior uninjured man in the squad, grabbed the intercom and told the Scooter commander to button up, that everyone assigned to the vehicle was aboard. The rear gate *clanked* shut and the Scooter twisted around on its center, then headed away from the charging Dusters.

Mackie, having pulled Martin aboard, and being the closest to him, shoved his rifle aside and clamped his hands on the wound where the Duster's projectile had found its way through a chink in Martin's body armor. Mackie was sickened by the feel of blood pulsing against his palms, trying to spurt out. "Stay with me, honcho! Don't you dare go into shock, you hear me?"

"Here's a field dressing," someone said, and shoved one at him. Mackie didn't look to see who it was, but the dressing was already open. He pulled a hand off Martin's chest to grab the dressing, then the other while he slapped the bandage onto the wound. "Another!" Then: "Talk to me, Sergeant," and reached for another dressing.

It took four field dressings, one stacked on another, to staunch the bleeding from Martin's chest.

"Is he still alive?" Corporal Button asked in a hushed voice.

"Yeah," Mackie said, feeling the side of Martin's neck for a pulse. "He lost a lot of blood, but he's still alive. Now we've got to keep him warm so he doesn't go into shock."

The Scooter jerked to a stop, and its ramp dropped down.

"Make room," a voice from outside called. "Four more coming aboard."

"Watch your step!" Mackie shouted, hunching over Martin to protect him from the four Marines in flight suits and helmets with side arms holstered on their hips who piled into the Scooter. They were the crew of Farsight Two; one had a bandaged arm.

"We're lucky, he's our only casualty," one of them said, pointing at the red-stained dressing. He looked down at Martin and the puddle of blood he lay in, and saw how much worse things could have been. They crammed in, giving Martin enough room.

The Scooter's ramp slammed shut and the vehicle lurched forward. Bullets from the pursuing Dusters *pinged* off the closed ramp. The Scooter didn't return fire; its guns couldn't reverse. But the Hogs' turrets could and did, sending streams of explosive twenty-millimeter rounds into the pursuing aliens.

The Marine vehicles gradually increased the distance between themselves and the enemy. After a few kilometers, the Dusters stopped chasing them.

15

Marine Corps Air Facility, Jordan, Eastern Shapland

During the short time Third platoon had been on its recon in force, the rest of India Company moved forward and occupied the minimal defensive positions that had been constructed on the west side of the air facility. They didn't only sit in place once they arrived, they engaged in building up the defenses. Combat engineers who came to bury the Duster corpses also brought wire and erected a barrier fence along the west side of the facility, and dug a broad but shallow trench on the inboard side of the fence. The wire was stacked three meters high, and the bottom of the trench was studded with short spikes intended to trip up and impale any Dusters who made it across the wire. And they dug a waist-deep trench fifty meters back from the barrier, a trench for the Marines to fight from. The company brought along a two-gun squad of M-69 Scatterers.

The armored amphibious convoy carrying Third platoon flowed through a section of the barrier fence that had been left unfinished awaiting their arrival, and the Marines immediately disembarked. Doc Hayden supervised moving Sergeant Martin and the platoon's other wounded to the hastily-repaired field dispensary where a flight surgeon who had come with India Company waited with a nurse and two more corpsmen.

"Mr. Commiskey, put your platoon in the trench, on the right flank," Captain Sitter ordered on his comm. "First platoon's in the middle, link with them. Then join me in the CP."

"Aye aye," Commiskey answered. He turned to Guillen and told him to put the squads in place, then headed for the command post.

"Vittori," Guillen shouted to the acting leader of first squad, "link up with First platoon on the left, and guns on your right. Two-man positions, five-meter intervals." After seeing that Vittori was positioning his men, he continued to the gun squad leader, "Kocak, put a gun to First squad's right. Linked with Third squad on its right. You hear that, Mausert? Your squad is in the middle. Same as First, two-man positions, five-meter intervals, with a gun team on each flank. Adriance, you've got the corner. Hold on to it, don't let the Dusters turn it."

In hardly more than a minute, Third platoon had taken position in the fighting trench. The engineers were busily closing the gap in the fence the convoy had come through, and completing the shallow trench inside it. Finished with the barrier to the front, the engineers began laying wire along the defensive flanks, enclosing the CP and medical dispensary.

Then they waited.

India Company's Command Post

"We lost contact with them twenty-two klicks back," Lieutenant Commiskey reported. "I don't know whether or not they continued following us after we broke off."

Captain Sitter nodded. "When they overran this facility they destroyed the satellite link. So until the link gets reestablished, which means a new antenna installed, we don't have the satellite view. Which means we need air. Colonel Chambers and Lieutenant Colonel Davis have convinced Major General Purvis to lean on Major General Bearss get us continuing air cover from MAG 14. Comments?" The question was directed at Commiskey.

"Sir, those Eagles from HMM 628 did justice by us," Commiskey said. "If we'd had an entire squadron, we could have put a serious hurting on the Dusters."

First Lieutenant Edward Ostermann, the company executive officer, snorted.

"A *more* serious hurting on them," Commiskey corrected himself.

"Sir, a message just came in," Sergeant Richard Binder interrupted excitedly as he turned from his comm unit.

"Tell me," Sitter said.

"Sir, MAG 14 is sending an AV 16 (E) from VMO 251 to give us some eyes." The AV 16 (E) was the electronic warfare version of the AV 16 Kestrel.

"Good!" Sitter said.

"I hope it has a shooter with it," Commiskey said. "The Dusters had anti-aircraft guns, and knocked two of the Eagles with us out of the fight. The Eagles tried, but they might not have killed all of the AA guns."

Sitter looked at Binder, who shook his head. "Sir, 14 didn't say anything about a shooter, just the Echo unit."

"Get their ops for me."

It took a few minutes, but Sitter was connected to the operations center at MAG 14.

"We really appreciate the Echo, it will be a tremendous help here," he told the operations officer. "But I'm concerned about its safety. The Dusters have triple-A. Without a shooter to give cover, the Echo will be a sitting duck."

The operations officer chuckled. "You must not be fully aware of the capabilities of the AV 16 (E). That baby's jamming set will screw up the Dusters' trip-A controller so badly it just might shoot itself. The latest 16 Echo doesn't need an escort to protect it against ground troops. And the bird on its way to scout for you has a primo driver. If anybody needs to be worried about this aircraft, it's any bad guys coming at you."

"You sound awfully confident."

"I am, I am. Now, if that's all, I've got other missions to run."

Sitter thanked the operations officer and signed off. The look he gave his officers and top NCOs gave no indication of what he was thinking. "You all heard the man, we don't have to worry about the Echo not having an escort."

Nobody else said anything, they didn't even look at each other. But every one of them had doubts.

AV 16 (E), call sign Troubadour, over MCAF Jordan

First Lieutenant Christine A. Schilt turned her Echo Kestrel in a lazy circle at one thousand five hundred meters above the air facility. Using her visual mags, she eyeballed the situation. What she saw made her whistle between tightly held lips and teeth. She'd seen the vids, of course, but pictures, even moving pictures, couldn't convey the enormity of the damage to the airfield. Everything was wrecked; aircraft were visibly damaged and unflyable, buildings were holed and partly collapsed, the runways were pocked with holes too big and close to each other to allow a fixed wing aircraft to taxi, much less land or take off. Debris choked the passages. And there was blood staining everything.

"India, India, this is Troubadour, above you at one-five hundred," she said into her local comm. "Do you copy? Over."

"Troubadour, this is India," said Sergeant Bender. "I hear you five by. Over."

"India, Troubadour, are you Six Actual? Over."

"Negative, Troubadour. Wait one."

A moment later, Captain Sitter was on the comm. "Troubadour, this is India Six Actual. Over."

"Six Actual, Troubadour. I'm at your disposal. What do you want me to do?"

"Troubadour, India Six Actual. We've got some bad guys out there. Last seen twenty-two klicks to our west. First thing is I need to know where they are now. Over."

"Six Actual, Troubadour, your wish is my command. On my way toward the setting sun. I'll let you know as soon as I see anything. Over."

"Roger, Troubadour. I await your report with bated breath. India Six Actual, out."

Troubadour, heading west from MCAF Jordan

First Lieutenant Schilt climbed to an altitude of three thousand meters and went thirty klicks west of the damaged air facility and the company of Marine infantry guarding it before she began her search for the Dusters. Her first step after turning on her ground-searching sensors was a leisurely, ten-kilometer-diameter, counter-clockwise circle back toward the MCAF. Her first sweep picked up nothing, so she did it a second time ten klicks farther east. Again no results, so she tightened the circle to seven klicks diameter and moved it ten klicks east, overlapping her first circle. At the easternmost arc of the circle she picked up something, but couldn't tell exactly what as it was at the very edge of her sensor range. She considered that it could be a small heard of ungulates, or a pack of wolf-like hunters.

Did Troy have such animals? She couldn't remember what the briefings had said about native lifeforms, or what Earth-animals might have gone feral. More likely, she thought, the traces she picked up were the Dusters she was looking for.

She tightened her circle to five klicks, moved it four more klicks east, and dropped to a thousand meters. At that altitude she might be able to get visual as well as instrumental identification of the trace.

The side-scanning radar showed several hundred man-size forms moving toward the MCAF. Schilt knew the Marines on the ground would need more information than that, so she had her comp make the necessary calculations and called in a report.

"India Six, Troubadour. Do you hear me? Over."

"Troubadour, India Six Actual, go," the reply came immediately.

"Six, Troub. I have approximately eight hundred, I say again, eight-zero-zero probable Dusters coming your way. They are twenty klicks to your west. At their current rate of movement, they should reach you in about seventy-five minutes. I say again, seven-five minutes. Over."

"Troubadour, India Six Actual. You say 'probable' Dusters. Can you confirm? Over."

"Six Actual, Troubadour. Wait one while I get a visual." Until now, Schilt had only used her instruments to check the movement on the ground. Now she used her VisMag.

The magnified visual image showed the distinctive bent-at-the-hip posture of the aliens, who seemed to be skittering more than trotting. She clearly made out the multi-pouched, leather-like straps that seemed to be their only garments, and the feathery structures that adorned their bodies and tails.

Tails and feathers on sentient creatures? Schilt shook her head in wonderment. But then, she only had humans for comparison. For all she knew, feathers and tails were more common on sentient creatures throughout the galaxy than were hair and sweat glands. What she did know was that sentience must have been fairly common in the universe. After all, in the small part of the galaxy so far explored by *Homo sap*, seventeen other sentiences had been found. Or the remains of their civilizations had, she wasn't very clear on the details. Hey, she wasn't an exobiologist or xeno-anthropologist to know such things.

She didn't notice that some of the Dusters looked up and pointed as she passed over them.

"Six Actual, Troub. I have made visual confirmation. They are Dusters. Over."

"Troubadour, Six, how are they armed? Over."

"Wait one, Actual. I'll swing over them again." She goosed her Echo to quickly circle back around to the mob of Dusters, checking her instruments as she went. "Six, Troub. I'm not picking up any electro-mag radiation. Going in for visual." After a moment she said in a low voice that probably wasn't meant for the Marines on the ground, "Ain't that cute. They see me." More loudly, she said, "Actual, Troub. I see small arms and some crew-served weapons including artillery pieces—maybe similar to pocket howitzers." She let out a short, delighted laugh. "It looks like they're aiming at me! No sweat. My jammers will send their missiles anyplace but at me. It's odd, though. I'm still not picking up any electro-mag. How the hell are they aiming?"

Puffs of black smoke appeared in the sky in front of her, and the AV 16 (E) shuddered as it ran into shrapnel thrown out by bursting aerial artillery—the dumb kind that humans hadn't used in centuries. Throw a bomb up in the air without guidance and let it explode. Maybe it'll hit something. The first one hit, peppering the skin of the Echo. That was really little more than cosmetic damage. What hurt the aircraft was the chunks of jagged metal that got sucked into its engines and tore them apart, screaming like lost souls.

First Lieutenant Christine F. Schilt would have screamed in the few seconds of her life that remained, but she couldn't believe that she was really being shot down.

The AV 16 (E) flown by Troubadour exploded in a fireball when it impacted with the ground. The impact was far enough away from the Dusters that none of them were injured by the flames or flying debris.

At their current speed, the Dusters were now little more than an hour away from MCAF Jordan. They picked up their pace. They had India Company outnumbered by four to one, if not more.

16

Observation post, three kilometers west of MCAF Jordan

"Shit, shit, shit, I don't like this," PFC Harry Orndoff muttered.

"None of us do, Harry," Corporal John Mackie said. "But this is what we're doing. Now shut up before you scare the new guy."

Mackie didn't have to worry about scaring the new guy, PFC Bill Horton was already scared. And with good reason. The fire team was in a four-man observation post in thin forest three kilometers away from the defenses at the air facility. They'd gotten there by way of a narrow farm road that hadn't been used in long enough that the forest was beginning to reclaim it. Their job was to provide early warning of the approach of the Dusters.

"Anyway, we've got a bug-out buggy," Mackie added.

The Major Mite they were given wasn't much of a bug-out buggy: a quarter-ton truck that strained when called on to carry four fully combat-loaded Marines. But it was a lot faster than running, and had a much better chance of letting the four Marines out-distance approaching Dusters.

Lance Corporal Cafferata leaned toward Horton and said *sotto voce*, "Ignore Orndoff, he's a chronic worrier. Don't mean nothing." He kept his eyes on the display of the motion detector console the fire team had been supplied with. Four individual detectors planted ahead swept the area to the OP's front, covering a width of half a kilometer. Cafferata had to watch the display carefully, as it was filled with static caused by leaves fluttering in the light breeze that wafted through the trees. Cafferata thought that, with a little bit of luck, they'd hear the Dusters before they were close enough for the detector display to pick up their motion.

"Luck is the final determinant in combat," Mackie had said when Cafferata earlier voiced his hope. "In the final analysis luck is more important than skill. But any Marine who relies on luck to accomplish his mission is a dead Marine."

Cafferata had sighed. He knew that, he just didn't like being reminded. He was on a mission that didn't require a tremendous amount of skill, and figured that made luck all that much more important.

Horton gave his fire team leader a worried look. He'd also heard what Mackie had said about luck. It didn't reassure him. He was entirely too conscious of the fact that there might be hundreds of Dusters closer to him than other Marines were. He'd also heard that the Dusters held a significant numerical advantage over the Marines at the MCAF, which also did nothing to reassure him.

Avians flittered and darted about in the trees, snapping up flying insectoids just like forest birds on Earth did. Somewhere a bark-boring avian *rat-a-tat-tat-ed* a tree, digging out insectoids that burrowed into tree trunks.

"That sounds just like the woodpeckers I saw back home when I was growing up," Mackie said. "How about you, Horton? Did you ever see woodpeckers?" He spoke softly, but kept his eyes front in case a Duster scout managed to slip past the motion detectors, and listened to the forest more than to Horton's answer.

"I—I don't know," Horton replied. He was too nervous to think about Earthly birds.

They sat quietly for a few minutes, Cafferata watching the display, the others looking into the forest, Mackie listening as well as looking.

Time drags when all you're doing is waiting. But wait was all they had to do—that and watch. The mind will drift after awhile. So it wasn't until the *rat-a-tat-tat* suddenly stopped that Mackie abruptly noticed the faint drumming of feet he'd been hearing for several minutes.

"Heads up," he called out, just loudly enough for his men to hear.

At the same time, Cafferata snapped, "Movement."

Mackie jumped up and ran to the movement detector monitor and studied the screen.

"They're coming," he said. He studied the display for a moment, read the numbers scrawling down one side of the screen, and said, "Two hundred meters and closing. Time for us to get out of here."

Mackie helped Cafferata close the control station and run with it to the Major Mite. The other two were all ready in it. Orndoff was at the controls, ready to go. As soon as Mackie and Cafferata were in, Orndoff gunned it. The Major Mite took off with a muted roar.

They'd barely started when wild *caws* and *skrees* echoed through the trees, and a few shots whizzed past, some thunking into tree trunks.

"Go!" Mackie shouted.

"I'm going, I'm going!" Orndoff shouted back. The smallish vehicle slowly picked up speed.

Mackie twisted around to look back and saw Dusters darting through the trees little more than a hundred meters to the rear. He took the most stable position he could in the moving, jouncing vehicle and raised his rifle to his shoulder. If any Duster got close, Mackie would attempt to shoot it. But his position wasn't steady enough to take the kind of shots he had when he'd faced them before.

More Dusters became visible, some running on the faint track the Major Mite followed. The vehicle hit a relatively smooth stretch of road and Mackie fired a three-round burst. A Duster tumbled, spraying red.

Cafferata was looking back and whooped. "Way to go, honcho! Got that bastard."

"Lucky shot," Mackie said back. "Just dumb luck."

Cafferata said dryly, "Right. I forgot. You only qualified as Expert." Expert, the Marines' highest level of marksmanship.

Belatedly, Mackie remembered he was supposed to notify the company when he saw the Dusters. He got on his comm and reported.

Defensive works, Marine Corps Air Facility, Jordan

"They're about two minutes behind us," Corporal Mackie shouted as PFC Orndoff skidded the Major Mite through an opening in the wire.

Corporal Vittori came up and grabbed Mackie's arm. "Get your men into the trench there." He pointed in the direction he was pulling Mackie.

Second Lieutenant Commiskey pounded to them. "How many are there?" he demanded.

Mackie didn't look at his platoon commander when he answered, but kept looking at the treeline where he expected to see Dusters bursting into the open at any second. "Sorry, sir. They were shooting at us, I didn't get a head count."

"But you shot one of 'em in the head," Lance Corporal Cafferata said from his position a couple of meters away.

"You killed one?" Commiskey asked.

Mackie nodded. "He was getting too close."

"One burst, Lieutenant," Cafferata said. "Right in the head. You should a seen it, that head burst like a melon, spraying blood all over the damn place."

"Did any get on you?" Commiskey asked, looking at Mackie's uniform.

Mackie shot a glare at Cafferata. "He wasn't *that* close, sir."

"Sixty, seventy meters," Cafferata said.

Commiskey glanced at the Major Mite. He'd ridden in them and knew how much they could bounce. "Damn good shooting at that range," he commented.

Mackie shrugged. "That was just one. There are hundreds more on their way. How much ammo do we have?"

Before Commiskey could answer, a siren sounded. A line of Dusters had appeared at the edge of the trees, five hundred meters distant. They jittered side to side, fore and back, but didn't advance.

"Lock and load!" the platoon sergeants called. "Lock and load!" It was an unnecessary command, as all the Marines on the line already had their rifles loaded and most were pointing them at the distant treeline. The better command at the moment was one taken up by some of the squad leaders, and repeated by many fire team leaders: "Hold your fire, wait for the command!"

"Get ready," Commiskey said to Mackie and slapped his shoulder. He stood and shouted out the same command to the rest of the platoon as he trotted back to his position. "Everybody, get ready." His voice didn't crack when he saw the number of Dusters appearing on the far side of the cleared area. But his throat tightened.

"Third fire team, take aim but hold your fire!" Mackie shouted. First platoon was on the company's right flank. Mackie couldn't see it from where he was, but the twenty Marines of the combat engineer platoon had also picked up their rifles and took positions on the trench's left flank, ready to fight off the attackers.

Captain Sitter came up on the all-hands freq. "Guns, strafe that line. Mortars, lob some into the trees behind the line. One gun on each flank, crossfire at the Dusters' flank. Everybody else, hold your fire until I say otherwise. Do it now."

From points along the defensive line, the M5-C machine guns of the company opened fire. Their tracers flew on a flat arc and danced side to side along the ends of the Dusters' line. Behind the Marines line came the distinctive cough of mortars firing. Arching high overhead, there was a noticeable time lag before the mortar bombs burst in the trees.

"Why aren't they charging?" Horton asked. "Why are they just standing there?"

"I don't know. Maybe they're dumb?" Orndoff said.

"They're sacrificing some soldiers to see what kind of weapons we have," Mackie said.

"Say what?" Horton squawked. "What kind of crazy man would do that?"

"First off, they aren't men," Orndoff said.

"There have been human armies that did that," Mackie explained, "as you'd know if you'd studied military history like I have."

"But that's crazy," Horton objected.

"I didn't say it wasn't."

"They aren't learning what kind of weapons we have, the Scatterers aren't firing. Why not?" Horton could see that the distant Dusters were taking casualties.

"Maybe the Skipper doesn't want them to know we've got Scatterers."

That was when the aliens charged.

"Hold your fire," Sitter again ordered on the all-hands freq. "Wait for my command."

The Dusters ran fast, but they jinked and dodged, running more side to side than forward, so they weren't closing the distance much faster than running men would. They fired as they ran, but nearly all of their shots were wild and went high or hit the dirt between them and the barrier wire—few struck near the fighting trench the Marines were in. The width of the charging mass was double the width of the Marines' defensive line.

Mackie picked a spot in the mass and aimed at it, gently caressing the trigger of his rifle while waiting for the command to fire. "Damn," he said. "That looks like a lot more than the eight hundred that jet jockey estimated."

"What's he waiting for?" Horton nervously asked.

"Be patient," Mackie said. "He wants more of them to come out of the trees so we've got a denser mass to shoot at.

When the leading Dusters were four hundred meters distant, Sitter called on the all hands, *"Fire!"* and everyone opened up. The two Scatterers threw their two thousand rounds per minute at the Dusters. Aliens started dropping in increasing numbers. Some of the fallen stayed down, others began crawling back toward the cover of the trees. A few rose and staggered after the charging mass.

Horton shook his head. "They're getting slaughtered!" he shouted. "How can they charge like that?"

While reloading, Mackie said, "There have been human armies that did that. They called it 'human wave' attacks."

"There's a difference," Cafferata added. "The first lines in human wave attacks often carried dummy weapons. These guys are *all* armed."

The leading line of Dusters reached three hundred meters from the wire barrier and dropped into prone positions to put aimed fire at the Marines. Bullets started striking the dirt close to the trench; some audibly *whizzed* past. The rest of the mass charged past them, still flipping backward or falling to the side when they were hit. Some flopped forward when their jinking carried them into the path of bullets from their comrades.

The first cry of, "Corpsman up!" was shouted.

At two hundred meters the leading aliens dropped to put aimed fire at the Marines. The first shooters leapt to their feet and rejoined the charge. The mass of attacking Dusters was thinner than it had been, and the Marines' fire wasn't knocking down as many.

Next to him, Mackie heard Cafferata yelp, and turned to the sound. Cafferata was slumped against the front wall of the trench. Pain made a rictus of his face, and he clutched his right arm above the elbow. Blood flowed from around it.

"Corpsman up! How bad is it?" Mackie asked Cafferata.

"Hurts like hell," Cafferata said through gritted teeth.

"Doc's on his way, he'll take care of that." Mackie pulled the field dressing from Cafferata's first aid pouch and ripped it open.

"Gimme that," Cafferata gasped, and let go of his wound to grab the dressing. "I'll hold it on until Doc gets here. Get back to killing Dusters."

Mackie gave him a searching look. The other's face was beading with sweat, but his complexion wasn't turning waxy. He pressed the dressing on Cafferata's wound and withdrew his hand so the lance corporal could hold it in place. He turned back to see the Dusters were closer.

"What do you have here?" Hayden asked as he dropped into the trench. His eyes took in the blood-stained bandage Cafferata pressed to his arm. "Let me put another one on that." He got another dressing out of his medkit to tie around the one Cafferata was holding. "Does it hurt?"

"No shit."

"I've got something for that." Hayden dipped back into his medkit for a pain killer and injected it into Cafferata's shoulder. "That'll hold you until I can get you to the med station."

The Duster leaders at one hundred meters dropped in turn and the others got up to resume their charge. There were still fewer of them, and fewer were falling to Marine bullets.

Then the leaders leaped onto the wire and the following Dusters clambered up them to pin themselves higher up on the wire.

Captain Sitter shouted on the all-hands freq, "Fix bayonets!" All along the line, rifles stopped firing for the seconds it took to attach the blades around the muzzles of the rifles, turning them into clumsy spears.

The third Dusters flung themselves onto the top of the wire, bending over it. The rest of the mass clambered over their bodies to the top and jumped to the ground. They'd been warned about the spikes in the bottom of the shallow trench inside the defensive wire, and didn't jump blindly into it. Most of them stepped around the spikes, although a few weren't as agile and shrieked when a foot was pierced. Some of them fell onto more spikes, and the Dusters who came behind used them as stepping stones.

"Remember, their necks are a weak spot!" Mackie shouted at his men.

Mackie fired three more bursts and saw a Duster tumble from one of them. Then they were in bayonet range. One ran straight at him. He stood and jabbed forward with his rifle, under the reaching claws of the alien, which had dropped its rifle in favor of using its talons and toothed beak on Earthly flesh. The man's arms were longer, and the bayonet impaled the Duster in its shoulder near where its long neck stuck out. The blade went deep, and Mackie rolled back, using the alien's momentum to swing it up and over. The Duster flew off the bayonet and fell to the ground behind the trench, with a bone-snapping thud.

Another Duster was almost on him, and he slammed the butt of his rifle into its beak, shattering it. The Duster fell back, shrieking in pain and clutching at its face.

Next to him, he heard the banging of Doc Hayden's handgun. A quick glance showed him Cafferata firing his rifle one-handed. Another Duster came at Mackie, too close for him to use his rifle. He used the same advice he'd shouted to his men—he used his rifle to bat away the Duster's reaching hands and grabbed its neck behind its head with his free hand. Again, he used the alien's momentum to swing it around, dropping his rifle in the process. He slammed the Duster to the ground, where its legs landed on the corpse of the one he'd bayoneted, leaped out of the trench to straddle it and gripped its neck with both hands. He wrenched the neck and twisted it, feeling bones snap. The Duster bucked with its head flopping on the end of its broken neck. He spun back to the trench and surged to his feet just as a speeding Duster reached him, aiming low with outstretched talons, expecting him to still be down. They collided, and Mackie was thrown back. He rolled to the side and jumped to his feet. The Duster was staggering backward and fell into the trench. Mackie jumped in after him and landed one foot on the Duster's chest, the other on its neck. The snapping of bones was clearly audible. Then the Marine had to toss the writhing alien aside to get to his rifle.

Once again armed, Mackie faced the front to fight more Dusters, but the only ones he saw were laying on the ground, either still or trying to crawl away from the fight. He turned around to see the Dusters who had gotten past the line of Marines racing deeper into the ruins of the air facility.

"What are they doing?" Horton yelped. "Where are they going?"

Mackie could only shake his head. He'd read about battles where a force had broken through a line and didn't know what to do next, because their commanders hadn't told them what to do beyond charge and keep going. It seemed that was what was happening here.

"I don't know, and I don't care," he shouted. "Kill them!" He added his fire to the fire of other Marines who were already putting bursts into the backs of the speeding Dusters.

A couple of hundred meters from the trench, the Dusters started milling about aimlessly in the debris from the original attack on the air facility. When they realized they were being shot at from behind, many of them ducked behind piles of debris, or larger chunks of wreckage.

"India Company!" Sitter shouted on his all hands, "Up! Get on line. We're going after them."

The Marines who were able climbed out of the trench and got in line, their rifles ready to shoot at any Duster that showed itself.

Mackie became aware of more cries of, "Corpsman up!" coming

from the trench.

"Watch your dress and stagger it!" the platoon sergeants shouted, the command echoed by the squad leaders.

"India Company, fast step, move out!" the company commander ordered.

As one, the able-bodied Marines started at a brisk walk toward the debris the Dusters were covering behind.

Mackie glanced at his sides to see that Orndoff and Horton were keeping pace, and weren't directly lined up with him or the Marines on their other sides. He blinked in surprise at what he saw.

"Hector, what are you doing here? You're wounded."

Cafferata grinned at him. "Doc patched me up and put my arm in a sling. I can still shoot."

Mackie shook his head. Cafferata had his rifle stuck through his sling, resting its forestock on his arm. *Doc must have given him a pain blocker*, he thought, *or that would hurt too damn much*. He returned his attention to the front, looking for any Duster foolish enough to expose itself. Here and there along the line he heard the sound of a three-round burst as another Marine saw—or thought he saw—a Duster poking its head out. He heard a shriek follow some of the bursts, indicating that not only had a Duster exposed itself, but the burst had hit home.

Fifty meters from the first debris pile the Dusters had taken cover behind, Captain Sitter gave a new command: "Slow fire bursts, keep their heads down." At ten meters he gave another: "Flush them out!"

The Marines sprinted to the piles of debris and bigger chunks of wreckage.

Mackie and his men dashed to what might have been the corner of a revetment roof, and turned to face it as they ran past. Mackie fired at the three startled Dusters hunkered down behind it. So did his men. The impact of the bullets threw two of the aliens back, blood spurting from sudden holes in their torsos and thighs. Missed, the third whipped around and raised its rifle. Before it could fire, Cafferata put a burst into it and it toppled backward, flinging its rifle up and to the rear as it fell dying.

More gunfire crackled, and more Dusters shrieked in deadly pain.

Deeper cries told of Marines being shot by the aliens.

Then India Company was beyond the area where the Dusters had taken cover, but they kept going, making sure none had escaped farther.

"India Company, back to the trench," Sitter ordered. "Stay alert in case we missed anyone, or anybody's faking. Fast march. Watch your dress and keep it staggered."

"Hey, Mackie," Sergeant Martin said when they reached the trench, "you're bleeding."

"What? Where?" Mackie looked at his front, turned his arms to examine them. "Where am I bleeding?"

"On your left side."

Mackie raised his left arm and looked. Sure enough, he saw blood staining his side, and a tear near his armpit. He poked the fingers of his right hand inside the tear and flinched when they touched a gouge in the muscle. "No shit. I got hit and didn't even realize it." He looked at his squad leader. "You're bleeding, too. Your leg."

"Why the hell did you think I was limping?"

"Orndoff," Mackie said. "Hold your arms out and turn around."

"Why for?" Orndoff asked, but did as he was told. He didn't show any blood stains.

"Horton, you too," Mackie said, and looked the other way.

Horton didn't raise his arms and turn around; he was leaning forward on the lip of the trench. "I think I got hit, too," he gasped.

"Corpsman up!" Mackie shouted at the same time Martin did.

The Butcher's Bill

Except for the wounded Dusters who had crawled back to the safety of the trees while they were charging across the half-kilometer of open land in front of the defensive line, the entire attack force had been killed.

The Marines suffered seven dead, one from first squad. Besides Martin, Mackie, Cafferata, and Horton, six other men from the platoon were wounded.

Camp Puller, Headquarters of NAU Forces, Troy,
near Millerton, Office of Commander, NAU Forces, Troy

Lieutenant General Bauer studied the After Action Reports not only from the division commands, but from the battalion and company commands as well. The various units of VII Corps, both Marine and Army, had acquitted themselves well in combat against the alien enemy. In almost all instances, the humans had severely damaged their foes. But their own casualties had mounted, and he had too few support troops that he could feed into the rifle companies to replace the dead or seriously wounded. And he had no knowledge of the number of aliens—or "Dusters" as the troops called them.

He looked again at the report from India/Three/One. In their latest action they had killed seven or eight hundred Dusters against only seven of their own kia and another eleven wounded.

But twenty casualties was ten percent of the company's strength.

In another action, the second platoon of Alpha, First of the Seventh Mounted Infantry had lost nearly half its strength. And the Construction Battalion detachment that was building their firebase was also severely injured. This against hundreds of Dusters killed.

How much did that damage the Dusters? Without knowing what the Duster strength was to begin with, he had no way of telling how badly his forces were hurting the enemy. For all he knew, the Dusters had the equivalent of two field armies on Troy—at least eight times as many troops as VII Corps had left Earth with. He reminded himself that not all of VII Corps had made it planetside; huge chunks of it were lost when the Dusters attacked ARG 17 after it exited the wormhole.

Task Force 8 was limited in the assistance it could provide the planetside forces; it too had been seriously wounded in the attack on ARG 17.

What could he do? He hoped his message to the Joint Chiefs made it through and that the President and the Secretary of Defense decided to act on it. He knew Marine Commandant Talbot would push to send a relief force, and was pretty sure Chairman Welborn would as well. He desperately needed the additional troops, and the shotguns and artillery canister rounds he'd requested would be extremely valuable in defeating the "human wave" attacks of the Dusters, if the Dusters were dumb enough to continue making them.

He called for his aide.

"Sir." Captain Upshur appeared in Bauer's office door in seconds.

"Captain, I want to conference my division commanders immediately. They don't have to come in, a vid conference will do. Pipe them in to my comp."

"Aye aye, sir." Talbot about faced and went to do his commander's bidding.

In moments Major Generals Purvis, Noll, and Bearss appeared in windows on his comp's display.

"Gentlemen, thank you for attending me so promptly. I trust the infantry divisions, Marine and Army both, have designated regiment- and brigade-level Whiskey Companies. Start distributing the troops. I want the line companies up as close as possible to full strength quickly, as quickly as possible.

Let me assure you, I have noted that your people have acquitted themselves in the highest tradition of the NAU military forces. But they are likely to face the enemy Dusters again and again before a relief force arrives.

With that in mind, I don't want any more company- or platoon-size outposts. You can use them, but only if they are in locations where they can support each other. My preference at this time is for battalion-size outposts.

"The Navy is still scanning for Duster concentrations, and looking for gravitational anomalies that could indicate underground spaces the Dusters might be using.

"Questions?"

"Sir," Purvis said. Bauer nodded for him to continue. "I just want to make sure that we should begin pulling our farthest outposts back, tighten up our lines."

"That is correct, General."

"Sir," 9th Division's General Noll said. When Bauer indicated he should speak, he asked, "Have you received a reply yet from Earth on your request for reinforces and additional weapons?"

"I'm sorry, General, but there hasn't been enough time for my message to reach Earth and a reply to come back. Rest assured, I will inform you as soon as I receive a reply.

"If there are no other questions, distribute your Whiskey Company people now.

"Bauer out." He broke his conference connection. *Ass*, he thought. *He should know that I wouldn't hold that information back.*

Ten days earlier

The War Room, Supreme Military Headquarters,
Bellevue, Sarpy County, Federal Zone,
North American Union

Secretary of War Richmond Hobson sat centered at the end of the wide conference table closest to the door. To his right was Fleet Admiral Ira Welborn, Chairman of the Joint Chiefs of Staff. General John C. Robinson, Army Chief of Staff, sat at Hobson's left. Arrayed along the sides of the table were sixteen Army Generals, eight to a side. A Marine general, a Navy Admiral, and a civilian were seated at the far end of the table. Other generals and admirals occupied chairs that lined the long walls of the room.

"As of fifteen minutes ago," Hobson growled, "we still don't know how much of Amphibious Ready Group 17 and VII Corps survived the enemy attack, or how far along the survivors are in reaching planetfall on Troy. We can only assume, and you all know what 'assume' does, that the Marines have the situation well in hand.

"You have a question, Mr. Gresser?" he asked when the civilian at the foot of the table cleared his throat.

"Ah, yes sir," Ignatz Gresser, the Special Assistant to President Albert Mills, "sort of, sir. I didn't mean to interrupt—" An imperious *spit it out* gesture from Hobson made him clear his throat again. "Sir, what does 'assume' do, that evidently everybody here but me knows?"

Hobson laughed, his first genuine laugh since Welborn and the Joint Chiefs' head of intelligence, Major General Joseph de Castro, brought him word of the alien invasion of Troy. Still laughing, he gestured to Commandant of the Marine Corps Ralph Talbot, who sat next to Gresser.

"Mr. Gresser," Talbot said with no trace of condescension in his voice, "of course, you never served in uniform. What we say is, 'Assume makes an ass of you and me.' It's an admonition that making assumptions is rarely a good idea. But in this instance," he glanced at Hobson for permission to continue and got a keep-going hand-wave in reply, "we lack the intelligence to do anything *but* make assumptions."

"Thank you, sir," Gresser said.

"If that's all the questions for the moment," Hobson finally said as his laughter died down, "our next assumption is that the aliens will soon send another invasion fleet to counterattack our limited forces on Troy. We must defend our colony, and save our people, both military and—if we can find them—civilian. To that end, Second Army will begin to mount out as soon as units and their equipment can board Navy shipping. Who's ready to go in the first wave?"

"Sir," Commandant Talbot said before anybody else could speak, "2nd and 3rd Marine Combat Forces are on two-hour standby and can be on the way to their assigned elevators as soon as orders to move are issued."

"Might have known the Marines would jump to the head of the line," Army Chief of Staff Robinson groused.

"The Marines *are* the door-kicker-inners," Fleet Admiral Welborn said calmly. "The NAU's force in readiness."

The corner of Robinson's mouth twitched, but he didn't say anything else.

"Which Army units can follow close behind the Marines?" Hobson asked, getting the discussion back on topic.

"I believe IV Corps is the most ready," said General George P. Hays, Second Army's commander, with a nod to Lieutenant General David S. Stanley.

"Yes, sir," Stanley said. "Each of my divisions has at least one brigade on twenty-four hour standby. Fifteenth Division is fully on standby. I can have the equivalent of two divisions ready to mount out in two days time. Give me a week, and I believe my entire Corps will be ready."

"Very good," Hobson said. "What about transportation?" He looked at Chief of Naval Operations Fleet Admiral James Madison.

Madison sighed the sigh of a man being put upon. "As you will recall, Mr. Secretary, much of ARG 17 was killed in the alien ambush en route to Troy. The surviving vessels haven't yet returned to Earth."

"We know that, Madison," Hobson snapped. "The question is, what *do* we have?"

"Well, in Navy shipping, I have enough transports immediately available to transport one MCF."

Hobson gave Madison less than two seconds to continue, then said sharply, "What about the civilian shipping you were to commandeer?"

"That's not all available yet."

"Well, how much of it is available?" The impatience was evident in Hobson's voice.

Madison shrugged. "Almost enough to transport an Army corps, but not quite enough for an MCF."

"And when will there be more civilian shipping ready for us?"

"I'm getting it in as fast as I can, Mr. Secretary. But understand, I am short on fighting ships to escort the transports."

"Most of Task Force 8 is still in fighting trim," Hobson said sourly. "Unless you don't believe the last dispatch?"

"Do you mean the one in which Avery said, 'Issue in doubt'?" Madison asked.

Hobson stared at Madison for a moment before replying. "I'm referring to the message from Lieutenant General Bauer." To himself he added, *I've had enough of this baffoon. There will be a new CNO by the time the Navy launches with another MCF for Troy.*

"Oh, yes, the *ground* commander's assessment of Navy status in Troy space," Madison said dismissively.

Talbot lifted a hand a few inches from the table top.

"Yes, Commandant?" Hobson said, giving the Marine permission to speak.

"Admiral," Talbot addressed Madison, "I have known General Bauer since he was a platoon commander in Lima Three/Four when I was executive officer there. It wouldn't surprise me in the least if he knew more about the strength and disposition of the task force supporting his efforts planetside than the admiral commanding the task force."

"That's preposterous!" Madison sputtered.

"It may be hyperbole, but it's not too far off the mark," Hobson said. "While you may disagree with the details, I think we can accept that TF 8 is still in fighting form, and needs reinforcement more than it needs replacing."

"Another assumption," Madison muttered, but softly enough that only those sitting next to him heard.

Ignoring Madison's mutter, Hobson said, "This is the problem we always have dealing with interstellar distances. Our most recent intelligence on Troy is nearly two weeks behind. We have no way of knowing what the true situation is. But we must act on the assumption—I know, there it is again—that our forces on Troy have the situation in hand and can use our help.

So, Admiral," addressing Madison again, how soon can the Navy board the Marines and launch to Troy? It seems that everybody is ready except you."

"Sir, if I may?" said an admiral seated against the wall behind Madison.

"I don't believe everybody here knows you, so state your name, rank, and command first," Hobson said.

"Rear Admiral William Moffett, sir. I'm commander, ARG 28. Sir, my ships have already begun moving to the elevator heads in anticipation of boarding the lead elements of Second Army, and can be ready to board them in three days."

"Excellent, Admiral!" Hobson said.

"Sir, by your leave," another admiral against the wall said.

"Speak."

"Sir, Rear Admiral Herman Stickney, commander Task Force 7. TF 7 is, as the CNO indicated, not yet fully up to snuff. However, it does have three dreadnaughts, three King class carriers, and seven other ships of the line. The lead elements of TF 7 can be in position to escort ARG 28 by the time it is ready to launch."

"That's thirteen warships," Hobson said. "TF 8 had thirteen warships. How does this make TF 7 less ready to launch than TF 8?"

"Sir, TF 7 has to escort an entire army, not simply a reinforced corps. It needs to be larger than TF 8."

"I see. Well, Admiral Stickney, coordinate with Admiral Moffett to escort ARG 28, and with General Talbot to get at least one Marine Combat Force on its way to Troy as soon as possible." He paused, looking at Madison, then said to Stickney and Moffett, "For purpose of this movement, you will report directly to Fleet Admiral Welborn."

Madison opened his mouth to protest, but shut it when he saw the glare Hobson gave him.

"That is all. Everybody, do it now." Hobson stood. In a moment, he was the only one left in the War Room. He headed for his office.

Command Post, Advance Firebase One,
Semi-Autonomous World of Troy

"Sir," Corporal Owen McGough, second platoon's communications man said, holding the comm out to Second Lieutenant Theodore Greig, "it's Six. Wants the Actual."

Greig took the offered unit and said into it, "Two-Six Actual. Over."

"Two Actual, wait one for Six Actual."

Greig held the comm, waiting impatiently. He had to reorganize his squads into something that could at least marginally function as a platoon. And where was that transportation he'd requested?

"Two Actual, This is Alpha Six Actual," Captain Harry Meyer's voice came over the comm. He and the rest of 10th Brigade had finally made planetfall. "Transportation for you and your boys is on the way. ETA, thirty minutes. I say again, three zero minutes. Can you hold out that long? Over."

"Six Actual, Two Actual. We are not currently under attack. What do you mean, 'transportation for me and my boys'? Over."

"Two, you are being withdrawn. I'll explain when you get here. Be ready to board when your transportation arrives. Bring your dead and the CBs. Alpha Six Actual out." With that, the transmission went dead.

"Platoon sergeant, to me," Greig shouted.

Sergeant First Class Alexander Quinn came pounding up to Greig from where he'd been checking the disposition of the remaining soldiers in the bunkers.

"Yes, sir," he said, panting slightly.

"Get the boys ready, we're pulling out," Greig said with a grimace.

"Really? Hot damn! I'll be glad to see the last of this place."

Greig looked at him grimly. "We paid for this patch of ground with a lot of blood, Sarge. It belongs to us. I don't like leaving."

Quinn looked back at his platoon commander just as grimly. "That's right, sir. We paid with a lot of blood. And if we stay here, we're liable to pay a lot more blood. Maybe all of our blood."

Greig had no reply to that. Instead he said, "Get me the CB boss. Then start getting our boys ready. Make sure our dead are ready for tranport."

"Yes, sir." Quinn ran off.

"What do you need, Mr. Greig?" Lieutenant Commander William Kelly Harrison asked when he reached the CP. "I don't have much time, my people have a lot of work to do."

"Sir, I have orders. Transportation is on the way. We're all pulling out."

Harrison looked around at the body bags that were lined up near the CP, and the bodies that hadn't yet been bagged.

"Probably a good idea. I don't think they'll give up with just the one assault."

"Instead of repairing and strengthening our defenses, I want you to prepare them to be blown as soon as we're out of here. I don't want any defenses left for the Dusters to use when we come back. Can do?"

Harrison nodded. "Yeah, we can. How much time do we have?"

"Less than half an hour."

"We can blow the bunkers in that time. What about the wire?"

Greig looked at the wire barrier, festooned with the bodies of the Dusters who'd sacrificed themselves to make bridges, and others who were killed trying to cross the once- living bridges.

"Leave it. The Dusters will be able to see the bodies hanging there from a long way off. It might give them pause about attacking humans again."

Harrison looked at the wire with the alien bodies hanging from it, and at the forest beyond. He nodded. "Either that or make them attack even more ferociously the next time." He took his leave and went to put his men to work arming the bunkers to be blown.

It only took a few more minutes for the soldiers to finish collecting and bagging the dead.

Quinn put them to work staging all of their gear and supplies to be put aboard vehicles when their transportation arrived. He hoped it wasn't those Marine Scooters again, although he did like the Hogs with their firepower.

All was ready when a convoy of six M117 Growler armored personnel carriers, the vehicles the platoon should have had to begin with, two five ton trucks, and two Marine Hogs as armed escort, arrived.

The soldiers and CBs tossed their gear and supplies into one truck, and hurriedly but reverently stacked the bodies in the other. Then the surviving soldiers and CBs piled into the Growlers. The convoy was moving five minutes after it arrived.

Firebase 17/10, under construction,
a few kilometers from Millerton

The temporary base for the First of the Seventh Mounted Infantry was bustling, with squad tents and larger being erected. Sergeants shouted orders, troops moved from place to place in groups or marching formations. Vehicles drove around raising dust. Heavy equipment was digging trenches and holes, and piling up berms, wire was being emplaced. Officers and senior noncoms moved about looking like they had important places to go and important things to do.

Captain Meyer greeted his Second platoon commander when Greig reported to the tent that temporarily served as the company command post. "Good to see you made it through, Greig. And damn sorry about your losses. First Sergeant Beaty is putting together a memorial service for them."

"Thank you, sir," Greig said, somewhat stiffly. He was thinking about how Meyer, Beaty, and the rest of the company were just arriving planetside when he and his platoon were fighting off hundreds of Dusters. He thought his platoon would have lost many fewer men if the entire company had been there. *Whose idea was it anyway*, he wondered, *to stick a lone platoon out in the middle of nowhere, with no more support than a Mobile Intelligence platoon that was somewhere else most of the time?*

"The Top is situating your boys. You've got a few days rest while you integrate new men from the Brigade's Whiskey Company." Meyer smiled crookedly "You hadn't heard about that, had you? The top jarhead ordered every division and brigade to assemble a Whiskey Company to provide replacements for combat losses. Anyway, I think you'll get enough cooks and bakers to reconstitute your platoon. In a few days, the battalion will be moving into a new firebase.

"Top Beaty will show your boys the chow tent, the latrines, and the shower point.

"If you have no questions, that is all for now."

Greig could think of many questions, but none of them were ones Meyer could answer to his satisfaction. So he said, "No questions, sir," saluted, and left the CP tent. Off to his left he saw the company first sergeant supervising the placement of a rank of bayonetted rifles being stuck in the ground, a helmet perched on each and a pair of boots below.

He told himself that dust thrown out by the vehicles and heavy equipment got in his eyes and made them water, that he wasn't really crying.

Marine Corps Air Facility Jordan, Eastern Shapland

When the call from battalion came in for India Company to pull back, Captain Sitter wasn't surprised, he'd expected as much.

"We'll blow our fighting works," he told his assembled platoon commanders and platoon sergeants at an officers' call. "We've already got our vehicles, so we won't have to wait for any to arrive when we're ready.

"How long will it take your engineers to ready the fighting trench to blow?" he asked First Lieutenant Alexander Bonnyman, Jr.

"We can have the trenches, wire, and the major debris piles ready within two hours, sir."

Sitter shook his head. "Leave the barrier wire and trench up. Only blow the fighting trench and the biggest piles and bigger pieces of wreckage. I don't want them to have much to block our fields of fire when we come back."

"In that case, maybe an hour."

"Good. The rest of you, put details to work moving our casualties and any equipment we aren't leaving behind into the vehicles. Have the rest of your Marines ready to fight off another assault, should the Dusters come at us again. And leave the alien bodies where they lay. Show those sonsabitches what happens when they tangle with Marines.

"Questions?"

There were none, Sitter's orders were clear.

"Then do it."

The platoon commanders and platoon sergeants left the command post to carry out the orders. Sitter turned to his executive officer, First Lieutenant Edward Osterman.

"Go to the dispensary and ask the surgeon which casualties are most ready to be moved. Ask if we need a triage to board them for removal."

"Aye aye, sir." Osterman headed for the makeshift dispensary.

Sitter called battalion and requested medevac for the most seriously wounded. Battalion made no promises, but promised to try. Two Pegasus SAR birds arrived to take out the worst wounded. They were escorted by two AT-5 Cobras.

The Dusters didn't come back

Firebase Zion, near Jordan

During India Company's absence, a platoon from Kilo Company had moved in to hold it. Battalion commander Lieutenant Colonel Davis was at Zion waiting for India Company's return.

"Well done, Captain," Davis said and shook Sitter's hand. He saw the company's other officers and NCOs moving the platoons into their assigned areas and nodded his approval. "I want your Marines to know that I think they did an outstanding job at the MCAF. I've seen vid. The Dusters' tactics are astonishing. I guess they just don't understand."

"No, sir, I don't think they have any idea of what they're up against."

"The question is, are they few enough for us to stand against until relief comes?"

Sitter perked up at that. "Has word come that a relief force is on its way?"

"Not yet. But I'm sure it will come shortly." Davis turned to the west. "Look over there. See the construction going on? That's a new firebase. Kilo Company's going into it. Then we'll do another to the east for Lima Company. The new firebases are each half a kilometer from FB Zion, close enough to provide mutual support. Another firebase will be to your rear. That'll have the headquarters and support company and an artillery battery."

He looked in the direction of the destroyed MCAF Jordan. "For all we know, the Dusters have shot their wad. But there's no way to know for sure. The Navy is still searching for Dusters, and any anomalies that could signal a cave where they're holing up. Word hasn't come down yet, but I strongly suspect that we'll be running search and destroy patrols.

"In the meanwhile, First Marines now has a Whiskey Company. Over there," Davis indicated a small formation of Marines standing nervously some meters to his rear, "are your replacements. Get them integrated as quickly as possible. There's no telling how soon you'll be going on patrol, and I want them to at least begin feeling comfortable in their new squads. With any luck, you won't have to go before your lesser wounded are well enough to go with you."

Sitter looked beyond the battalion commander at a dozen Marines standing at ease, if not with ease, in two ranks. They were all armed, and each had a ditty bag at his feet and a pack on his back.

"I see their weapons. Do they have all their gear?"

Davis nodded. "All you have to do is provide them with platoon assignments. They've got everything they need."

"Thank you, sir. I'll get right on it."

"Once more, Captain, you and your Marines did an outstanding job at the MCAF. It's just too bad we had to abandon it."

"It was."

"Carry on. And remember to tell your Marines I know what an outstanding job they did." With that, he headed for his vehicle and back to where his headquarters firebase was under construction.

The platoon from Kilo Company piled into its vehicles and returned to the rest of their company.

Sitter looked for his first sergeant, and saw him heading in his direction.

"Well, Top," he said, "we've got replacements from Whiskey Company. Let's meet them."

"Sounds like an excellent idea, sir," the Top said. He followed Sitter a pace to his left and rear as they walked the few paces to the dozen new men, who came to attention, uncertainty on all of their faces.

"Marines, I'm Captain Carl Sitter. This is First Sergeant Robert Robinson. I'm sure you know why you are here. But in case any of you didn't get the word, India Company has just returned from a substantial engagement with the Dusters. They had overrun MCAF Jordan, and we went to fight them. The aliens used human wave tactics to attack us. They weren't successful, we killed hundreds of them. We don't believe they've given up. You are here to replace the seven Marines we lost, and five of our worst wounded. The first sergeant will assign you to platoons, and the platoon commanders and platoon sergeants will put you in squads.

"Don't worry about what you're going to do. No matter what your MOS is, you've all had training as infantrymen, and you've fired your rifles for qualification—more than once if you've been in the Corps for longer than a year. When you're in your squads and fire teams, pay close attention to what your NCOs tell you. They've all gone up against the Dusters several times and beaten them every time.

"I'm sure you will do well. We are Marines. Marines always win their battles."

He turned to face Robinson. "First Sergeant, the detachment is yours," and walked off.

As he left he heard Robinson barking at the new men, putting a little fear of god into them. As if they needed more fear. *Damn, I hope we don't have to fight again very soon. If we do these cooks and bakers and clerks are liable to get killed.*

Camp Zion, near Jordan, Western Shapland

A WEEK AFTER INDIA COMPANY FOUGHT THE DUSTERS AT MCAF JORDAN, Sergeant Martin, Corporal Mackie, Lance Corporal Cafferata, and PFC Horton were recovering from their wounds. Cafferata was back with the squad, although on light duty. The others were mostly recovered. The only member of First squad to be killed in the action had been Lance Corporal John Dahlgren from first fire team. Lance Corporal Edwin Appleton, a clerk from the battalion's S-1, personnel section, who had been assigned to Whiskey Company, replaced him.

None of the Marines would admit it, but the lack of action—or threat of action—was making them bored.

"You're lucky John," Corporal Joseph Vittori said when the squad's fire team leaders had a chance to relax, sitting against the face of a bunker, looking out over the surrounding landscape. They weren't doing it consciously, but they were watching for anything out of the ordinary, anything that could signal the approach of danger from the front. Their rifles looked like they'd been placed without a care, but all three could grab their weapons and have them in fighting positions at an instant's notice.

"What do you mean, lucky?" Mackie asked. "Me and two of my men were wounded at the air facility. How's that lucky?"

"For one, you didn't get anyone wasted. I lost Dahlgren."

"You say 'For one.' That implies a 'For two.' Spit it out."

"My newbie? He's a pogue. He was a clerk in S-1." Vittori grimaced and shook his head. "A goddam pogue."

"Hey, man, I got a pogue to replace Zion." Mackie shrugged. "No big deal, you just have to supervise him more closely than anybody else in your fire team, that's all."

"More closely," Corporal Bill Button said. "You know what that means, don't you? It means more than your other men combined. It means so closely that you maybe don't pay enough attention to what you're doing yourself and get *your* young ass blown away." He ducked away from the slow round-house punch Vittori threw at him.

Mackie laughed and Vittori glared at him.

"Horton's a fucking PFC. He's your bottom man. Appleton's a goddam lance corporal. That makes him my number two. I can't afford to spend all of my time supervising him, I have to rely on him to help me with my other men." He spat at his feet and scuffed some dirt over it. "And I almost had Dahlgren up to where he wasn't a liability."

"Better you than me," Mackie said.

"Come on," Button said, ignoring what he'd said about Vittori's new man needing more supervision. "The man's a lance corporal, he's gotta know something. How much supervision can he need?"

"I had to show him where to put his bayonet so he could get to it in a hurry if he ever needs it, that's how much."

"*Jesu gott*," Button swore. "I feel for you, brother."

"Hey, Joe," Mackie said, "you're senior fire team leader. You've been a corporal longer than either Bill or me. Hell, you're next in line in the platoon to make squad leader. You can deal with it."

Button slowly shook his head. "I hate to say it, Joe, but it sounds like you've been screwed, blued, and tattooed."

Their subconscious minds were so intent on watching for danger from the front that none of them noticed Sergeant Martin approaching from behind. The squad leader listened for a while before interjecting himself.

"You're all corporals," Martin said. They all jumped at the unexpected voice. "You're all fire team leaders."

"Oh, hi there, boss," Vittori said, looking up.

"Skootch over, let me get in there," Martin said. The others made room for him and he joined them sitting against the bunker's front, favoring his right leg which was still mending.

"See anything out there?"

"A few avians," Vittori said.

"I saw a dust devil," Button added.

"There's no cover for a Duster within three hundred meters," Mackie said. After a few seconds he added, "Of course, that didn't stop them from coming up underneath us in that house on Clover Sugar Place."

"You sure know how to make a man feel good about where he is," Button said.

"He's right, though," Martin said. "We're in a combat situation here. You can't assume anyplace is safe. You know, I ought to smack each of you upside the head for the way you let me come up behind you."

"We knew you were there," Vittori protested.

"We heard you coming," Button said.

Mackie stayed quiet, he remembered how all of them reacted to Martin's first words.

"Sure you were," Martin said dryly. "Then tell me, how long was I there?"

They didn't say anything at first, but Vittori finally said, "Long enough to hear what we were talking about."

"That's right," Martin said. "And about that, all three of you are corporals, fire team leaders. The Marine Corps has entrusted each of you with the lives of three valuable assets, the lives of three Marines. The Marine Corps believes you can do the job. Corporal Vittori, are you going to make a liar of the Marine Corps by not giving Appleton the supervision and training he needs if you get taken out tomorrow and he has to take over the fire team?"

"Uh, no, Sergeant," Vittori said sheepishly.

"I can't hear you, Corporal."

"No, Sergeant," Vittori said in a normal speaking volume.

"I still can't hear you, Corporal!" Martin said just short of a bellow.

"No, Sergeant!" Vittori shouted.

"That's better." Martin put a hand on Vittori's shoulder and used it to push himself up. On his feet, he looked down at his three fire team leaders. "Now figure out how you're going to deal with pogues who don't have experience or recent training. If I didn't think you could do it, I wouldn't tell you to." He paused and gave them a firm look. "I'd replace you." He cast another look at the landscape, then turned and walked away.

Shocked, the three didn't say anything, either to Martin or to each other. They knew he didn't have the authority to replace them on his own. But they knew his word carried enough weight that he *could* have any of them replaced if he thought they couldn't do the job. And the only way any of them was willing to give up being a fire team leader was to be moved up to squad leader. Not that any of them thought he was particularly ready for the added responsibility of squad leader. Still....

They put their heads together to figure out a way to bring Appleton up to speed, so he could take over the fire team if necessary.

The next day

Mackie was standing in front of the bunkers that had been built to defend Firebase Zion. Vittori stood next to him. The two of them were taking a break from giving Appleton the training he needed to get up to speed, ready to take over the fire team if necessary.

Slowly, Mackie shook his head. "Three hundred meters. That's all we've got between us and the trees."

Vittori spat into the dirt by his feet, and scuffed dirt over the sputum. "I wish we had five hundred meters cleared, like at the air facility. Hell, a full klick would be better."

"Yeah. Think of how many Dusters we could waste before they reached the three hundred we can see now."

"A shitload."

"And that's why I've got a job for you," Martin said from behind them. They both spun about with their rifles at the ready on hearing the unexpected voice.

"Boss," Vittori said, turning to look at the squad leader, "you've got to stop sneaking up on us like that. One of these times somebody's reaction will be too fast and your ass will get blown away."

"And you need to be more aware of your surroundings, not just your front. I've told you that before. Then I wouldn't be able to catch you sleeping like this." He joined them, looking over the open ground.

"So what's the job you've got for us?" Vittori asked warily.

"Not just you, it's for the whole squad. We're going out there and plant motion detectors."

"How far out there?" Vittori asked.

"Who's going with us for security?" Mackie wanted to know.

Martin shook his head. "Just First squad. Nobody's going with us." He glanced at the two fire team leaders. "We're going a half klick into the trees. I've already briefed Button."

"How many detectors are we humping?" Vittori asked.

"Forty. But we aren't humping them. A Scooter is going along to carry them for us, along with repeater stations for us to plant. We'll be able to ride on the way out."

"You said 'on the way out'," Mackie said. "Does that mean we'll be humping back?"

Martin shrugged. "Depends."

"Depends on what?" Vittori asked.

"Depends on the situation when we come back. The Scooter will return to base after it disembarks us and offloads the equipment. If we've got Dusters coming at us, a Scooter will meet us on the way back in. No Dusters, no Scooter. Is that clear enough to you?"

"Yes, Sergeant," Mackie reluctantly said.

"Our call sign is Purple People. Get your people saddled up. Full ammo allotment. Make sure your people's camelbacks are full. I'll issue one meal ration before the Scooter arrives for us. Do it."

"Yes, Sergeant," Mackie and Vittori said.

A half kilometer into the trees

"You know, you didn't have to come," Martin said to Cafferata. "You're still on light duty."

"You already told me that, Sergeant," Cafferata replied. "Twice. But, dammit, I'm bored. I've already read everything in my library at least twice. And just about everything in the battalion library. Hell, I believe I've read more than Mackie has! So until Regiment sends down more books, going out with the squad is the only thing I can do, short of going totally bugfuck."

"I hear you, Hector, I hear you." He turned to his Third fire team leader. "Mackie, Cafferata doesn't hump any of the detectors. The battalion surgeon said he's not supposed to do any heavy lifting. Got it?"

Mackie looked at the stack of detectors and rolled his eyes, he estimated they each weighed half a kilo. "No heavy lifting. Got it."

Cafferata looked away, trying not to smile.

"All right, everybody," Martin said. "I've got the location for every detector programmed into my GPS. We start here and go west. Vittori, place the first one. The rest of you, come with me." He looked at his GPS and began following its directions.

The Scooter had gone back after dropping them off. Along the way it had stopped two hundred meters in to drop off the repeater units.

✪

"Look sharp," Mackie told his men, all except PFC Orndoff, who was troweling out a shallow hole to plant a detector in. The lower part of the detector was bulb-shaped, and had several thin spines protruding fifteen centimeters around its greatest circumference. The spines had to be placed carefully, parallel to the surface of the ground. They would pick up the vibrations from footsteps. The neck of the detector stuck two centimeters above the surface and could detect the heat radiating from the body of any lifeform larger than an Earth rabbit. An aerial out of the rear of the neck sent its data back to a repeater, which in turn would send it to the master unit at Firebase Zion.

"Ready," Orndoff said, sitting back on his knees.

Mackie knelt next to him and examined the detector's placement. "That's why I have you doing the digging, Harry. You do it right. Now cover it."

Orndoff carefully scooped dirt back into the hole, covering everything except the neck. Then he scattered fallen leaves and twigs over it to conceal it from view.

"Let's go," Mackie said. He and his men rose to their feet and headed toward the rest of the squad. They passed First fire team and continued to Second, where Martin waited.

"Follow me," the sergeant said, and looked at his GPS for direction.

It took the better part of three hours to emplace all of the detectors.

"Now we hump," Martin said. "First fire team, Third, Second. I'll be between Third and Second." Cafferata was still on light duty, Martin didn't want him at either of the most exposed positions. He put himself near the rear of the short column because that was the direction he thought any trouble was most likely to come from; normally he'd be closer to the front of his squad.

Even moving cautiously, it took little more than half an hour for the squad to reach the cache of repeaters. They repeated the earlier exercise, leapfrogging as the fire teams individually planted repeater units.

They were just starting to put in the last of the ten units when the call none of them wanted came over the comm: "Purple People, Purple People. This is Homebase. Over,"

Martin put his comm to his mouth. "Homebase, this is Purple People. Over."

"Purple People, Homebase. Repeaters one through six are showing massive movement in this direction. You are hereby instructed to come home. Over."

"Homebase, we will begin movement as soon as we finish planting the last repeater, it's almost in. Over."

"Purple, that could be too late. Strongly advise you leave now." There was a brief pause during which Martin heard indistinct voices in the background. "Purple People, a Scooter and two Hogs are being dispatched to your location. Meet them. Do you understand? Over."

Martin looked at Vittori, who was inspecting the placement job PFC Simanek had just finished. "Homebase, I understand. We are moving now. Over."

"Purple People, Homebase. We will see you soon. Out."

"We gotta go," Martin told his squad. "Somebody's coming this way, and we're going to be picked up along the way. Same order as before. Move out."

Vittori kicked some leaves over the repeater's antennas and said, "Harvey, point. Let's go at a trot. Move now."

The squad formed into a column as they ran, Martin took a place near the rear. They'd only gone a few meters before they heard the muted roar of the vehicles coming for them. In the distance, to their left rear, they heard the first *caws* of the Dusters.

Camp Zion, near Jordan

"INTO YOUR BUNKERS, MOVE, MOVE, MOVE, MOVE!" STAFF SERGEANT GUILLEN roared as soon as the Scooter carrying First squad dropped its rear ramp and the Marines started rushing out with Sergeant Martin and the fire team leaders echoing him. Guillen was the only Marine standing in the open.

The Scooter and both Hogs took position to fire on the aliens when they came into sight.

As Sergeant Martin ran to his bunker, he looked at his men to make sure they were all headed to the right bunkers. Before he ducked into Third fire team's bunker he paused to look out across the open ground. He didn't see any Dusters.

Inside the bunker, he took a position at the aperture and got on the sound-powered phone and called the command group. "Where are they? I don't see them."

"Company says they stopped a hundred meters inside the trees," Sergeant Binder replied. "The Skipper's called for artillery. Maybe we'll wipe them out before they begin their charge."

"Yeah, maybe." But Martin didn't believe it. He told Third fire team what Binder had said, and got on his comm to pass the word to the rest of the squad.

"What the hell are they waiting for?" Lance Corporal Cafferata asked.

"That's something new for them," PFC Orndoff said.

Corporal Mackie shook his head. "We don't know that. For all we know, when they attacked before they held a prayer meeting inside the trees to psych themselves up."

Horton snorted. "A prayer meeting. Yeah, sure."

"Mackie could be right," Martin said. "Sort of. We don't have any audio pickups in the trees. Their CO could be giving them a pep talk, telling them they've only got a short run and they'll be able to overrun us. All we can do now is wait."

"And hope nobody gets the idea that we should go out there and see for ourselves," Mackie said softly.

"Wait a minute, how do we know where they are?" Horton suddenly asked. "The motion detectors are farther out and shouldn't be able to see them."

"It's the seismo detectors," Martin answered. "They pick up vibrations three-sixty through the ground."

"Oh. Right."

To the rear, muffled by the walls of the bunker, they heard the *booms* of artillery rounds being fired.

The Marines all looked at the trees, and barely heard the rearward *booms* that told of another artillery salvo being fired. Seconds later, six explosions blossomed in the trees. The explosions themselves weren't visible through the trees, but the sudden swaying of foliage and thrown up debris was. All along India Company's line, the Marines cheered. They just knew that the Dusters had lost a chunk of their power, and were probably thrown into disarray. Hey, they might even be running away.

No such luck.

Word came down from the company CP. As soon as the first salvo was fired, the Dusters moved two hundred meters to their right.

The second salvo hit in the same place as the first, and must have done as much damage to the enemy as the first. Which is to say, little or none.

A third salvo was fired after an aiming adjustment.

This time word of the Duster's movement came sooner.

"Damn, they're just inside the trees," Martin swore. Then he muttered to himself, "Where the hell's our aircraft?"

Another salvo came in, once more hitting the place the Dusters had just vacated.

There wasn't a fifth salvo.

The Dusters burst from the trees in their by-now expected jinking and jiving, more side-to-side than to the front charge. Constant unexpected movement to confuse the foe and throw off aim.

"Open fire!" Captain Sitter shouted into his all-hands freq. "Everybody, blow them away!"

Along the line, every Marine began shooting. Not only with rifles, but the machine guns and Scatterers as well. The Scooters and Hogs added their fire. The mortars were silent.

"Why aren't the mortars firing?" Mackie shouted.

His answer came seconds later when a division of AV16 C Kestrels zoomed across the mass of Dusters, from one flank to the other, dropping Scatter-Blast cluster bombs. The Scatter-Blasts flew open fifty meters above the ground flinging their hundreds of bomblets in a pattern that covered the length and width of nearly the entire Duster formation. The bomblets erupted individually, looking like nothing so much as popcorn on a griddle. Chunks of flesh and bone and feathers were tossed into the air. Too far away for the Marines in the bunkers or manning the crew weapons, to see how bloody the pieces were.

The Kestrels turned around and swooped low, less than fifty meters above the Duster mass. The powerful wind of their near-mach passage roiled the bits and pieces of what had moments before been living, charging, alien fighters. The Kestrels gained altitude and orbited, their pilots and instruments searching the carnage for movement. They didn't see anything that couldn't be accounted for by random air movement. They turned again and overflew Camp Zion, wagging their wings in salute.

The killing ground in front of Camp Zion

"Goddamn shit!" Mackie swore. He tried to be careful where he put his feet, but he'd just stepped with both feet in offal. He breathed through his mouth to cut down on the stink.

"Shit is what it is," Cafferata said, laughing. He made no attempt at fastidiousness, yet his boots weren't any more befouled than Mackie's. He also breathed through his mouth.

The killing ground smelled as badly as the words Mackie and Cafferata used to describe it. Third platoon was prowling through the area seeking Dusters who had survived the bombing and low-level, high-speed passage. Nobody expected to find any living aliens. Most wondered why they'd been given this shit job, what genius thought looking for life in a cesspool was a good idea.

"I hope S-4 has boots in store," Mackie said. "We're going to need new ones after this. I don't believe this stench will ever come out."

"You just might be right," Martin said, coming up behind them. "And if you are, you'll need new utilities, too."

Mackie flinched at the unexpected voice. "I hope not," he said with a grimace that was partly directed at his squad leader for sneaking up behind him again. "But why?"

"You haven't seen the back of your legs." His lips were closed, though not sealed.

"What?" Mackie twisted around to look down behind himself. He swore again; the backs of his trouser legs were spattered with Duster blood and offal.

"I suggest you shitcan your gloves before you return to your bunker."

All of the Marines were wearing gloves to protect their hands from anything that might contaminate them in this search for survivors.

Cleanliness no longer mattered to Mackie. Now he kicked through piles of flesh and bones and feathers, no matter how splashed with blood they were, no matter how covered with the contents of erupted guts.

"I'm taking this one home," he said, bending down to pry a Duster rifle from the disembodied hands that still gripped it.

"Don't you dare take that into the bunker!" Orndoff yelped. "You'll stink us out if you do."

Mackie snarled at him.

After half an hour of fruitless searching for survivors, Third platoon was called back in. As soon as First Sergeant Robinson got a whiff of them, he ordered the entire platoon into the showers.

"Don't take off your uniforms and boots," he ordered. "Scrub them down on your bodies. *After* you've cleaned the crud and corrosion off them, strip down and scrub it off your scuzzy-ass bodies."

They did their best to follow the Top's orders without too much objection.

Mackie managed to get enough of the stink off the rifle he'd claimed as a souvenir that nobody seriously insisted he not take it into the bunker.

Firebase Gasson, under construction,
a few kilometers from Millerton

A week had passed since Alpha Troop's First platoon had been pulled from Advance Firebase One. New personnel had been brought in from Whiskey Company to replace its losses. One of the toughest for Second Lieutenant Greig to take was Sergeant Gasson. So, with the agreement of the other survivors, he named the new firebase after the late fire team leader. He'd been a brave and steady small unit leader, he'd be difficult to replace. But he would have to work with what was available. Fortunately, none of the replacements were sergeants. Sergeant First Class Quinn agreed with him that Specialist Abner Haynes was the best man best to replace Gasson. Greig put in a request to promote Haynes to sergeant. He expected the request to be granted promptly; the Army wanted its junior leaders to hold the rank their positions called for.

Firebase Gasson was called "under construction," and indeed there was building going on. But the little that remained to be done wasn't much more than cosmetic. Heavier construction was taking place at the two firebases to the left of Gasson, which the troop's other platoons would occupy. Temporarily, Captain Meyer had his command post co-located with First platoon.

And Meyer wanted the new men to get fully integrated into the platoon quickly.

Alpha Troop's temporary HQ

"Ted," Captain Meyer said when Greig reported to him, "your new boys need to get up to speed as quickly as possible."

"Yes, sir," Second Lieutenant Greig fully agreed. "Yes, sir."

"Short of coming under fire, which I sincerely hope doesn't happen any time soon, I think the best way of doing that is for your new boys to go on patrol out there." He waved a hand at the farmland outside the firebase, and distant forest beyond. "The Navy hasn't reported spotting Dusters in this area, so I suspect it's clear. I want you to take your platoon out on a ten-hour patrol tomorrow. One of the other platoons can hold Gasson during your absence. I'll come up with a proper patrol order for you by evening chow. You can brief your platoon after morning chow tomorrow.

Any questions?"

"No, Sir. That seems clear enough."

Meyer smiled wryly. "Any doubts?"

"If it's as quiet as the Navy says, there shouldn't be anything to cause a doubt."

"Of course, we all know the Navy sometimes misses something."

Greig didn't say anything to that.

"Then that's all until this evening."

"Thank you, sir." Greig saluted and left the HQ tent.

Farmland and into the forest

Second platoon followed a dirt tractor-track. The farmland was checkerboarded with different crops. First was a broad field of something that looked like knee high grass, turned brown and gone to seed. It may have been Earth's wheat for all the soldiers knew. Beyond it was something much lower and leafy, perhaps soybeans. Then something stalkier, which might have been the greens of potato plants. None of the soldiers of Alpha Troop's First platoon had been farmers and didn't know. But this had been farmland used by the human colonists of Troy, so whatever the crops were, they were likely Earth-evolved food plants, perhaps genetically engineered to grow healthy in this alien soil. At its edge, the forest was already beginning to reclaim the farmland; saplings and other forest undergrowth were sprouting among the probable potato plants.

Just inside the trees, the undergrowth grew thick and was reclaiming the roadway. It thinned out as the tree cover became denser, blocking more and more sunlight. Avians chirped and sang in the canopy, swooped among the branches. Insectoids buzzed and clicked all around. They all ignored the column of humans passing in their midst, even the insectoids, some of which had been actual Earthling insects imported as pollinators, left the men alone. Again, none of the men in Second platoon knew or cared. Although Greig saw an avian that looked like a blue jay and an insectoid that might have been a bee buzzing about looking for a a patch of nectar-bearing flora.

And none of the soldiers were comfortable about taking a walk in the woods.

Particularly not the new men from Whiskey Company, soldiers who days before had been manning comps or comms in headquarters units, or maintaining vehicles, or issuing stores, or moving the materials the heavy equipment operators needed to build up firebases. One had been working in a medical station in Millerton, treating the minor scrapes and bruises that afflicted rear area personnel. He was particularly uncomfortable humping the field medical kit he'd been issued when he reported to Whiskey Company.

The order of march was Third squad, Greig, Second squad, SFC Alexander Quinn with the medic, First squad.

"Make a comm check," Lieutenant Greig said when the platoon was fully under the trees.

PFC Charles H. Marsh spoke into the comm he carried. "Goal Line, this is Red Rover. How do you read me? Over."

The answer came immediately, "Red Rover, Goal Line. I read you five-by. You me? Over."

"Goal Line, Red Rover. I read you five-by. Over."

"Roger, Red Rover. Goal Line out."

"Sir, comms read five-by," Marsh reported.

"Good." Greig turned on his map and studied it for a moment. It was linked into the orbiting warships; his position showed up as a glowing blue dot on the barely noted track through the forest. His assigned patrol route was a purple dotted line. Clearings were hashmarked green, and water courses were blue lines. Dusters, if the warships picked any up, would show up flashing red.

He saw all the colors except red.

Greig went to the head of the column where he found Staff Sergeant O'Connor behind his point fire team.

"Sergeant O'Connor"

"Yes, sir."

Greig showed him the map. "I want you to go fifty meters off the right side of the trail, and proceed to this blue line," he pointed at a thin line that indicated a stream cutting across the direction in which the platoon was headed.

O'Connor studied the map for a moment, then nodded. "What do you want me to do then?"

"Hang a right and go far enough for the entire platoon to be along the water course.

Again, O'Connor nodded, and he asked, "Do you want us on the bank or back from it?"

"Stay inside the trees. I don't want to get surprised on the bank."

"Got it."

"Go."

O'Connor nodded and headed for the point, he'd lead the squad until it was time to make the turn.

This had all been covered in the squad leaders' briefing before the platoon left the firebase, but repetition was always helpful.

The blue line on the map was only a few hundred meters away, but it took the platoon most of an hour to get there. Part of the slowness was due to the frequent times the more experienced squad and fire team leaders had to spend instructing their Whiskey Company replacement on silent movement. The avians and insectoids gave proof of their noisiness by falling silent as the platoon passed; the noise disturbed them in a way their more quiet passage on the dirt road hadn't.

The platoon stopped when all its members were in the trees parallel to the stream that showed on the map. Greig called for a squad leaders' meeting. They edged through the trees to where they could see the waterway. It was a stream only two or three meters wide, that softly gurgled over a pebbly bed. The trees on the other side looked as quiet and empty as the woods they were in.

"How are they doing?" Greig asked *sotto voce*.

"They're learning," O'Connor said. "Slowly, but my squad isn't making as much noise as it did when we first got into the trees."

"I wish we had time in the rear to drill them," First squad's Staff Sergeant Alphonso Lunt said.

"We don't," Platoon Sergeant Quinn snarled, equally unhappy about taking out a patrol with so many untested men into possible enemy held territory. "So let it go."

Lunt looked across the stream and didn't reply.

"They'll get there," said Second squad's Sergeant Charles Breyer with a shrug. "At least there aren't any Dusters near us."

"Listen," Greig said, holding up a finger and looking up into the canopy. The avians and insectoids on their side of the stream were resuming their calls.

"If the birds and bees start talking again this quickly after we stopped moving, any ambush set over there has been in place long enough for them to start up again. We need to stay alert. I don't want to totally rely on the Navy for intelligence."

"The LT's right," Quinn said in a lower voice than he'd used before.

"Look." Greig held out his map. "We're only a couple of hundred meters from the nearest part of the road we came out on. We'll sit here in ambush for a couple of hours. Then we'll go beyond it maybe three hundred meters farther, then head back in, using a different track through the fields." The map showed the stream made a slight turn to the left, so the way back in would be a bit longer than the way out had been. "When we start out again, keep instructing your boys on silent movement. Let's see if we can move without causing undue distress to the fauna. Order of march will be First squad on the point, Third, tail end. Now see to your boys, and take a rest."

The squad leaders acknowledged the orders with nothing more than grunts, and headed back to their squads.

Two hours later, Second platoon was once more on the move. Enough of the soldiers whispered among themselves about how relieved they were to be on the move out of the forest that the avians and insectoids went silent once more.

When they pulled out of the ambush, Quinn kept Second squad in the middle because Breyer was his least experienced squad leader, and he wanted as much experience as possible front and back.

The return to the firebase was as uneventful as the trip out. Almost.

Halfway across the fields Greig glanced at his map again, then did a double-take. He thought he saw a brief flicker of red at the far edge of the map. He turned to look back the way they'd come, but didn't see any pursuers. He gave the entire treeline a quick scan and still didn't see any sign of Dusters. Nonetheless, his map had shown that faint flicker of red. He resisted the urge to have the platoon pick up speed.

He didn't know how many Dusters might be in the forest, or whether they would attack. But the flicker of red told him positively that Dusters were still in the area, despite their heavy losses.

Combat Action Center, NAUS Durango,
flagship of Task Force 8, in geosync orbit around Troy

As was usual, the lighting in the CAC was dim, the only illumination coming from the display screens at the workstations scattered about the compartment, spaced and angled so that their lights didn't interfere with each other. The only sounds were the muted sussurus of air circulation and occasional reports from the techs at the stations.

"Chief, I'm picking up something odd," Radarman 3 John F. Bickford suddenly said, a bit louder than anybody else's reports.

"What kind of odd?" Chief Petty Officer James W. Verney asked, taking the two steps from his station to Bickford's. He looked over the radarman's shoulder to see what was so odd. "That's not odd, son," he said when he saw it, "that's downright anomalous." He turned toward the station where the division head oversaw the entire operation. "Mr. Hudner, we got us a problem."

Lieutenant Thomas J. Hudner, the radar division head, glanced at the chief to see which display he was looking at, dialed his screen to show the same image, and quickly saw what Bickford had spotted. He swore softly, then said only loudly enough for Verney to hear, "We've been expecting something like this."

Verney nodded. "Yes, sir, we have."

Hudner picked up the comm and pressed the sensor that connected to the bridge. "Bridge, CAC."

"CAC, Bridge. Go," replied Lieutenant Commander Allen Buchanan, the bridge watch officer.

"Bridge, it looks like a fleet is approaching from the scattered disc. Roughly four AU out. Two-seventeen, three degrees above ecliptic."

"Show me," Buchanan said, all business. He peered at the display that popped up on the bridge's main board. "I will inform the captain," he said as soon as he saw the display of approaching bogies. He toggled his comm to the captain's quarters. "Captain, Bridge."

Captain Harry Huse answered immediately, but sounded groggy as though suddenly awakened from a deep sleep. "Captain. Speak."

"Sir, CAC has spotted what appears to be an unknown fleet approaching. Range, four AU."

"I will be there momentarily. Notify the admiral's CAC."

"Aye aye, sir," Buchanan said, but Huse had already signed off.

Bridge, NAUS Durango

"Captain on deck!" Petty Officer 2 Henry Nickerson shouted as the *Durango*'s commanding officer stepped into the bridge.

"Carry on," Captain Huse snapped, ignoring the fact that nobody had stood to attention at the announcement that he had entered the bridge. He took the command chair and strapped himself in. Buchanan, who had vacated the seat as soon as Huse said he was coming, stood by its side. "Details," Huse said as he began studying the big board.

Buchanan gave his report. "Sir, the bogeys were first spotted as an anomalous smudge coming from the scattered disc during a sweep for any missed survival capsules."

During an attempt to intercept and destroy a swarm of enemy missiles aimed at Amphibious Ready Group 17, many of the SF6 Meteors off the fast attack carrier *Issac C. Kidd* were killed. The fighter craft were built around a "survival capsule" intended to keep the pilot alive in the event the craft was severely damaged or destroyed. The surviving starships of ARG 17 had been conducting a rescue mission for them and survivors of the starships that had been killed by the missiles that had gotten past the Meteors and defensive fire from the ARG's escort of warships. The *Durango*'s radar had been aiding in the search for survivors.

"CAC estimates there are at least forty spacecraft in the approaching fleet. ETA at current velocity, ninety-seven hours. Composition of fleet not yet determined. CAC thinks that determination will be possible in approximately twenty-four hours."

"Thank you." Huse toggled his comm to the admiral. "Sir, did you get that?"

"Yes I did," replied Rear Admiral James Avery, commander of Task Force 8. "I have ordered the remaining ships from ARG 17 and the escort to move at flank speed to Troy orbit. And I am notifying the forces planetside to prepare for company."

Huse thought about the report. The scattered disc was exactly that; scattered. The wormhole the fleet came from must have been in line with a clump of the icy dwarf planets and cometary objects that made up the scattered disc.

Not that it mattered. More of the aliens were on their way.

Headquarters, NAU Forces, Troy, near Millerton

"Sir," Captain William P. Upshur stood in the doorway of Lieutenant General Harold W. Bauer's spartan office. He held the control of a surface-orbit comm in his hand.

"Yes, Bill?" the commanding general of the human ground and air forces on Troy said, looking up from the reports he'd been going over, showing where the elements of the 1st Marine Combat Force and those elements of the VII Corps that had made it to planetside were deployed.

"Admiral Avery wishes to speak with you at your earliest convenience."

Bauer cocked an eyebrow at his aide. The last time he'd talked directly with Avery, it had been face to face. On that occasion, he'd had to talk the commander of Task Force 8 out of resigning on the spot; falling on his sword, as it were. "Make the connection." He gestured for Upshur to stay, but be out of sight.

"Aye aye, sir." Upshur manipulated the control in his hand and a display on the office's side wall came to life, showing the interior of the Admiral's Bridge on the NAUS *Durango*, in orbit above Troy. Avery was centered in the image.

"General, thank you for replying so rapidly," Avery said.

"Of course, Admiral. When the Navy shield wants to speak to the planetside commander, the wise ground commander complies as rapidly as possible. What can I do for you?"

"You can get ready. We have detected an unidentified, forty-plus spacecraft fleet approaching Troy. Estimated arrival, slightly more than ninety-six hours." He paused before adding, "The fleet's vector makes it being from Earth unlikely."

Neither felt it necessary to mention communication—or the lack thereof—between the approaching fleet and the humans in orbit around Troy. Had there been contact, Avery would have said so. Attempts to make contact were standard operating procedure.

"How firm is that ninety-six hours?" Bauer asked.

"It's at current velocity. We have no way of knowing at what point they will begin to decelerate, or whether they will overshoot before braking.

More, we cannot yet determine how many are combat ships, or how many are transports or other support vessels."

"What is the disposition of the outlying ships of ARG 17?" Bauer asked.

"Not good. Four wounded transports plus the *Kidd* have resumed their voyage to Troy orbit. They're all limping badly, but they should arrive in orbit within two hours of the soonest arrival of the unidentified fleet."

"A wormhole is out of the question?" Bauer's question was almost a statement, and Avery didn't bother replying to it. They both knew that a wormhole from Earth wouldn't open in that direction.

"I am drawing plans to counter any hostile action by the unknowns," Avery said.

"The Army brought limited surface-to-orbit defensive weapons. I will make sure they're all operational by the time the unknowns arrive. Do you have anything else?"

"No, sir, that's everything for now. I will keep you appraised of developments as they arise."

"And I will inform you. Thank you, Admiral. Bauer out."

Upshur touched a sensor on his control and the display blinked out.

"Notify my staff and component commanders. A vid conference will do. Meet in thirty minutes."

"Aye aye, sir." Upshur left to do his commander's bidding.

✪

Upshur had a conference screen set up in Bauer's small office. It took up a side wall of the room, from front to back, and gave the small office a claustrophobic feel. Bauer's desk had to be moved to make room for it. The screen was divided into twelve windows, one for each of the MCF's primary staff, and the commanders of the NAU Force's major components. Two of the windows were for Admiral Avery and Captain Huse, or their representatives.

Thirty minutes after Bauer called for the meeting, Brigadier General Porter, 1MCF's Chief of Staff, standing in the doorway for lack of space inside the office, turned on the screen. All twelve remote attendees expectantly looked out of their windows.

"Gentlemen," Bauer began, "thank you for appearing so promptly, I'm sure you've all come from important duties. Many of you are going to have to change your planning as result of what I have to tell you.

"The day we've all been expecting is upon us. Two hours ago, TF 8 detected a large fleet approaching Troy from a direction that disallows it being from Earth. At its current estimated velocity, it will arrive in ninety-four hours." He looked at the admiral and captain for confirmation. They nodded. "At this time we don't know the composition of the fleet, except it's likely a mix of warships, transports, and support vessels. We have to be prepared for a hostile assault within days. Possibly simultaneous on TF 8 and a landing.

"Task Force 8 is down to nine warships, one of which is severely damaged. The Navy will need as much help as we can provide. Marine artillery and aircraft will be essentially worthless in the space battle. General Noll, Colonel Ames, what about your artillery?"

Major General Conrad Noll, commanding general of the 9th Infantry Division, said, "Colonel Ames, kindly take the question."

Colonel Adelbert Ames, commander of the 104th Artillery Regiment cleared his throat before answering. "General, sir, my regiment is fortunate enough to have all four of its battalions on Troy, none were lost in the attack on Amphibious Ready Group 17."

Bauer made an impatient *get to it* gesture.

"Ah, yes, sir. Each battalion has a laser battery, consisting of four companies of twelve lasers that are capable of striking orbital targets."

"Are they currently deployed for planetary defense?"

"Ah, no, sir."

"Well, get them so deployed. You have less than four days to have your lasers positioned to support TF 8 in its battle. Deploy the other batteries to do maximum damage to a landing force, and then support infantry and armor once the hostiles make planetfall.

"General Purvis, have your artillery regiment do the same once the enemy commences planetfall.

"Admiral Avery, can you put TF 8 in geosync so that we can concentrate our fire to assist you?"

"Yes, sir. Most of TF 8 is already in geosync over the locations held by NAU forces. I can quickly have the rest of the task force join up. It's better for the Navy anyway to be together, so we can concentrate our fire on the enemy."

"General Purvis, General Noll, I want you to locate your forces where they can support each other, I doubt that when the Dusters make planetfall that they will ever attack in numbers small enough for a company to defeat. General Bearss, liaise with the ground commanders to provide air support. Colonel Reid, have your Force Recon company ready to conduct recon missions, and to fill gaps in our defenses.

"Brigadier General Porter is your primary point of contact.

"If there are no questions, gentlemen, you have your orders."

None of the generals or admirals had any questions, they all understood the commander's intent. One by one over a few seconds, all the windows closed until Bauer was alone in his office with Porter.

"This may be what we expected to find when we first made planetfall," Porter said.

"Except then we expected to have an entire Army corps at our back, not a reinforced division."

Combat Action Center, NAUS Durango,
Flagship of Task Force 8, in geosync orbit around Troy

THE DIMLY LIT QUIET OF THE CAC WAS BARELY DISTURBED BY RADARMAN 3 JOHN F. Bickford's murmured, "Chief, they're decelerating."

Chief Petty Officer James W. Verney took the two steps from his station to Bickford's and looked over the junior man's shoulder at his display.

"So they are," he affirmed. "I wonder what kind of couches they have." That was a reasonable query; the apparent deceleration of the alien spacecraft was greater than human ships ever achieved—fast enough to injure human passengers. "They aren't going to fly past us after all," he murmured as he turned toward Lieutenant Thomas J. Hudner, the radar division head. "Mr. Hudner, they're slowng down—fast."

Hudner glanced at Varney to see which station he was at, and dialed his monitor to display Bickford's view, examined it for a few seconds, made a couple of mental calculations, and whistled under his breath at the result of his calculations. He toggled his comm and signaled the bridge.

"Bridge, CAC."

"CAC, Bridge. Go," Lieutenant Commander Allen Buchanan answered.

"It looks like they're slamming on the brakes. Here's the data." Hudner sent the data from Bickford's display.

"Is that accurate?" Buchanan asked after studying it briefly.

"Yes, sir. I make it twelve Gs." At twelve gravities of deceleration, it wouldn't take long at all for a human to be rendered unconscious. And not much longer to burst enough blood vessels in the brain to bring about death.

"I will notify the captain," Buchanan said. He switched his comm to buzz Captain Huse, *Durango's* captain.

Huse had been napping, but woke and sat erect immediately on hearing the beep of his comm. "Huse."

"Sir, the bogeys are making their move," Buchanan reported. "They should reach high orbit within fifteen hours."

"Not flying past," Huse said. It was merely an observation, so Buchanan didn't reply. "Notify the Admiral. I will be on the bridge in a moment."

"Aye aye, sir."

Huse was in his combat quarters, a small cabin directly adjacent to the bridge. He slipped his feet into shoes, tugged his uniform straight, and was through the door to the bridge before Buchanan finished notifying Rear Admiral James Avery of the development.

Task Force 8, deployment around Troy

The fast attack carrier *Rear Admiral Isaac C. Kidd* was still limping in when Rear Admiral Avery began issuing orders for the screening formation. In total, Avery had one carrier, an injured fast attack carrier, three destroyers, three frigates, and one battleship to combat twenty or more enemy warships of unknown capability, and impede the planetfall of a similar number of transports—if their guess about the enemy fleet was right.

The situation might not be that dire; some of the approaching spacecraft could be support ships rather than combatants or transports. Still, there were forty-plus enemy vessels to the nine of TF 8.

The frigates were the fastest warships in Avery's task force. He placed them high to the port of the oncoming fleet's vector, ready to strike at its flank. The three destroyers made a thin screen ahead of the *Durango* and the carrier *Rear Admiral Norman Scott*—and the *Kidd*, if she arrived in time. The *Scott* prepared to launch her four space-combat squadrons; her atmospheric combat squadrons, which wouldn't be of use in the coming fight, were already planetside.

As soon as Avery issued his preliminary orders, he had Lieutenant Julius Townsend, his aide, contact the planetside headquarters of the 1st Marine Combat Force—he needed to talk with the planetside commander.

Camp Puller, Headquarters of NAU Forces, Troy

"Sir," Captain William P. Upshur said, standing at attention in the doorway of Lieuteant General Bauer's tiny office.

"Yes, Bill?" Bauer, looking up from the map display he was studying, waved Upshur in.

The captain took a step inside and stood relaxed. "A message from geosync, sir. 'Rear Admiral Avery would like to speak to the General at his earliest pleasure.'" He restrained the smile he felt coming.

"That was Townsend?"

"His words verbatim."

Bauer nodded. "Tell him it's my pleasure now," and went back to his map display.

"Aye aye, sir." Upshur left, and was back a moment later. "Sir, the admiral is on." He handed Bauer a surface-orbit comm unit.

Bauer waited for Upshur to leave and close the door before he picked up the handset of the comm.

"Jim, Harry here. Good to hear from you. How's orbit treating you?"

"Not as well as one might like, Harry. We're about to get very busy."

Bauer straightened, this was the report he'd been waiting for. "Tell me."

"The alien fleet is decelerating, very rapidly. We anticipate their arrival in high orbit in less than fifteen hours."

"Any change in their composition?"

"Not that we can tell. Forty-plus spacecraft, probably half and half combatants and transports, perhaps a few support ships in the mix."

"How much damage will TF 8 be able to do to them?"

"We'll try to stop their transports, but my main effort will be killing their combatants."

"Understood. How much damage can you do to them?"

Bauer could hear Avery swallow; the man hadn't been quite the same since he'd lost a significant part of TF 8 and an even larger part of ARG 17, when Bauer had needed to talk him out of relinquishing command of the Navy forces.

"Sir, we still have no idea of the strength of the combatant vessels. All we know of their weaponry is the leviathan that attacked Troy to begin with had a laser."

"So do you, Jim. And your gunners are better. I know my Marines and soldiers are better shots than the Duster infantry." Bauer had deliberately used Avery's first name, to draw him back from the formality of calling him "sir." As the higher ranking officer, Bauer was in overall command of the operation, but he needed Avery to be in top form when he fought the alien spacecraft. "You know where the Army's laser batteries are. Their primary targets will be the transports once they start to make planetfall, but you know I'll give you as much support as I can against the warships before then. Between us, we can handle them."

Avery audibly took a deep breath. "You're right, Harry," he said, sounding more confident. "We can do this."

"You know it. Now, let me get my troops ready to do some serious ass kicking. Bauer out."

He'd considered asking Avery to copy him on the orders to his fleet, but decided against it out of concern that Avery might misinterpret the request, might think it indicated that Bauer lacked confidence in his abilities. Anyway, he knew that Captain Edwin Anderson, TF 8's operations officer, would keep him appraised.

"Bill," Avery said loudly enough for his voice to carry into the outer office, "get my staff and component commanders on the horn."

"Aye aye, sir."

Ten days earlier

The War Room, Supreme Military Headquarters,
Bellevue, Sarpy County, Federal Zone, North American Union

"Admiral Stickney," Secretary of War Richmond Hobson growled, "how soon can Task Force 7 launch for Troy?" His tone suggested the only acceptable answer was *immediately*.

"Sir," Rear Admiral Herman Osman Stickney answered, "we will finish provisioning tomorrow morning, Omaha time, and TF 7 can launch immediately thereafter." A thin smile cracked his face. "Or I can begin sending my ships piecemeal to the wormhole now."

"Begin moving them." Hobson turned his attention to Rear Admiral William A. Moffett. "How soon can Amphibious Ready Group 28 launch?"

"Sir, ARG 28's ships are already positioned at the elevators. We can leave as soon as the Marines board."

It was Lieutenant General Edward A. Ostermann's turn. "How soon can Third Marine Combat Force board the ARG?"

"Sir, the elements of 3 MCF are prepositioned at Jarvis Island, waiting for the order to embark." His mouth curved slightly in a grim smile. "I've already given orders for them to begin staging at the elevator lobby."

"Sir." Moffett raised his hand.

"Yes, Admiral?"

"Sir, I request that ARG 28 begin launching as soon as the first two starships are loaded."

"No, I can't authorize unarmed transports leaving before the entire TF 7 has launched."

Moffett grinned. "But, sir, the first two transports I want to launch are the *Enterprise* and the *Tripoli*." Seeing a lack of understanding on the faces of a couple of the Army generals, Moffett explained, "The *Enterprise* and *Tripoli* are amphibious battle cruisers—troopships with combat capability equivalent to a light cruiser. Between them they can carry an entire Marine division."

Hobson stared at Moffett for a moment, then looked at Osterman. "Can do, General?"

"With pleasure, sir."

"Outstanding. Get those Marines aboard immediately. Now all of you, you have your orders. Go."

The three component commanders rose and left the War Room, on their way to fight a war.

Briefing room, Headquarters 1st Marine Combat Force,
Camp Puller, Semi-Autonomous World Troy

"Attention on deck!" Brigadier General David Porter, the 1st MCF chief of staff, boomed out. The sudden silence in the largest interior space in the 1st MCF HQ as conversation abruptly stopped was punctuated by the scraping of chair legs on the floor, and the clicking of buttons on commanders' comps as the assembled staff and commanders rose to their feet.

"Seats, gentlemen," Lieutenant General Bauer said as he strode into the room. The assembled senior officers took their seats, facing the small stage set at the front of the room. Bauer stepped onto the stage and turned to face his staff and major subordinate commanders—the Marine commanders on Eastern Shapland attended by conference vid.

"You all know Major General Noll of the 9th Infantry Division, but you may not know the man with the oversized stars on his collars. He is Brigadier General Rufus Saxon. He runs the Army's 10th Brigade, and is a welcome addition to our force. His soldiers, as you know, have already taken on the Dusters many times—and just as often defeated them."

Heads turned to look at the Army general. Many of the Marines nodded at him. A few said, "Welcome aboard." None followed up on Bauer's remark about the size of Saxon's rank insignia, they simply accepted that Army officer rank insignia, for unknown reasons, was larger than the insignia worn by Marine and Navy officers.

"More survivors of the attack on ARG 17 are on their way and will be joining us in defense of Troy," Bauer said. "And they can't get here too soon. The Duster fleet approaching Troy's orbit is decelerating. It has been coming at speed, and decelerating more rapidly than human spacecraft can. The fleet should be overhead engaging TF 8 in little more than twelve hours. Navy's best estimate at this time remains the same, the alien fleet is half combatants, half transports. If they operate anything like we do, we can anticipate that they will bombard the surface prior to making planetfall with their ground troops. But, they're *alien*, so we can't safely make that assumption. We must be prepared to be in a fight by this time tomorrow. In the meanwhile, we won't be sitting on our thumbs playing switch. We will work on improving our defensive positions. The Cee Bees are busy on that, right?" He looked at Captain Mervyn S. Bennion, commander of the 44th Construction Regiment.

"Yes, Sir," Bennion answered. "My engineers are working with army engineers at ten different locations, mostly on Shapland. A couple of the platoons are working with Marine combat engineers on Eastern Shapland."

"Outstanding. We all know what excellent work your people do." Bauer looked around the room. "Revise your plans, and be prepared to revise them again as we get more intelligence about enemy action. Lieutenant Colonel Neville—" the 1st MCF intelligence chief—"will keep you updated with developments. I want all of you to keep Brigadier General Shoup appraised of all changes in your plans.

"We have an invasion to defeat. Let's do it."

With that, he stepped off the stage and marched out of the room to Porter's shouted, "A-ten-*hut!*"

Firebase Gasson, near Millerton, Shapland,
Semi-Autonomous World Troy

CAPTAIN PATRICIA H. PENTZER, THE COMMANDING OFFICER OF FOURTH PLATOON, H Battery, 1045 Artillery Battalion (Laser), stood on the mount of laser 2 and looked around with disapproval. *Firebase Gasson is just too damn small*, she thought. *It won't take much at all for a counter-laser attack from orbit to take out all three of my guns. Even one gunboat can do the dirty deed in minutes.*

Such an attack would wipe out that Leg platoon that was there to protect her guns as well. As if a Leg platoon could defend a position from an orbital attack. She shook her head and made a face. And assigning a Mobile Intelligence platoon to Gasson made as much sense as tits on a bull. What were they thinking?

It was that Jarhead three-star who did this, no Army general could be dumb enough to order a cock-up like this. Hell, she needed a base the size of Gasson for each of her lasers—and they should be separated by a minimum of a klick, better yet three klicks. One gunboat would have a hell of a time taking them all out before it got killed itself. Even a lone destroyer couldn't survive trying to get all three if they were properly spread.

Damn dumb Jarhead. Has to be his fault.

She craned her neck, looking at the sky overhead. A futile motion, she knew. But, damn, she had to take a look after the sitrep that sent her climbing the laser's mount. A presumably hostile fleet rapidly approaching Troy. She had to have her battery ready to aid TF 8 in combating the enemy warships, or to blast landing craft if they attempted to make planetfall.

Now, where was that Leg lieutenant—what was his name, Cragg or something—in command of her security? She looked around until she saw him walking the perimeter.

"Hey you, Leg LT!" Her shout was loud enough to be heard all through the small base, even if not understood at its farthest reaches.

Lieutenant Greig didn't even turn his head.

She glared at his back and filled her lungs to shout again.

"You, Leg LT!"

Again, he didn't react to her, even though a soldier poked his head out of the bunker the Leg lieutenant was standing next to and up looked at her.

"Him!" she shouted, and pointed at the Leg. The soldier said something to the Leg, and pointed at Pentzer.

The Leg turned to look at her and mimed, "Are you talking to me?"

"Yes, you!" She pointed emphatically at the base of the laser mount, and hopped to the ground. The Leg ambled over to her.

"Yes, ma'am," he said when he reached her. "What can I do for the captain?"

"Mister, I should put you on report," she snapped. "You deliberately ignored me when I called."

Greig blinked innocently. "Ma'am? I'm sorry, but I didn't hear you call me. I did hear you call some Leg LT, but I didn't realize you meant me—I'm not a Leg."

Her face turned red and she shoved her face up into his. "You're infantry, right? That means you're a Leg."

He sauntered to her, shaking his head. "*Mounted* infantry, ma'am. There's a difference."

"Is that a fact, now?"

"Yes, ma'am. It's a distinction we take very seriously."

She ostensibly looked around, "I don't see any vehicles. If you're mounted infantry, where are your vehicles?"

Greig went rigid. "Ma'am, most of Alpha Troop's vehicles were lost when the Dusters almost killed the *Juno Beach*. The few that survived are with a platoon that is conducting patrols."

Pentzer flinched and the red in her face washed out. The 1045 Artillery Battalion (Laser) had been on the *Wanderjahr*, which had not been hit during the Duster attack on ARG 27. The battalion had suffered no losses, but she knew that many of the soldiers on the *Juno Beach* had been killed.

"I'm sorry, Lieutenant. Did you lose many people?"

"No, ma'am. I managed to get my entire platoon into a stasis station in time to save everybody."

"Outstanding. Now," she reddened again, but with embarrassment this time, "I'm sorry, but what's your name? I know we exchanged names when I arrived, but I had other things on my mind then."

"That's all right, I sometimes have trouble remembering names myself. I'm Theodore Greig."

She extended her hand. "Patricia Pentzer." They shook, all business now, "Have you heard the latest? A fleet, probably alien, is approaching Troy. It'll reach orbit in a matter of hours. My lasers are going to be involved perhaps as soon as they're in range. I strongly suggest that you move your people at least a kilometer away from my guns before then."

He blinked. "Why?"

"Counter-battery fire will take out this entire base, that's why. Where's that MI platoon that's supposed to be here?"

"They're out running recon patrols. If you're concerned about counter-battery fire, why don't you spread your lasers out more?"

"Because we're assigned to Firebase Gasson, and we're spread out as far as its dimensions allow, that's why."

Greig hesitated before speaking again; what he was about to say could be insulting. "You've never fired your guns in anger, have you? You haven't come under fire yet."

If Pentzer was insulted, she managed to control it. "That's right. Both counts. You have?"

He nodded. "Not only on the *Juno Beach*. We've had plenty of action." He turned in a circle, looking over the landscape beyond the perimeter. "You know, if you keep one gun here and move the other two to the other platoon firebases, you won't have to worry about counter-battery fire taking you all out at once."

"But that's outside where I'm supposed to be."

He looked down and nodded, as though thinking, then back at her. "Ma'am, your CO didn't come here, did he? He doesn't know how confined you are in this firebase. You're the commander on the scene. The placement of your guns is your tactical decision to make. I'll talk to my company commander. I'm sure he'll agree."

She studied him for a moment, then said, "I do believe you're right, Mr. Greig. We just have time to move my guns before they'll probably have to fire." She looked for her platoon sergeant, and began giving orders to move two of the lasers.

Captain Meyer's only reaction to Greig's request was an astonished, "Hell yes! Move those things."

NAUS Durango, Fleet Combat Action Center;
in geosync orbit around Troy

In the dimness of the CAC, Lieutenant Commander Rufus Z. Johnston scowled at the images on his status board. "Get me the Admiral's Bridge." His voice cracked like a whip over the soft pings emitted by the comps, and the muted voices of the techs manning the stations..

"The Admiral's Bridge, aye," said Radioman 2 Edward A. Gisburne. Then into the fleet comm, "Bridge, CAC."

"CAC, Bridge," Radioman 3 Matthew Arther immediately answered.

Gisburne saw Johnston adjust his speaker and told Arther, "CAC wants to speak to the admiral."

"CAC wants to speak to the admiral, aye," Arther said.

Seconds later Johnston heard, "Avery, CAC. What do you have for me?"

"Sir, the leading elements of the unidentified fleet are now within extreme range of the *Durango*."

"Let me know when they are within range of the *Scott's* Meteors." The fast attack carrier had almost closed to range; the slowing down of the Duster fleet had given her time to get close.

"Let the admiral know when the bogeys are within range of the *Scott's* Meteors. Aye."

"Avery out."

Johnston went back to peering at the board. How many of these vessels were warships? How many were transports? Or support ships? Those were the questions he most needed to answer. But the North American Union Navy had no information on the alien spacecraft. Even if they were close enough to make out details, he had no way to know for certain.

But, if the Dusters' navy was organized along lines similar to human, then he could assume—and, yes, he knew what "assume" did—that the ten ships in the front were similar to human frigates and destroyers, forming a screen for the eight ships following them, possible cruisers and battleships, even carriers. He wasn't about to assume that none of them were carriers—just because the Dusters didn't use any aircraft planetside, that didn't mean they had no space fighters, analogs to the NAU Navy's SF 6 Meteors. If he was right, that meant that the score-plus ships farther back were transports and, possibly, support ships.

Although as profligate as the Dusters had been with the lives of their troops planetside, he wasn't going to assume that they were any more concerned about the repair and rescue of their own damaged ships. He was willing to go only so far to risk making an ass of himself.

He changed the board's scale to close up on the bogey fleet, enlarged the view again to include the warships of TF 8. He wondered how much good the *Kidd's* remaining Meteors could do when they launched a flank attack on the bogeys.

An hour later Johnston contacted Avery again.

"Sir, I have tentative identification of the bogey ship types."

"Give me," Avery said.

Johnston's earlier estimate hadn't changed; ten frigate/destroyer types, eight cruiser/battleship types, one or more of which might or might not be a carrier, twenty-four transports and/or support ships.

"Range?"

"Sir, they will be in range of the *Scott's* Meteors in fifteen minutes. Ten minutes after that they will be in range of the *Durango's* lasers, and in five minutes more the destroyers will be able to strike them. The *Kidd* should be close enough for her Meteors to strike their rear."

"Avery out."

Admiral's Bridge, NAUS Durango

"If it pleases Captain Huse, I would like to speak with him," Avery said into his comm. Task Force 8 belonged to Avery, but the *Durango* belonged to Huse, and his position must be acknowledged.

"Huse here, Admiral," the captain's voice came back seconds later.

"Captain, I am shortly going to have the *Scott* launch her meteors to strike at the bogey fleet. When the Meteors are halfway there, I want the *Durango* to give the fighters covering fire."

"Give the Meteors covering fire when they are halfway to the bogeys, aye."

"Avery out." He turned to Lieutenant Commander George Davis, his communications officer. "Get me Captain Rush on the *Scott.*"

"Captain Rush on the *Scott*, aye aye," Davis said, and got on the ship-to-ship radio.

It took twenty seconds for the message to go from the *Durango* to the carrier *Rear Admiral Norman Scott* and a reply to come back.

"*Scott* Actual," Rush's voice came came over the ship-to-ship.

"*Scott*, how soon can your SF 6 squadrons launch?"

"The crews of two squadrons are in the ready room now. How soon they can head for the flight deck depends on the length of time it takes to prepare and deliver the operation order. Once they get the 'go' order, they can begin launching within ten minutes."

"The op order is brief. The bogey fleet is five hours from Troy orbit. The front row is a screen of frigate and destroyer analogs. Kill them. *Durango* and the destroyers will provide covering fire. Send all four of your SF 6 squadrons."

The pause before Rush replied to the operation order was longer than before. When he spoke again there was a thickness in his voice. The operation sounded to him like a suicide mission for his space fighter group. "Aye aye, sir. The *Scott's* entire space fighter group will launch and attack the screening ships of the bogey fleet."

"Good hunting, *Scott*. Avery out."

Avery studied the big board, which covered most of the forward bulkhead and displayed all the elements on both sides. He watched the tiny flecks that indicated the SF 6 Meteors launching from the *Scott* and forming up, then heading for their targets.

Distance between the bogey fleet and TF 8 was closing rapidly. But the Dusters hadn't begun firing. *Don't they see the small fighter craft yet?* Avery wondered. *Or maybe they don't see such small things as a threat. They're alien, and we don't have a grasp on how they think.* He didn't see any specks that would indicate Duster fighter craft. *Maybe they don't have any carriers.*

Time seemed to drag as Avery watched the fighters getting closer to the bogeys.

Finally, the four squadrons were halfway to their targets, and the *Durango* opened fire with her lasers. A moment later, TF 8's three destroyers did as well. They didn't aim at where they *saw* the bogey fleet, but where they expected the ships to be in several seconds; what they saw when they fired was not where the ships were *now*, but where they had been a few seconds later.

Lasers suddenly lashed out from the second rank of bogeys, the rank Johnston had tentatively identified as cruisers and battleships. The front rank didn't fire.

Avery looked to where his three frigates were stationed, high and to the left of his main formation, and ordered them to move in and attack the flank of the second rank.

Glowing red began to appear on the bogey ships—hits from TF 8!

Enemy lasers converged on the destroyer *First Lieutenant George H. Cannon*, and she erupted, her spine split through and her missile magazine exploded. Debris scattered everywhere.

Avery felt the *Durango* shudder as she suffered multiple laser hits. Horns sounded throughout the warship, calling damage control crews to action.

The Meteors finally got close enough to the first rank of bogeys to fire their missiles. A squadron concentrated its fire on one, and it burst open. The rest of the screening warships seemed to suddenly notice the small craft, and began flinging missiles at them. Avery watched stone-faced as six of the dots representing the SF 6's blinked out, killed by enemy fire. He doubted that any of their pilots survived.

"Bridge, CAC," the call came.

"CAC, bridge," Davis answered.

"Kindly inform the admiral the bogey fleet is accelerating."

"The bogey fleet is accelerating, aye." Davis turned to Avery. "Sir—."

"I heard." *Why did they do that*, Avery wondered. He watched as lasers and missiles killed another destroyer, the *Rear Admiral Herald F. Stout* and a frigate, the *Sergeant Major Daniel Daly*. The first rank blinked out another dozen Meteor dots, but the only significant damage to them was one that lost acceleration, and drifted, evidently powerless. The remaining frigates scored a kill on the left-most ships in the second rank.

Firebase Gasson, near Millerton, Troy

The lasers of fourth platoon, 1045 Artillery Battalion (Laser) had begun attempting to lock onto the approaching enemy fleet as soon as they were emplaced in all three of Alpha Troop's platoon firebases. Finally, the warships were close enough to fix on a target; they all locked on one craft in the front row. Had it been a human warship, Captain Patricia Pentzer would have identified it as a frigate. Her three lasers should be able to kill it, even at this extreme range, a distance that would spread their beams.

"Fourth platoon," Pentzer ordered, "commence countdown to fire in five seconds."

Five seconds later, the air above the three lasers flashed with the heat of the beams they shot heavenward. Watching through her glasses, Pentzer saw three lines of light converging on the designated target. When they struck the warship she saw a red glow sprout in its center, and spread outward. Before the edges of the red could begin to dull, a second salvo hit, and the warship split in two.

A cheer went up from everybody in Firebase Gasson who was looking up and saw the distant death.

"New target," Pentzer ordered, and gave the coordinates to what she tentatively identified as a destroyer.

H Battery fired.

Admiral's Bridge, on the Durango

"Sir, another message from CAC," Lieutenant Commander Davis said.

Avery turned his head to face his comm officer.

"Twenty-two of the trailing starships are falling behind. They appear to be going into low orbit around Troy."

Transports, Avery thought. *Planetfall will commence shortly.* "Notify Commander NAU Forces, Troy."

"Notify Commander NAU Forces, Troy, aye," Davis said, and got on the orbit-to-surface comm.

The bogey warships were almost on TF 8 when lasers blasted up from Troy. Another of the enemy's first rank died, and a second, larger warship staggered and lost weigh.

All the warships on both sides were firing; lasers, missiles, and guns, as well as the remaining Meteors off the *Scott*. The *Kidd's* Meteors launched and joined the frigates attacking the left-most ship in the Dusters' second line.

The planetside lasers ceased fire as the Duster fleet zoomed past TF 8, but picked up again as soon as there was space between the front rank and TF 8.

The frigate *Gunnery Sergeant John Basilone* died in the close up exchange, and the *Durango*, the *Scott,* and the destroyer *Hospitalman 3 Edward C. Benfold* were injured. Half of *Scott's* Meteors were gone. Two warships from the Dusters' second rank died as well, and three others appeared to be damaged.

The Duster fleet was losing more warships than TF 8, but the odds were still heavily in the aliens' favor.

"Bridge, CAC," another report came in. "The bogeys are beginning to decelerate and are arching in an evident attempt to begin a parabolic orbit around the planet."

"How long before they come back?" Avery asked.

"Best estimate at this time, six hours."

Avery looked at the big board. By then, the *Kidd* would link into the task force's formation.

"Instruct the *Scott* to retrieve her SF group and the *Stout* to begin retrieval rescue and operations," Avery said ordered. "*Durango, Butler,* and *Benfold,* knock out those transports that are moving into low orbit."

Camp Zion, West Shapland, near Jordan,
Eastern Shapland, Troy

"Look alive, Marines!" Staff Sergeant Guillen bellowed. "We don't know when or where or how many, but we know they're coming, and we had best be ready when they get here. Or be ready to go out and find, fix, and fuck them, whichever comes first."

The other platoon sergeants were shouting similar orders at their Marines throughout the firebase. So was Gunnery Sergeant Hoffman, while First Sergeant Robert G. Robinson stood watching, crossed-armed.

There wasn't the hustle and bustle one might normally expect in a Marine company when its senior NCOs, under the watchful eye of the company's top sergeant were shouting orders. They'd known for a few days that a counter-counter-invasion was coming. It was only a question of when, where, and how many. So when they weren't out running patrols in search of Dusters who might or might not—but often were—out there someplace, they'd been busily engaged in building up Camp Zion's defenses. By this time, there wasn't really all that much that still needed doing. Marines on the perimeter looked through the sights of their weapons, making sure they had clear views of their fields of fire. Fire team leaders checked their men's positions. Squad leaders oversaw the fire team leaders and inspected their men's equipment and weapons, making sure they all had everything they might need and all was in proper working order. The machine gun and mortar crews checked and rechecked their weapons.

Being expeditionary, the Marines didn't have the same heavy-lift capability that the Army did. One thing that meant in practical terms was the biggest artillery pieces, including laser guns able to fire on orbiting targets, belonged to the Army. Where the Army had lasers powerful enough to augment the Navy's "shore batteries" in attacking enemy ships in orbit from the planetary surface, the Marine lasers couldn't. The Marine lasers were most useful against ground armor, as anti-aircraft guns, and to shoot down enemy shuttles on their way planetside from orbit. A four-gun laser platoon from 2nd Marine Air Wing's base defense squadron had joined India Company in Fire Camp Zion.

Captain Carl Sitter came out of the command bunker and joined Robinson, looking over the company. "What do you think, Top?" he asked.

"They look ready right now, sir," Robinson answered. "But if something doesn't happen soon, I think they'll get over-wound."

Sitter nodded. A high level of readiness couldn't be maintained for a long period of time without the readiness falling off drastically. "Suggestions?"

"An inspection never hurt."

Sitter chuckled. He'd been an enlisted man before he got his commission, and remembered how he hated company commanders' inspections in the field. "You know, that'll piss them off."

Robinson nodded. "Yes, sir, it will. And they'll take it out on the next Dusters they see."

"One platoon at a time. Have First platoon in formation here in fifteen minutes. Shift everybody else to cover their section of the perimeter. I think twenty minutes per platoon will be enough."

"Will you flunk anybody, sir?"

"Not unless somebody has a weapon fouled badly enough it's liable to misfire. I'll have an officers' call to inform the platoon commanders. You tell the platoon sergeants. Do it."

"Aye aye, sir," Robinson said to Sitter's back as the CO returned to the CP bunker. Then at the top of his lungs, "Platoon sergeants up!"

Nobody in First platoon was happy about having to stand in a parade ground formation for a company commander's inspection, not even the platoon's top people, who knew and understood the reason for it. But nobody complained. Not out loud, anyway.

★

"Are your people ready, Mackie?" Sergeant Martin asked while Second platoon was being inspected, when there were only a few minutes left before Third platoon had its turn.

Corporal Mackie grimaced. "Shit, ready. Look at this." He gestured at the bare ground of the firebase, at the thin clouds thrown up by gusts of wind. "You can't do spit-and-polish in this. No matter how clean you wipe something down, half an hour later it's coated with dust again."

"At least it's not raining," Martin said. "Spit-and-polish would be impossible then."

"Maybe not the spit part," Mackie said with an ironic laugh.

Martin had to laugh. "Got that right. But that doesn't answer my question."

Mackie grimaced again. "Depends on how hard-ass the Skipper's going to be."

Martin looked toward the Marines of First platoon. None of them seemed upset at the results of their inspection. "I believe the inspection is nothing more than ass-busting make-work. Something to take our minds off of when are the Dusters going to make planetfall."

"You're probably right. But there are other things we could be doing if all he's looking for is make-work."

"Could be. But he's the boss, so it's his decision. Besides, it gives him something to do to take *his* mind off the waiting."

Then Sitter finished his inspection of Second platoon and Third was called to stand in ranks in front of the CP bunker to be inspected.

The company commander wasn't hardass at all.

Second Lieutenant Commiskey stood at attention in front of Mackie, but looked through rather than at him, while Captain Sitter inspected Private Frank Preston, on Mackie's right. Sitter's only comment to Hill was, "Keep it that clean, Preston," when he returned his rifle after giving it a visual once-over.

Mackie sharply raised his rifle to port arms as soon as Commiskey stepped away. Out of boredom as much as anything else, Mackie let go of his rifle as soon as his peripheral vision showed Sitter's hand moving to take it.

Sitter had to move fast to catch the weapon before it fell to the ground. He leaned close and whispered, "Corporal, we've both been around too long for you to pull that kind of crap."

"Sorry, sir," Mackie whispered back. But he didn't sound apologetic.

Sitter gave the rifle more of an inspection than he had Preston's. He wiped a finger along the barrel guard, picking up a faint smudge of dust. "Clean it again, Mackie," he said as he returned the rifle. To Commiskey, "Inspect him again after he's cleaned it."

"Aye aye, sir," Commiskey said, and gave Mackie a disgusted look.

They moved on, which put Guillen directly in front of Mackie. The platoon sergeant gave Mackie a barely perceptible headshake and mouthed, *Later*, at him.

Later came and Guillen wanted to know, "What was that about, Mackie?" Martin stood at Guillen's left side, arms folded across his chest, glaring at Mackie.

Mackie stood at his tallest and defiantly looked Guillen in the eye. "An inspection in the field, when we're expecting the bad guys to make planetfall at any minute, is mickey mouse, that's what it was about."

Martin snorted and looked away.

Guilllen snarled. "Junk-on-the-bunk in garrison is mickey mouse. In the field, when we expect a fight soon, is maybe the best time for an inspection. An inspection is necessary then, to make sure everybody's weapons and gear are ready for the fight. Now, you've got fifteen minutes to clean your rifle before Lieutenant Commiskey comes to inspect it.

You know, I really do expect better from you, Mackie." Guillen spun about and stalked away.

Martin stayed and watched to make sure Mackie was cleaning his rifle instead of sulking.

After Mackie's rifle passed Commiskey's inspection, the lieutenant marched him to the company HQ bunker, where Captain Sitter inspected it again. This time, Mackie didn't let go of his rifle until Sitter's hand touched it. He passed.

Watching the sky

The battle above began on the night side of Troy, which also happened to be during Camp Zion's night. The first thing the Marines of India Company saw were three lights moving across the sky; the impulse engines of the three frigates as they crawled into higher orbits to intercept the lights of the Duster fleet, which had been visible close to the horizon, and rising toward the zenith since sundown. The frigates' movement was followed moments later by the larger lights of the *Durango's* and *Scott's* engines as the battleship and carrier followed them. The ground observers couldn't see any lights showing that the *Scott* had launched her fighters—they didn't flare brightly enough.

There were abrupt flashes in the night sky, as the warships launched missiles and fired lasers at each other and each other's missiles. Larger flashes erupted as lasers slashed through missiles, igniting their warheads.

"It's like a far away fireworks display," PFC William Horton murmured, awed. "I wonder what it sounds like up close." He was sitting cross-legged on top of the fire team's bunker.

"It doesn't sound like anything, Horton," Corporal Mackie said. His voice had a trace of fear instead of awe. He understood better than the younger man what the lights in the sky foretold. This was merely the preliminary, the Duster fleet would soon enough turn its attention to the ground. Followed by alien ground forces making planetfall. "They're in vacuum up there. There's no sound." He was laying supine on the bunker's top.

Horton looked at the shadow that was his fire team leader and considered. "Right," he said, remembering his nearly-forgotten basic science studies. "You need air for sound waves to propagate." After a further moment's reflection he added, "I think I'm glad I can't hear it."

Mackie's nod went unseen in the night dark. "When a missile hits a ship, everybody onboard will hear it. And for many of them, it'll be the last thing they hear."

There was another moment of silence before Horton whispered, "Right."

Throughout Camp Zion, the Marines watched the battle in the sky. For the most part, they didn't say anything as the warships continued moving closer to one another. They watched and some cheered as the three frigates made their move, coming in on the flank of the Duster formation and sending missiles and laser beams flying at the enemy. The sharper-eyed of the Marines picked out tiny flashes of Navy fighters being hit by Duster weapons. The Marines cheered again when lasers from Shapland struck a Duster warship and broke it in half. The cheering didn't last long, not once it became clear that there were only three ships hitting the Duster flank. They could see the NAU ships were badly outnumbered.

"What are they doing now?" Lance Corporal Cafferata suddenly asked, sitting bolt upright.

It looked like the human task force and the Duster fleet were merging.

"Whadafug?" was all Mackie could say.

Then the Dusters were through the task force and seemed to be gaining velocity. Another of their warships tumbled from being hit by Army laser fire.

Laser fire from orbit and Shapland chased the Duster fleet for a short while before stopping.

"Why aren't they chasing them?" PFC Orndoff asked.

"Maybe because they're waiting for more Duster ships to come," Sergeant Martin said from behind them.

"Goddam it, Sergeant Martin!" Mackie snapped. "You've got to stop sneaking up on us like that."

"And you've got to—" Martin started.

"Yeah, yeah, I know," Mackie said, interrupting him. "We've got to have all around awareness. But, man, you're a Marine, you're quiet."

Martin crained his neck looking up. He pointed toward the sky above the eastern horizon. "That's why they aren't pursuing."

The others looked where he pointed in time to see lines of light from TF 8 zipping at large, barely seen shadows in the sky. Small flashes of light shot out from from the shadows and began dropping, plunging planetward.

"That's the invasion fleet," Martin murmured.

Shadow-ship after shadow-ship rolled past the horizon. Half of them dropped shuttles and altered their trajectories, maneuvering out of the way of the lasers from TF 8. The others headed onward, aiming for Shapland, to drop their invaders on the elevator, and the Army positions near Millerton. Here a shadow-ship spun as laser bolts slashed through its hull and vented its atmosphere. There a shadow-ship broke in half when lasers sliced its spine in twain. Another burst apart when lasers penetrated to its power core. A shadow-ship began limping with its power reduced, another staggered and lost way.

The diving Duster shuttles glowed red as Troy's atmosphere ablated their heat shields.

"They aren't making planetfall near us," Mackie observed.

"Over the horizon," Martin agreed. "Be ready to move out, we might go out to meet them."

"Shit," Cafferata said. "That'll leave us without defensive works."

Marine anti-air laser artillery began lancing beams at the distant, plummeting shuttles, too far away for explosive artillery. Some beams hit the shuttles, some beams missed. And some were too diffuse to kill by the time they struck their targets.

A few shuttles were broken open by hits. A few more were tossed so their heat shields no longer protected them from burning up. Most passed through the barrage of killing-light lances to drop below the horizon.

Headquarters, NAU Forces, Troy,
near Millerton, Shapland

"If their shuttles carry the same numbers as ours, we can expect the equivalent of a reinforced corps to make planetfall. More on Eastern Shapland than here, because the transports coming west are subject to more fire from TF 8 and the Army's laser artillery," was the gist of Brigadier Shoup's operational assessment. "That's opposed to a battle-weary Marine division and wing on Eastern Shapland, and an even more battle-weary Army division here. Navy air assets are here to give the Army support, as well as two AV16C squadrons.

"Do you want to go after them, sir?"

Lieutenant General Bauer hardly had to think about his answer. "The best defense, and all the other clichés aside, they can overwhelm our ground forces if they catch us in the open. Make sure all our defensive positions are as strong as possible—especially the Army's."

He turned to Captain Upshur, standing ready in the doorway of Bauer's office.

"Get me Admiral Avery, if you please."

Upshur was back a moment later. "Sir, the admiral is on the surface-to-orbit."

Bauer took the comm. "Admiral, I see TF 8 acquitted itself well against the Duster warships."

"Thank you, General," Avery replied after a few seconds lag for the surface-orbit transmission. "What can the Navy do for the ground forces?"

"We have large numbers of Dusters making planetfall in locations remote from our positions. I don't believe they'll stay at a distance. It would be very helpful if you could keep us appraised of their locations, directions, and speed of movement, as well as their formations and armor, if any."

"General, I will bend every asset the Navy has to that task, provided it doesn't reduce TF 8's ability to defend itself."

"That is understood. Jim, the Marines and the Army thank you. We also offer our sympathies for your losses. TF 8's actions here will go down in Navy lore."

There was an audible lump in Avery's throat when he said, "Thanks, Hal. I appreciate that. I will pass it on to my task force."

"Bauer out." He set the comm aside and looked at Upshur, who still stood ready to do his commander's bidding.

"Bill, we have a fight on our hands. A big one."

Camp Zion, West Shapland,
near Jordan, Eastern Shapland

First Lieutenant Bonnyman came back with his platoon of combat engineers.

"Not good news, is it Captain?"

"It could be worse," Captain Sitter said. He looked eastward, toward where the Duster shuttles had touched down beyond the horizon. "It's still pretty bad. The Navy says they cram more than twice the number of soldiers in a shuttle than we would in the same similar size vessel." He shook his head.

"Two corps coming at the First Marine Division," Bonnyman said. "Eight to one odds."

"Marines have faced worse odds in the past and won. I don't see why we can't win again. They throw their soldiers' lives away."

"Yeah, they do. And we're here to help them throw away more. My people are enlarging the spiked trench inside your platoons' wire and adding another outside it. They've already done that for Kilo Company. Lima is next."

"It'll help."

"I better see how progress is going. By your leave, sir?"

"I'll go with you." Sitter donned his helmet and led the way out of his command bunker.

"Hey, Skipper!" Corporal Mackie called when the two officers were parallel to his fire team's bunker. "Does this mean we aren't going hunting?"

Sitter paused to look at him. "We've got beaters out there, driving them toward us. Turkey shoot, Marine!"

Mackie threw a thumbs-up at his company commander.

Firebase Gasson, near Millerton, Shapland

"A corps and a half?" Sergeant First Class Quinn yelped. "Are you kidding?"

Second Lieutenant Greig shook his head. "I could only wish." He'd just returned to his platoon's area from a battalion officers' call, where battalion commander Lieutenant Colonel Hapeman had delivered the latest intelligence from Navy surveillance. The majority of the alien transports and shuttles had made it through the gauntlet of orbital and surface missiles and lasers to land their counter-invasion force. The Dusters had landed the equivalent of seven human infantry divisions.

"But all we have is a single division," Quinn said. "And it's worse than that—the division was assembled from bits and pieces of other units!"

Greig smiled crookedly. "It's more like a reinforced division. Besides, it could be worse."

"How could it possibly be worse?" Quinn demanded.

"The Marines don't have as many troops or armor as we do, and they're facing two full corps."

Captain Patricia Pentzer and her platoon sergeant, James H. Bronson, joined Greig and Quinn after giving her own noncoms basic information.

"I can depress my guns," she said. "They can knock out armor if it comes here. But they won't be a lot of use against infantry."

"The foot soldiers present targets that are too small for you to hit?" Greig asked. "I can always use more riflemen on the line if that's the case."

"They aren't too small, it's just that a laser beam will only hit one at a time, unless they're lined up."

"You can't sweep the beam side to side?"

"Very little. Just so you know, I'm not putting my crews on the line until I know the Dusters aren't bringing armor at us."

"We'll do what we can with what we have."

Surveillance and radar section, NAUS Durango, in orbit

"Chief," Radarman 2 Peter Howard said over the susurration of soft voices and gentle pings that were the only sounds in the darkened compartment.

"What do you think you see, Howard?" Chief Petty Officer William Densmore answered.

"I *know* I see maneuvering," Howard said.

Densmore stepped close to bend and lean in to study Howard's screen over his shoulder. The screen showed a view from the side-looking radar of a section of the surface of Eastern Shapland east of the positions of the 1st Marine Division. After a moment he sucked on his teeth and stood straight.

"Sir," the chief called to Lieutenant George McCall Courts, "we've got something for the Jarheads, or for CAC. Your choice."

"Zero it in for me," Courts ordered.

Densmore bent back to Howard's station and reached for the controls. In seconds, an enlarged image of Howard's screen appeared at Courts's command station.

"Oh, my," the lieutenant whispered. He got on the comm to the bridge.

"Bridge," Lieutenant Commander Buchanan replied.

"I'm sending you coordinates. It looks like the Dusters are making a move at the Marines."

Buchanan only took a couple of seconds to study the display before whistling. "Keep an eye on it," he told Courts, "and have somebody take a close look at the Dusters west of Millerton. I'll notify the Skipper."

"Keep watching, and put someone on the Dusters west of Millerton, aye," Courts said.

As soon as he was off the comm to S&R, Buchanan called the captain.

"Huse," the *Durango's* skipper answered immediately.

"Sir, Bridge. It looks like the Dusters are maneuvering. The Marines should know."

"I'll be right there. Notify the Admiral."

Huse was on the Bridge before Buchanan could finish notifying TF 8's commander.

Admiral's Bridge, NAUS Durango

Rear Admiral James Avery took almost no time at all to understand import of the side-looking radar images he was sent.

"Get me General Bauer," he told Lieutenant Commander George Davis.

"Get General Bauer, aye," Davis said, and made contact with Headquarters, NAU Forces, Troy. "Sir, General Bauer's office," he said, and handed the comm to Avery.

Avery waited a few seconds before he heard Lieutenant General Harold Bauer's voice.

"Jim, it's good to hear your voice," Bauer said.

"And yours as well, General." Avery used Bauer's title to make it was clear this was an important call.

"What do you have, Admiral?" Bauer asked, taking the hint.

"Sir, the Dusters are moving on Eastern Shapland. We are tracking them, and will feed you our intelligence as we get it. Your G-2 can expect the first data burst in fifteen minutes."

"What about the Dusters on Shapland?"

"We are checking on them now."

"How is your situation?"

"The majority of the alien transports managed to get away, although many of them were damaged. We estimate eight hours before their warships return. Good hunting, General."

"Good hunting to you as well, Admiral. Bauer out."

Surveillance and Radar Section, NAUS Durango

"Chief, I have movement," Radarman 3 Michael McCormick said in the quiet of the *Durango*'s Surveillance and Radar Section.

"Show me," Chief Densmore said. He leaned over McCormick's shoulder to study his screen. "Sir," he called to Lieutenant Courts, "we've got them. I'm dialing you in."

Courts looked at the data and saw the alien army's movement toward Millerton and the Army division surrounding it. He notified the Bridge, where Captain Huse was still in his command chair.

Fifteen minutes later, Headquarters, NAU Forces, Troy had all the available information on Duster movement on both continents.

The staff began to change the plans based on this new intelligence.

Headquarters, 9th Infantry Division,
near Millerton, Shapland, Troy

Major General Noll, commanding general of the 9th Infantry Division, which he was beginning to think of as the Frankenstein Division, as it was pieced together from those elements of the 9th that had survived the missile attack and other units that had made planetfall, looked wonderingly at the situation board hanging on the wall behind him. Red smudges moved on it, showing the movement of the alien army as they moved at the white dots, rectangles, and circles that represented the NAU forces.

They've got to be crazy, he thought. *I don't care how badly they have us outnumbered. This is insane, they won't be able to concentrate their forces enough to break through our lines.*

His G-3, Lieutenant Colonel Henry Merriam, had worked closely with Brigadier General Shoup, the acting NAU G-3, to arrange defenses around Millerton and the McKinzie elevator station. *But this?*

He looked from his sitboard to his assembled staff and major element commanders. "When they get in range, our artillery will begin to shred their formations. We have," he said proudly, "the artillery with the greatest range and power of all human armies. So far the aliens haven't shown that they have any artilllery other than dumb anti-air artillery. Don't discount that, even dumb anti-air artillery can be highly effective against armor and hardened defensive positions. Past wars have clearly demonstrated that.

"They're going to hurt us badly, I have no doubt of that. But if we fight our best, I have absolute confidence that we will defeat the alien army.

"You all know what to do. Now do it."

There was a clattering of chairs as the assembled generals and other senior officers rose to their feet. Someone, Noll didn't see who, gave out a *huzzah!* In seconds, so did the rest of them. Some pumped their fists in the air.

Camp Zion, 3rd Marine Regiment complex, near Jordan

Major General Purvis, commanding general of 1st Marine Division, put the 6th Marine Regiment in a triangle of mutually supporting battalion firebases five kilometers northeast of Jordan, and the 7th Marine Regiment, also in mutually supporting firebases, an equal distance to the city's west. The 1st Marine Regiment, similarly placed, went three kilometers north of Jordan. He divided his artillery regiment, the 12th Marines, among the three firebases. He based his headquarters battalion, along with the division's armor, reconnaissance and other units, just outside the small city, adjacent to the 1st Marines.

When the Navy's latest intelligence reports were passed on to the regimental headquarters, and from there to the companies, platoons, and squads, it caused surprise, and not a little consternation among the junior officers and the enlisted men.

"Say what?" Corporal Mackie yelped when he heard. "Are they out of their ever-loving minds?"

"They're aliens, Mackie," Sergeant Martin said patiently. "Who knows what goes on in their minds? I sure don't. And if anybody higher-higher knows, they aren't telling me."

Mackie shook his head and looked at his men. They were staring at him and their squad leader as though they were crazy. Or at least like the Navy intel report was.

"We're Marines," Martin said. "When we're surrounded, all that means is, now we can shoot in all directions." He left, headed for the platoon CP bunker. He hadn't said it, but he agreed with Mackie; the aliens had to be out of their fucking minds.

✪

Not long after, the Dusters for the first time made a coordinated attack. Their combat fleet completed its circuit of Troy and fell on Task Force 8. At the same time, their ground forces, having completed their encirclement of the NAU forces on both Shapland and Eastern Shapland attacked.

Combat Action Center, NAUS Durango

"Chief," Radarman 3 John Bickford said, "I'm picking up another anomaly from the same direction that Duster fleet came from."

Chief Petty Officer Verney rushed to Bickford's station and looked over his shoulder.

"Damn," he swore, "they've got more coming!"

NAUS Durango, Fleet Combat Action Center

Lieutenant Commander Rufus Z. Johnston sat in his command chair, peering at the display on the big board, showing the warships of Task Force 8 maneuvering into position to take on the invaders. The display's scale was small enough to show the slow approach of the wounded Fast Attack Carrier Kidd, and the far faster approach of the enemy fleet. It was clear that the enemy would arrive first. The display also showed the remnants of Amphibious Group 17 in its ongoing rescue and recovery operation for survivors—and the remains of those who didn't survive—from the missile attack that had devastated the ARG.

And there, on the far edge of the display, beyond ARG 17's operation.,..

Johnston toggled his headset to signal Rear Admiral Avery. "Sir," he said after Avery's gruff, "Speak," acknowledged him, "Sir, someone else is coming into range from beyond ARG 17."

"Identification?" Avery demanded.

"Not yet, sir." Johnston's fingers danced over the keypad on the right armrest of his chair, signaling the comm shack, ordering it to attempt to contact the newly detected spacecraft. "Comm is working on it."

Lieutenant Commander Davis's excited voice intruded. "CAC, comm."

"Comm, go. The admiral is on," Johnston answered.

"Sir, we just received a message from Earth via drone. Task Force 7 is en route. It should reach the Troy wormhole terminus within a day."

Within a day. The new arrival CAC detected beyond ARG 17 must have been the lead elements of TF 7. At flank speed, the warships were still more than two days out.

"Comm, attempt to contact TF 7 and extend my compliments on their timely arrival. Tell them I request they come to Troy high orbit at flank speed. I will instruct Captain Anderson to prepare a brief for you to transmit to TF 7 so they will know what to expect when they get here. Do it."

"Aye aye, sir," Davis said, and dropped out of the communication link to obey Avery's orders.

"Avery out."

"CAC," Avery said, sounding much stronger and more confident than he had at any time since the attack from Minnie Mouse, "I anticipate two days for TF 7 to reach us. Stand by for revised orders. Perhaps we will still be here to greet them when they arrive." That last sentence was said so softly that Johnston wasn't sure Avery intended him to hear it. He told Davis to contact the ground commander, so he could give him the news about the relief force.

An hour later

The Admiral's Bridge, NAUS Durango

"Sir, a message," Lieutenant Commander Davis said excitedly.

"Speak."

"Sir, the unidentified starships are the van of TF 7 and ARG 28! The warships are the battleship *Nebraska*, cruisers *Grandar Bay* and *Suvla Bay*, the carrier *Vice Admiral Theodore S. Wilkinson*, and the amphibious battle cruisers *Enterprise*, and *Tripoli* with the Second Marine Division on board."

"Outstanding!" Avery said. "If we survive the next day and a half, we may live through this war. Notify the commander, NAU Forces, Troy."

ABOUT THE AUTHOR

DAVID SHERMAN IS THE AUTHOR OR CO-AUTHOR OF SOME THREE DOZEN BOOKS, MOST of which are about Marines in combat.

He has written about US Marines in Vietnam (the Night Fighters series and three other novels), and the DemonTech series about Marines in a fantasy world. The 18th Race trilogy is military science fiction.

Other than military, he wrote a non-conventional vampire novel, *The Hunt,* and a mystery, *Dead Man's Chest*. He has also released a collection of short fiction and non-fiction from early in his writing career, *Sherman's Shorts; the Beginnings*.

With Dan Cragg he wrote the popular *Starfist* series and its spin off series, *Starfist: Force Recon*—all about Marines in the Twenty-fifth Century.; and a Star Wars novel, *Jedi Trial*.

His books have been translated into Czech, Polish, German, and Japanese.

His short story "Chitter Chitter Bang Bang" is set in the world of *Starfist: Double Jeopardy*.

He lives in sunny South Florida, where he doesn't have to worry about hypothermia or snow-shoveling-induced heart attacks. He invites readers to visit his website, www.novelier.com.

CPSIA information can be obtained
at www.ICGtesting.com
Printed in the USA
LVHW041205180623
750100LV00003B/378

9 781942 990444